# REICH OF RENEGADES

Published by David J Publishing 2016

First David J Publishing edition 2016
www.davidjpublishing.com

Cover Design: Copyright © Jacqueline Stokes
www.yannadesignstudio.co.uk

A CIP catalogue record for this book is available from the British Library
ISBN: 978-0-9934591-7-7

**Also by Mark Lynch**

Insurgent Town
American Nemesis
The War of Zero Sum
The Rogue Colony

# Dedication

To my wife Jackie, my parents,
my publisher, my editor, cover artist
and to all who have supported and
encouraged me over the years.

*"I believe the common denominator of the Universe is not harmony, but chaos, hostility and murder."* Werner Herzog

*"The war against Russia will be such that it cannot be conducted in a knightly fashion. This struggle is one of ideologies and racial differences and will have to be conducted with unprecedented, unmerciful, and unrelenting harshness."* Adolf Hitler, 1941

**Definition of Renegade –**
*"A person who deserts and betrays an organisation, country or set of principles."*

# REICH OF RENEGADES

by
Mark Lynch

DAVID J
PUBLISHING

# PROLOGUE

## END OF EMPIRE

# PART 1

## 'AT THE CROSSROADS'

IT HAS OFTEN BEEN said that there are only a few occasions in a man's life, just a couple of monumental events, which will determine how his life will turn out. A man will reach a crossroads, if you will, and he must decide which way to go. Some say there are few free choices in life; that our decisions are so heavily influenced by social conditioning, and our destinies are pre-determined by the unpredictable chaos of the universe. Certainly there is some truth to this philosophy. Nevertheless, sometimes a man will have a clear choice between two divergent courses of action, and the decision he makes will change his life forever.

For John Preston one such momentous occasion did occur on the 22nd July 1946. The summer of '46 marked the sixth anniversary of Britain's wartime defeat at the hands of Hitler's Germany. John had been a part of this immensely significant event. His role was small; just one of thousands of foot soldiers fighting in a huge war which spanned a continent. He had been there to the bitter end, fighting the Hun until the very last hours, when their mighty Panzers and fanatical storm troopers had all but pushed Britain's Army into the sea. Six long years, but to John it still seemed like yesterday.

The summer of '46 was an important one for other reasons too. Just two weeks before, the US government had successfully tested a terrible and potentially devastating new weapon out in the hot and empty deserts of New Mexico. Manhattan had been announced to the world by President Truman on the 4th July – Independence Day, to be exact. John had listened to the wireless announcement along with millions of others across the civilised world. He, like most others, knew next to nothing of the science behind the new bomb. Nevertheless, the accounts of Manhattan's immense destructive power were impossible to ignore. John had the impression that this new weapon was a harbinger, summoning the dawn of a terrifying new world.

But, on the morning of 22nd July, the atomic bomb was the last thing on John Preston's mind, because, on this date, he had more important business to attend to.

It was a boiling hot day in central Jerusalem, the administrative capital of the British Mandate of Palestine. John had been on sentry duty the night before, and so he had slept late that morning. He awoke in his pokey barracks room at around 11am. His body was drenched in sweat and his back ached as a result of the hard and lumpy mattress beneath him. The small window beside the bed was ajar, and John could clearly hear the hustle and bustle of the city beyond. He groaned as he sat up on his single bed, his back creaking as he rose. John slowly adjusted his eyes to the bright daylight. He shook his head as he took in the surroundings of his small and untidy bedroom. He was lucky in a way. As an NCO he was at least entitled to his own digs. The lower ranks had to share bunks, and the Arab auxiliaries slept in cramped and primitive accommodation that was little better than stables.

Officers had better digs, of course. John had been a sergeant in the Army. This had been his rank at the point he was demobilised by the War Ministry. John had known that he could never aspire to rise any further. He would never be an officer, not in the British Army...not with his working class upbringing and his lack of formal education.

He got up off his hard mattress and reached across to his wash bag and his wrinkled and dusty uniform. It was difficult to maintain cleanliness and to dress neatly in this hot and muggy climate. But still, John Preston had to make the effort. Appearances were still deemed important by the British ruling classes, even in the middle of a warzone. He would wash himself and acquire a clean shirt from the laundry room. Afterwards he would tuck into a Mediterranean breakfast of figs, dates and olive bread, washed down by a strong Arabic coffee. And then Sergeant John Preston would report for his afternoon's duty.

John had been in the Holy Lands for almost a year now. He served in the Palestine Police Force, an armed colonial paramilitary unit which served alongside the regular British Army. The mission of both armed forces was nominally to 'support the civil power'. John himself had come over with his younger brother Andrew. It had been John's idea to volunteer for colonial service. There was little in the way of work back home in England. John had been a soldier for 15 years, and soldiering was all he knew. But Britain had no need for veterans in 1946. The country had been 'at peace' since the Allied victory over Japan in 1944, and there wasn't enough money to maintain a large peacetime army, not when the economy was in such dire straits. But an ex-soldier could still find work out in the Empire, where rebellions were brewing in a dozen or more colonies, and the near bankrupt British government was struggling to cope. The transition was easy enough for John, but less so for Andrew. In spite of all Andrew's macho posturing he had never served in the military and he'd never been to war. John had needed to carry his younger brother through the first couple of months of their tour.

Palestine was a dangerous country to be in during the hot summer of '46. The situation was highly volatile, and often violent. The security forces prime mission was to maintain order and keep the warring communities from tearing each other apart. It had started out this way, but the Army and Police increasingly found themselves in the firing line.

The Arabs and the Jews had been at each other's throats for over a decade now. John had only arrived in the country in '45 but he had an interest in history and so he knew something of the centuries old conflict in the Holy Lands. The current fight had spiralled off somewhat after the Arab Uprising was put down in 1939, but the situation had escalated during the early 40's, when

15

Jewish refugees had flooded into the Mandate in a seemingly endless stream. Almost all came from Europe. The smart ones had got out before the Nazis became so powerful. Others had been lucky to escape after their respective countries were invaded by the German juggernaut.

The refugee boats had continued to land on the Palestinian coast until about 1942, but then they had slowed to a trickle, before stopping altogether. The last Jews to arrive had spoken of unimaginable horrors occurring in Europe, but few in the British Administration had believed them, and no one knew the truth for sure. The Nazis controlled the continent, from the English Channel in the West to the Volga in the East, from the Arctic Circle in the North to Malta in the South. Europe was under Hitler's control, and his oppressive regime controlled all news coming out of the countries under their occupation.

There were about 600,000 Jews living in the Mandate today. This was the figure the censors gave, but the real number was probably higher, since many of the Jews were still living here illegally. Nevertheless, the Jews were still outnumbered by about two-to-one by their Arab neighbours. This fact didn't seem to deter the Zionists from their consistent and now violent campaign for a Jewish homeland.

John's brother Andrew was a rabid anti-Semite and he blamed all Jews for this conflict, and indeed for just about every other war and great evil throughout human history. John didn't believe this himself, but he was disgusted and sickened by the Zionist terrorist campaign. He didn't understand why Haganah, Irgun and the Stern Gang attacked the British Army and Police. What the hell did they hope to achieve? John would ask. The British had offered the Jews sanctuary, both here in Palestine and back home in England. If these bastards wanted to fight, John asked, why don't they go to war against the bloody Germans? John just didn't understand it, but he had seen a lot in his time, and there was little that surprised him anymore.

Sergeant John Preston was clean shaven, fed and reasonably well turned out by the time he left the barracks. He wore the khaki uniform and bush hat of the Colonial Police. In contrast to the traditional English 'bobbies' back home, the Palestine Force was fully armed. In reality it was more of a gendarmerie than a constabulary.

As he walked out of the fortified barracks John carried a .303 Lee Enfield rifle slung across his right shoulder. The .303 was standard issue for the British Army, and therefore the rifle was so familiar to John that it was like an extension of his own body. In addition to the Enfield, John also carried a .455 Webley revolver in a holster hung around his waist. No policeman was allowed to leave the barracks these days unless they were well armed. It was too dangerous now, as the Zionist terrorists had unleashed a cowardly campaign of cold blooded assassinations. Walking out on the streets alone wasn't exactly safe either, but John reckoned he would be alright, as it was only a short walk through the town to his destination.

John strolled through the town centre. He tried to retain a cool and casual composure, but in reality he was on alert, keeping his eyes peeled for any potential trouble; such was the instinct of a Jerusalem policeman. Anyone who met his eye would be considered with suspicion, as it was nearly impossible to tell the difference between a civilian bystander and a terrorist.

The street was bustling with market stalls; assorted Arab street vendors selling silks, rugs, cheap jewellery, figs and dates, and a dozen other local products of all descriptions. The vendors accosted potential shoppers in the street, as they tried to persuade the passers-by to purchase their produce. Those who stopped were given the hard sell, but the local customers knew the score, and they would engage in prolonged haggling before a price was finally agreed.

Several of the Arab vendors attempted to gain John's attention by speaking to him in broken English.

"Good price, sir...Good price...sir."

"Englishman, you buy...you buy..."

John smiled politely at the locals but he rushed on by without stopping. He was due on duty soon and had no time to browse. John Preston wasn't buying today but nevertheless he did enjoy the whole experience of the Bazaar, the colours and smells, the hustle and the bustle. In a way the street scene reminded John of his home, the East End of London. Perhaps he was homesick for England, yearning for the Green and Pleasant Land.

John kept walking and soon he reached the end of the line of market stalls. The last vendor on the street was a middle-aged and short Arab man, with a bushy grey beard, yellow teeth and wrinkled brown skin. He smiled at John as he approached, turning on the charm for the benefit of a potential customer.

"Hello sir," he said in decent but heavily accented English. "Good day to you, sir. Please come and see my inventory...Fine gold and silver. Perfect for your lady friend. She will be grateful to you forever after..."

"No, thank you." John answered politely. He kept his head down, only taking a fleeting glance at the collection of jewellery neatly lined up on the man's stall.

In all likelihood, a load of cheap imitations, John reckoned. Still, the Arab's mention of 'a lady friend' did get John thinking about the nice young woman he was courting. He had first met Elaine two months ago, up at the hotel where she worked. Elaine was a Somerset girl, the daughter of a country solicitor. She worked for the Governor's office in Jerusalem. She was an attractive girl, with her long and dark flowing hair and soft, pink skin. It wasn't just a physical attraction. Elaine was also kind hearted, with a good deposition and a sunny outlook. A fine young woman indeed, and she accepted and liked John in spite of his 'inferior' social background.

John had been nervous when he'd first asked Elaine to step out with him for dinner. He was afraid that she would reject him out of hand, but Elaine had not. It seemed she had a soft spot for grizzled ex-soldiers. They had got on well during that first dinner and had been courting ever since, seeing each other whenever possible. John was surprised at how much he had in common with the girl. He was very fond of Elaine and had already made the decision to ask for her hand in marriage.

It would be a while yet before John was in a position to do so. He could afford to buy a cheap engagement ring from one of the

Arab stalls, but this didn't seem right. He wanted to save up his pay and get her something decent. Elaine deserved this much at the very least. And the ring was the least of John's concerns in this regard. A proposal in Palestine just wouldn't do. He wanted to do things properly, and this meant asking her father, Mr. Davies, for his permission. John and Elaine's next home leave wasn't until Christmas and he couldn't hope to meet the man before then. He could write, of course, but this seemed just too impersonal. And John didn't expect an easy time from Mr. Davies. The Somerset solicitor was unlikely to take kindly to a cockney ex-squaddie courting his only daughter. At the very least the old man would want to know how John intended to keep his daughter in the manner she was accustomed to. This was a problem. The Colonial Police paid fairly well, better than the Army anyway. Nevertheless, John's term of service wouldn't last forever, and he had little prospect of finding a well-paid job back in England.

Financial security was a concern. But surely money didn't matter, if he and Elaine really loved each other? But did he really love her?

This was the nagging doubt in the back of his mind. John was certainly very fond of Elaine, but he couldn't say for certain if he was in love. In truth, he had never felt such a thing in his life. There had been few prospects for marriage in his life thus far. The existence of a professional soldier wasn't particularly harmonious with married life. But John was 33 now, and he didn't want to grow old alone. He saw what his brother Andrew had, with his beautiful and sophisticated wife Yvonne, and his two fine children; Edward, handsome and athletic, and Julie, smart and fearless.

John was jealous of his young brother's family. He wanted what Andrew had. But still, John reckoned there was little love left in his brother's marriage. Andrew bullied and controlled his wife, and John suspected his brother also beat Yvonne, although she would never say. Yvonne herself was deeply unhappy; this much was obvious to John. She loved her children and put up with her miserable marriage for their sake.

Come to think of it, John and Andrew's parents had been much the same. Their father's mind had never recovered from his stint in the trenches. He drank heavily and beat them often, usually for little or no reason. John had lived a tough life and he was no mug. He knew life wasn't a fairy tale, and perhaps all marriages became unhappy compromises between two people, who stayed together due to a lack of options, rather than an undying love. He was a cynic at heart. But still, Elaine was a good woman, as good as he would ever find. She would make a good wife and mother. John was sure of this. And, if she accepted his proposal, he would do everything in his power to protect her and to make her happy. He could grow to love her, over time.

By the time John Preston had finished his musings he had walked to the end of the street, and was approaching the front entrance of the building. In front of him, in all its grandeur, stood the King David Hotel.

The large hotel had been built in the early 1930's and the architecture was a typical colonial mix of western style with eastern influences. The building was built from pink limestone, and its strict symmetry marked it out as recognisably European in design. Nevertheless, the archway sitting above the front entrance was evidently Arabic. As usual, the hotel was busy, and John could see a congregation of people milling around in the front lobby. The hotel was the best in Jerusalem and so was a popular destination for both local elites and foreign visitors.

More importantly, the establishment also served as the central office for the British civil administration of the Palestine Mandate, and was also the Headquarters for the British military garrison. Elaine worked here, and John and Andrew's police platoon would frequently be deployed on security details in the immediate vicinity of the hotel. This afternoon would be such an occasion, as the squad had been ordered to set up a road block further up Julian's Way. John wasn't looking forward much to standing out under the hot sun all afternoon and so he decided to begin his day's patrol with a stiff drink in the hotel's bar.

He proceeded up the exterior staircase and marched confidently towards the front door. A young, clean shaven Arab boy stood attention by the entrance. He was dressed in an immaculate white uniform and he greeted John respectfully, as he opened the door to allow his English master entry to the hotel.

"Good afternoon, sir," said the lad. "We are pleased to see you again, sir."

John nodded curtly but did not speak to the doorman. He wondered whether the Arab had mistaken him for an officer. Or maybe the boy was just used to acting with deference to all Englishmen, such was the legacy of Empire.

John proceeded through the busy lobby, pushing his way past the assorted crowd of British soldiers, civilian support staff and Arab hotel workers. He took only a cursory glance at the décor of the hotel's interior, which he had seen many times before. The decorations were impressive, spectacular in fact. The walls were filled up with religious symbols and inscriptions, evoking something of a Biblical style. Christianity wasn't the only architectural influence, however. John had been told that the public rooms were decorated in motifs influenced by Assyrian, Hittite, Phoenician and Muslim artwork. This was a true meddling of civilisations, the symbols of fallen Empires, now adopted by the current masters of the Holy Lands. But how long would the British continue to rule? John wondered.

He proceeded into the public bar at the back of the hotel. This room was not as well decorated as the others, with its hard stools, plain tiled floors and dark booths complete with gun metal plates, used for striking matches. The enlisted men and the clerks drank and socialised in here, while the officers and senior officials drank in their own private club in a different part of the hotel. John Preston had served in many different colonies during his military career, so he knew that the strict social divisions of British society were evident in all corners of the Empire.

He proceeded to the bar and greeted the barman, who he knew by name. The young man was a friendly Russian Jew called Lev.

Lev was apparently a loyal Jew, as opposed to a Zionist. He seemed to have little interest in politics and was more concerned with playing cards and chasing girls. John spoke briefly to the young man, cracking a joke as he ordered a double gin and tonic.

When served by Lev, John lifted his glass and walked across the tiles to take a seat in an empty booth in a quiet corner of the room.

He laid his .303 rifle down on the wooden table in front of him and balanced the holstered revolver against the outside of his thigh. The close proximity of the guns made John feel a bit like a gunslinger drinking in a 'spit and sawdust' Western saloon. And, given the state of Jerusalem these days, perhaps this was an accurate comparison.

He was looking forward to enjoying his gin in peace, and sitting for fifteen minutes before he had to meet with his squad and go out onto the streets. Maybe he'd take a couple of minutes to visit his girl Elaine, who was working in the office upstairs. This was what John had planned, but his hopes were to be dashed. He had only been sat down for a minute before his brother walked into the bar and sauntered over to his table.

Andrew was two years younger than John. The brothers looked alike, although Andrew was more handsome; John had to give him that. At age 31, Andrew still had his cheeky boyish grin, deep green eyes and skin as smooth as a baby's. It was as if nothing could touch him. And Andrew had always been more popular with the girls.

Back when they were still in their teens, Andrew had liked to dress up smart, slick back his hair and get the tube up to the West End, where he'd bluff his way into the dance halls and bars, even though he was still underage. This hadn't been John's scene. He had lacked the self-confidence and charm of his younger brother. John had always been the sensible one, and he'd spent much of his teenage years in the cadets, before joining the Army at 18.

Andrew had a few girlfriends back then, but he married young. His charms had won over Yvonne, a middle class girl from West London, whose father owned a garments factory in Ealing. The bride's family were worth a few bob and they were considered a 'better class' of people than the working class Preston's.

John had always reckoned this was part of the reason why his brother had married Yvonne. Andrew had wanted to raise his social standing.

John put these thoughts to the back of his mind as he reluctantly stood up from his bar stool and greeted his sibling. Andrew coolly glided across the tiled floor, whilst blatantly ignoring the Jewish barkeeper, Lev. John noted that his brother was dressed in a khaki uniform, almost identical to his own. He had a Webley revolver holstered around his waist and a Sten sub-machinegun slung across his shoulder. Both brothers were armed and ready for their afternoon patrol. Andrew grinned as he held out his hand to greet his comrade.

"Good afternoon, brother dearest," said Andrew, in a sarcastic tone. "Out of your scratcher, I see."

John reluctantly shook his galling brother's hand, as he answered him. "I was on sentry duty last night, as well you know. Our shift didn't end until four in the morning."

Andrew nodded his head in acknowledgement as he took a seat in the booth.

"Boy," he called out towards the bar. "Yes you, Jew boy...get me a glass of tonic water, with ice and a lime. Be quick about it too, you bloody Yid!"

John glanced wearily over at the bar. He saw that young Lev was furious, but the boy reluctantly went about the business of preparing Andrew's drink. John didn't approve of his brother's outspoken anti-Semitism. The Zionist terrorists were their enemy, but not all Jews supported them.

"You shouldn't treat the lad like that," he said, in a fairly tame rebuttal. "Lev is a good lad. He deserves some respect."

"Respect!" Andrew spat out in an angry response. "What the hell do those people know about respect? Murdering scum, they are! You shouldn't trust that swine...How do you know he's not a Zionist spy?"

"He's alright, I tell you," said John. "He's worked in the hotel for two years. Lev never has a bad word to say about us British."

"Bah!" Andrew replied dismissively. "That proves nothing. They're sneaky ones, those Jews. Very underhand in their dealings. You never can know what they're up to. The Yids invented Communism, you know. Thank God the glorious Wehrmacht beat

23

the Bolshevik-Jews in Russia. If not, the vermin would probably be ruling all of Europe right now. And they still rule in New York...the filthy swine own Wall Street. They use their money to buy off the corrupt Yankee politicians and push forward their sinister agenda. And it was Jewish scientists who built this new bomb...Talk about crimes against humanity! The Fuhrer had the right idea...crush the Jews...drive them out. That's what we should be doing out here...but our government is weak. No wonder we lost the bloody war!"

John listened to his brother's hateful rant in complete silence. He broke off eye contact with his brother and drank his gin. He wanted to block out Andrew's arguments, but the hate speech always seeped through, as if the very words were corrupting his mind. John had long given up trying to argue with his brother. There was simply no point. Andrew Preston was a man beyond reason. Luckily, the rant ended when his brother removed a packet of cigarettes and a lighter from his inside jacket pocket. He lit up his fag, and promptly began to smoke.

Andrew was a fascist and an unashamed Nazi sympathiser. He'd been a notorious member of Mosley's Blackshirt movement during the 1930's, fighting against Jews and socialists out on the streets of the East End. When the war came, there was little doubt as to where Andrew's loyalties lay.

He was arrested during a violent protest outside the House of Commons on 4 September 1939, the day after Britain's declaration against Germany. Andrew got six months for riotous behaviour. He was released from prison in early 1940 but was only a free man for a matter of weeks before he was arrested again. Andrew was identified as a suspected enemy sympathiser and was interned under emergency wartime laws for the duration of the conflict.

John was furious with his brother when he heard the news, and, at the time, he had vowed never to speak with Andrew again. Obviously, his anger had cooled over the years and now the brothers were reconciled, up to a point at least.

Germany invaded Western Europe during the late spring of 1940. John was serving with the British Expeditionary Force in

Northern France and so he was soon thrown into the thick of the battle. The German Panzers were seemingly unstoppable. John's division kept being pushed back and back, until they were finally encircled at the Channel port of Dunkirk. John was wounded and taken prisoner by the Wehrmacht. He became a POW, along with about a quarter of a million other British servicemen.

It was ironic he supposed, because both of the Preston brothers were prisoners at the exact same time; John a loyal soldier captured by the enemy, and Andrew imprisoned as a traitor to his own country. But all this was a long time ago now, and much had changed in the six years since.

Just then, Lev arrived at their table with a glass carried on top of a circular tray. He carefully placed the drink down upon a cork coaster on the table.

"Your drink, sir," said the barman, in a subtly scathing tone.

"About bloody time too!" sneered Andrew, as he stubbed out his cigarette. "What is it with you people? You're not keen on hard work, are you?"

John watched as Lev struggled to contain his fury. It was a credit to the young man that he was able to swallow his anger and walk away from the table with making any comment. John felt extremely embarrassed by his brother's behaviour. This wasn't the first time Andrew's conduct had mortified him, nor would it be the last.

He watched as Andrew sipped his cool drink. His brother never drank alcohol, a fact he prided himself on. John finished up his own G&T before glancing down at his wrist watch. It was only five minutes to midday now. They had been sitting in the bar for too long.

"Best drink up, Andrew," John said. "We need to find the squad and set up the roadblock."

"Yeah, yeah," Andrew answered, with little enthusiasm, as he nursed his tonic drink.

Andrew wasn't exactly the model policeman, and he lacked dedication to his duties. It took a few more minutes until John could 'persuade' his brother to move, as Andrew insisted on smoking another fag before he would shift from the table. But, soon enough, the two brothers were up on their feet.

As he walked through the lobby, John realised he had missed an opportunity to see Elaine. But, no matter, as he was meeting her tonight for dinner. The brothers marched out of the hotel's front entrance and made their way through the hot and dusty streets of Jerusalem.

# PART 2

## 'TIPPING POINT'

HALF AN HOUR LATER the Preston brothers were standing in the middle of the busy, hot and dusty road, along with eight other armed men. All but one were fellow Brits, dressed in khaki uniforms and sun hats or helmets. The eighth man was a local Arab auxiliary and was there primarily to act as a translator for the police squad.

The unit manned a hastily arranged road block which blocked access both ways on the narrow street. The men stopped cars and trucks, questioning the drivers and asking to see their papers. If a civilian didn't give a good account of their coming and goings, the men would search his vehicle. Pedestrians, bicycles and camels were allowed to pass uninhabited, unless they looked particularly suspicious or nefarious.

The task was tedious and the temperature was unbearably hot. The policemen sweated and grumbled under the relentless Middle Eastern sun. John's rank was sergeant, so he was nominally in command of this afternoon's patrol.

It took all his efforts just to keep himself from keeling over in the intense heat. The job was fairly pointless. In theory the men were meant to be looking out for suspects on the wanted list; the terrorists and Zionist extremists who were the primary targets of the British security forces. John knew that the chance of them catching anyone on the list was about one in a hundred thousand. There was a slight prospect of finding weapons or contraband this afternoon, but even this was improbable. At best, the colonial policemen would discover a few political pamphlets or stolen goods, material that was technically illegal but was of little interest to the security forces.

Tensions were high at the moment. Just a few weeks ago, the British Army and the Colonial Police had launched Agatha, the Mandate government's biggest military operation to date. Raids, arrests and arms searches were carried out across the territory; in Jerusalem, Tel Aviv and Haifa. The scope of the operation was huge. Thousands of troops and police were deployed and around 2,500 arrests were made. Andrew and the hardliners in the security forces said the crackdown was well overdue. John was not so sure.

The operation had some success in apprehending terrorists, but many of those arrested were moderates of the Jewish Agency. Some of the European Jews had claimed the British were no better than the Nazis. To John's great shame, his younger brother had openly mocked the Jewish prisoners, raising his arm in a Nazi salute and shouting, 'Heil Hitler!'

The Jewish population was angry, and John just wondered how long it would be until they struck back. That was the way of it out here; an eye for an eye.

The street was busy. Vehicles slowly drove down the narrow street, their drivers blowing their horns and shouting out in frustration towards the British police, who were slowing their respective journeys to a crawl. Pedestrians, Arabs and Jews alike, walked the street, going about their business. The smell of spices and cooked meats filled the air. The din of numerous languages could be heard. Soon all voices would be drowned out, as the loudspeakers would produce their mighty sound, as the Islamic faithful were called to their mosques, for Zuhr, afternoon prayers.

Jerusalem was a hot, noisy and colourful city; full of diversity, history and cultural richness. Andrew hated it here. He called it 'the Modern Babylon', if he was being polite. Most of the time, Andrew would simply rant incoherently about how this city was a 'mongrel hell-hole, a hive of sub-humans and degenerates'. John's brother hated the Arabs almost as much as the Jews. He despised their food, mocked their religion and treated the Force's Muslim auxiliaries as if they were little better than slaves.

He didn't care about the momentous history of this great city, the birthplace of three global religions. He didn't believe in any religion, only in National Socialism. A city thousands of years old was of no interest to him. Instead, he only ever spoke of the 'great' city of Berlin, which even now was being rebuilt by the Nazis, as grotesque and monstrous monuments where built to celebrate their psychotic leader.

John despaired when he thought about his brother, but blood was blood, and there was no changing that. His thoughts allowed him little respite from the boredom and the near overwhelming heat. Another Ford truck rolled by, as the young driver flashed his license and his papers. The lad was carrying fruit and vegetables across to the other side of the town. John didn't bother searching the back of the van. The vehicle slowly drove forwards, past the roadblock and up the street.

At that very moment, they heard the first explosion. A loud bang startled John and his men. For a moment he was thrown back in time, back to the bloodbath at Dunkirk, cowering in a cellar while the Wehrmacht howitzers and Luftwaffe dive bombers pounded the British lines. But Sergeant Preston soon returned to reality.

He was in Palestine, not France. There had been a single blast, relatively small but evidently close.

The explosion had surely been caused by a bomb. Women screamed on the streets, and grown men fled in panic. The police officers all instinctively took cover, crouching down behind vehicles and walls whilst preparing their weapons to fire.

John used his Lee Enfield rifle to scan the horizon. He stared down the gun sights, looking for targets amongst the scrum of frightened civilians. The policemen all expected to come under attack at any moment, but several tense minutes passed, and nothing happened. The street soon cleared, and the eight armed men were on their own. But all was not quiet out on the streets. John and the others could hear shouts and screams, sirens and vehicles, all of them very close. It soon became obvious that the epicentre of the attack had occurred only a few hundred yards from where they stood.

John was the commander here. All of the men, even his brother, looked to him for leadership. His orders were to maintain the roadblock. This task seemed more important now, since the terrorists would be attempting to escape the scene, and they may flee in this direction. Nevertheless, he didn't feel right just standing here, not when there were surely wounded people who needed his assistance.

In an instant, John made an executive decision. He turned to the man on his right hand side, crouching behind an overturned cart. This was Corporal Macintosh, a hard faced Glaswegian who was a veteran of the Burma campaign. He was the man John trusted most in the whole squad.

"Mac," he shouted out, in an authoritative tone. "Take over command. Keep the road closed, water tight…And, if any of those bastards come down this way, leave them bloody well have it!"

Mac nodded in a stern acknowledgement. "Right!" he cried out in his thick Scottish accent, whilst addressing the other men, "You all heard the sarge. Get on your feet and back to your posts. Stay on your toes. The Yids could be here any bloody minute now!"

John stood up. He motioned over to his brother Andrew, who was striding across the middle of the road, clutching his Sten gun tightly as his eyes lit up in anticipation of the battle to come. His sibling's bloodlust brought a cold chill to John's spine. But still, he wanted…needed Andrew by his side.

"Constable Preston," he yelled. "Come with me!"

Andrew grinned sadistically as he raised his submachine gun and jogged to his brother's side.

"Lead on, sarge," Andrew said, sarcastically, in an open mockery of his older sibling's authority. John chooses to ignore him, and soon they were both on the move.

A moment later the two brothers were tearing down the now virtually abandoned Jerusalem city street. John felt a painful twinge emanating from the old bullet wound in his thigh. He ignored it and ran on. They reached the corner, and heard the gunshots. The heavy crack of rifles was punctuated by the popping of pistols and revolvers. A small but intense gun battle was occurring very close by. John pulled back the hammer on his .303, forcing a round into the chamber. The gunshots surely meant that the bomb had not been a one off. They were in the midst of an all-out attack. The man felt a raw panic deep inside, as he suddenly realised the terrorists' target. They were attacking the hotel. They must be…what else? John's jog turned into a sprint, and Andrew was close behind him.

The two brothers sprinted around the street corner. They could see the hotel now; its pink limestone walls illuminated by the intense midday sun. The street in front was packed with people; locals and colonials who were sent into a blind panic, as they sought cover from the explosion and the gunfire. John and Andrew were quickly approaching the south side of the hotel. In spite of the immense danger John could only think about getting to Elaine. She was working on the third floor of the building, and John knew she would be frightened. The young woman wasn't used to bombs and bullets. She would be terrified. John had to get to her side; he wanted to protect his woman.

John was running fast, but suddenly he hit a brick wall. He saw a flash of light, so powerful that he was temporarily blinded. Only then did he hear the deafening sound of the explosion. The sudden surge was so intense that John was physically lifted off his feet and thrown backwards. He fell down hard onto the concrete, feeling a sharp and sudden pain rushing up his spine. He lay on his back and tried to look upwards, but all he could see was darkness. For a terrifying few seconds John actually believed he was blind. But then he realised that his eyelids were still shut. He opened them slowly and saw the blue sky above. His whole body ached and his ears were still ringing. With some difficulty he managed to move his arms and legs, and he fought the pain to push himself up off the concrete.

Suddenly, John became aware of a figure standing directly above him. He looked up and was relieved to see his younger brother. Andrew's face was covered in a layer of grey dust, and there was a nasty gash on his forehead. Other than this, Andrew appeared to be unhurt. His brother was shouting down at him. John could see Andrew's lips move but he couldn't hear a word he was saying. He must still be deaf from the blast. John just hoped that the damage to his hearing wasn't permanent.

His brother held out his right hand. John took it and slowly got to his feet. He was shaky on his legs, but John soon realised he wasn't seriously injured. He was only winded.

He warily looked towards the hotel, or rather what was left of it. John was horrified when he saw the carnage. The building which had stood tall just seconds ago was now reduced to rubble. It looked as if the entire southern side of the structure had fallen in on itself. John was in total shock. The destruction was as bad as anything he had witnessed since the war. He felt a raw fear rising up inside him when he remembered that Elaine had been in this very building. He imagined her sitting in her typing pool. A mundane and dreary office room. The King David Hotel had been a sanctuary from the chaos and dangers out on the streets. It had been safe, until today.

John looked to the rubble strewn street directly in front of the demolished hotel. The injured were sprawled across the blood soaked concrete. The brothers stood still for a moment, watching on in awestruck horror as the wounded and mutilated walked or crawled away from the blast zone. Some of the injuries were horrific and reminded John of soldiers caught up in artillery attacks during the war. But these people weren't soldiers. They were unarmed civilians; innocent men, women and children who were in the wrong place at the wrong time, torn apart by what could only have been a terrorist bomb. John's hearing was yet to return, so he could not hear the screams and the cries of pain. For this he was grateful.

Instinctively, both brothers knew that they needed to help. They were policemen after all, and it was their job. Their guns were of no use now, so they both slung their weapons over their shoulders as they prepared to use their hands to tend to the wounded.

The minutes which followed seemed like an eternity, as John descended back into the depths of Hell. He witnessed many terrible sights during that nightmarish afternoon. He saw a young boy, perhaps only 10 years old, with both his arms blown off by the blast. The poor boy's eyes were filled up with pain and fear. He screamed frantically as the rescuers made a vain attempt to administer first aid. The child eventually lost consciousness. Then, his eyes closed and the screaming stopped. The boy would never wake up again.

Next, a middle aged white woman, probably a Jew, emerged from the rubble and walked out onto the street beyond. She was shaky on her feet and was clearly still in shock but, at first glance, the woman appeared to be unhurt. But then she turned around and, to his abject horror, John saw that the left hand side of her face was a bloody mess. The skin had literally been ripped off, exposing her jawbone and cranium. They did what they could for the woman and resolutely refused to speak of her horrific injuries. She would probably survive, but her terrible facial disfigurement would last forever.

After some indeterminate period of time, John's and Andrew's ramshackle team of rescuers succeeded in clearing the street of the dead and wounded. The many casualties were loaded onto a fleet of ambulances, Army trucks and even commandeered civilian vehicles. But the rescuers did not rest. There were still wounded people buried under the stone and rubble, and John knew Elaine was amongst their number. And so they began to dig.

At first they used nothing except their bare hands. John and Andrew lifted heavy heaps of rubble and passed the debris down a line of other policemen, soldiers and local volunteers. The men worked in unison as they went about their grim task. They hardly spoke a word, except to bark instruction and orders, or to make observations or suggestions. They worked like this for hours and hours. The job was exhausting, but their stubborn determination and frantic adrenaline kept them all going.

Later that afternoon the Royal Engineers arrived on the site, bringing with them heavy lifting equipment in the back of their armoured vehicles and massive trucks. After this, the rescue operation became more organised and efficient, but progress was still painfully slow. The Preston brothers continued to work long into the night.

John felt a terrible sensation of foreboding doom build up inside. They pulled a couple of dozen bodies from the rubble. A few were still breathing, but most were dead. They found Lev just after dusk. The barman had been literally torn in two by the sheer force of the blast. They found his torso on one side of the bar and his legs on the other. John was appalled to witness the pointless taking of yet another young life. Andrew was unsurprisingly indifferent.

They discovered Elaine's body just after midnight. By this time, John had already resigned himself to the fact that his girlfriend was surely dead. Nevertheless, he retained just a glimmer of hope, which was why he insisted on staying on the rescue mission, even after the relief team of Army sappers arrived to take their place. The two brothers dug the young woman's cold corpse out from under the rubble and gently carried her out to the cordon on the roadside. It was strange, because John could not see a single wound on her whole body. Elaine looked as if she'd simply drifted off to sleep, like her passing had been entirely peaceful. Her face and her body were untainted. She was still young and beautiful; even in death.

The brothers carefully laid the stretcher on the ground. John kneeled down beside her body and brushed his right hand against her soft cheek. Elaine's skin was ice cold. He took his hand away and stood up, averting his eyes from his beloved's corpse. His eyes filled up with tears and he felt as if his head was going to explode. He looked up to the dark night sky above and he cried out in agony, as all his pent up rage was finally let loose. After he stopped screaming, he instinctively looked to his brother, faithful and loyal Andrew...the man who had stayed by his side all through this hellish day. John's hearing had now returned, but still his brother did not speak. Andrew did not say a word. He did not need to...the man's eyes said it all.

*I told you so.* That was what Andrew Preston was saying to his older brother. *I told you that the Jews can't be trusted. I told you they are all cold blooded murderers.*

The Zionist terrorists had committed this atrocity. This much was certain. They had taken the life of the woman John loved, and for that, he would hate them forever.

34

# Book One

## Crossing the Rubicon

# 1/ 'A Woman's War'

YVONNE PRESTON KNEW THERE was going to be a row this evening. She could just tell. Maybe it was a woman's intuition, or perhaps she just knew her husband too well. Andrew had always been an ill-tempered man with a violent rage.

Yvonne hadn't seen it until after their wedding, all those many years ago. Or maybe she had always seen Andrew's bad side, even before they got married. But Yvonne had been a silly and foolish young girl back then, and she was blinded by what she thought was love. The woman knew better now. She had learned the hard way.

Andrew was a thug and a bully, and he made Yvonne's life a constant misery. She just knew there was going to be trouble tonight. There had been a glint in her husband's eye this morning, the kind he got whenever he was planning to spring something horrible on his wife. Yvonne knew how to cope with her husband's anger, up to a point. It was best not to provoke him, although sometimes Yvonne couldn't help herself. But she didn't want a fight today. Tonight, Yvonne would do everything in her power to pacify Andrew.

She had spent all afternoon cleaning their small terraced house top to bottom, making sure their home was pristine and spotless.

The Preston's lived in a rundown part of Whitechapel in London's notorious East End. Yvonne herself had come from a good family. Her father owned a factory in Ealing and she had grown up wanting for nothing. But that was before she had met Andrew. Back then, Andrew had seemed charming, handsome and exciting. She had fallen for him, but her parents hadn't approved of the union. Andrew had wanted to elope…to run away to Gretna Green and get married without her family's consent. He was very persuasive. He almost always got want he wanted. And Yvonne was just a teenage girl with romantic illusions. She had been swept up in the moment and had eagerly agreed to Andrew's proposal. It was the worst mistake she'd made in her whole life.

Yvonne's misery had been confounded by her father's furious reaction to the news of her marriage. He had disowned his only daughter and refused to have anything to do with the couple. It had been years before Yvonne was able to reconcile with her father, after bad feelings had finally cooled. Her parents had come round because they wanted to know their grandchildren, Edward and Julie. Yvonne was grateful for this, although she knew her father still despised Andrew. She could hardly blame him.

Yvonne had sent her children to their grandparent's house to stay for the evening. She didn't want them to witness yet another fight between their parents. Edward and Julie were growing up fast. They were both teenagers now, and Yvonne could no longer protect them from learning the truth about their father. The best she could do was to try to shield her offspring from the worst excesses of Andrew's violent temper. This she would do, even if it meant becoming her husband's punching bag. She could live with his abuse because the love she felt for her children was so strong.

Yvonne had finished her housework by late afternoon. The whole house was spotless. She had put fresh linen on the beds and had ironed and neatly folded all of her husband's shirts. Andrew liked a tidy home, and he would be angry if his wife didn't maintain a high standard. Next she began to prepare her husband's dinner, a stew made of tough and stringy beef, mixed in with a couple of potatoes and carrots. This was the best meal she could produce with the food she had in the larder.

The war with Germany had ended eight year ago, and the Japs had surrendered back in the winter of 1944. Nevertheless, there was still a strict rationing system in operation. Britain was a hungry nation in 1948, and there was never enough of anything to go around. The news was full of reports of strikes and bread riots in towns and cities across the United Kingdom. Conditions were bad in this country, and there was little indication that things were getting any better.

After putting the pot in the oven, there was time to enjoy a few minutes rest at the kitchen table, as she awaited the inevitable return of her husband. She took some time to collect her thoughts and to consider her current grim situation.

This time last year, Yvonne's life had been much happier. Her husband had been stationed abroad, serving in Palestine as a policeman of all things! Andrew had gone out there with his brother during the summer of 1945. Yvonne had been anxious for the brothers' safety. She wasn't heartless after all. But, after a few weeks of uncertainty, she began to enjoy her new found freedom. For only the second time in her adult life, she was free to do whatever she wanted, without her bullying and controlling husband breathing down her neck.

She started to make friends for the first time in years. She would socialise with other local mothers, accepting invitations to come over for a cup of tea and a natter. She'd even taken the odd night out in the dance halls of the West End, reliving her days of youth. Yvonne had also started a secretarial course at a local technical college. She liked the idea of being a modern woman, earning her own money for her family, rather than relying on her errant husband or begging for hand-outs from her disapproving father.

Those had been happy times, but, inevitably, they did not last. Yvonne remembered receiving that letter in the post. In the back of her mind she imagined that it was bad news. She thought that Andrew may have been killed out in Palestine. She wondered how she would react to such news, and she realised that she'd be secretly relieved to hear of her abusive husband's demise. But the letter contained even worse news than this. The correspondence was from Andrew himself, and he was coming home.

The Preston brothers' tour had lasted over two years, and they'd only had a couple of periods of home leave during that time. But, by late 1947, the war in Palestine was petering out, and the colonial government had eventually managed to negotiate a peace settlement between the Arabs and the Jews. Naturally, Andrew didn't support the peace, which he considered 'a shameful and inexcusable surrender to Zionist terrorism'. Nevertheless, Andrew and John had been demobilised from the police force and they were being shipped back to England.

Yvonne's heart sank when she read the letter. She remembered sitting down at the dining room table and bursting into tears. She knew what her husband's homecoming meant. His return spelt the end of her short-lived freedom, the death of her modest dreams for a happy life. She knew this would all be over as soon as Andrew came home…and there was nothing she could do.

She thought back on these days with a sad regret, but she didn't have long to dwell on her memories. Her husband arrived home at about 5pm, which was earlier than she had expected him. She almost jumped out of her chair when she heard the key turn in the door. Suddenly, her husband came busting through the front entrance, nosily slamming the door shut behind him. He always liked to make an entrance. He barged into the kitchen, and Yvonne winced whenever she saw his face. She had once found his looks irresistible, but now she could hardly retain eye contact with her husband for more than a few seconds.

"Evening, love," she said, in as amicable a tone as she could muster.

He merely grunted in acknowledgement without looking at her and she watched on wearily as his dark green eyes glanced around the room, as he carefully considered every detail of the décor and surfaces. It was almost as if he was conducting an inspection, looking for any minor discrepancy. Yvonne held her breath. She knew that her husband would kick off at the very slightest of grievances. Eventually, Andrew finished his silent inspection. He appeared to be satisfied at the state of the kitchen, or at least he couldn't find anything to criticise.

"Where are the children?" Andrew asked, in an accusatory tone.

"They're at my parents tonight," Yvonne answered nervously. "I told you this morning, don't you remember?"

"I'm sure you never told me any such thing," he spat back angrily, as he shot his wife a look.

"No, sorry, love," she answered. "I must have forgotten."

Andrew nodded in acknowledgement at the admission. Yvonne knew she had told him, but it was best not to push the point. Andrew hated her father, but he reluctantly allowed his children to spend time with their grandparents. Yvonne didn't want to give him an excuse to revoke this privilege.

Next, Andrew sat down at the kitchen table; he kicked his feet up and lifted his copy of the Daily Mail, which Yvonne had carefully placed out for when he got home. Soon after, he extracted a Lucky Strike from the packet in his jacket pocket, and proceeded to light it. Yvonne regarded smoking as a filthy habit, but she said nothing in protest. After a minute or two of tense silence, Andrew suddenly sighed aloud, before saying, "What a bloody day! Make us a cup of tea, woman."

Yvonne meekly complied with the order, filling the kettle with water from the tap and placing it on the heating stove. She knew how her husband liked his tea, builder's strength with two lumps of sugar. She got it exactly right, not giving him any opportunity to complain.

She recalled that he had been out looking for work today, or at least that's what he had told her he was doing. Andrew had been employed as a senior clerk before the war. Not the best paying job, but enough money to support their family. But Andrew's political activities had tainted them all. Yvonne remembered when her husband first became involved with Mosley's lot, the so called British Union of Fascists.

That had been back in the mid 1930's, and Yvonne had hoped it would just be a passing fad. But Andrew loved being a

Blackshirt; he enjoyed wearing the uniform, barking out orders to subordinates and using his imagined authority to bully and intimidate others. Fascism was right up Andrew Preston's street, no doubt about it.

Andrew had been imprisoned for a brief period during the war because he was considered to be an enemy sympathiser. Those had been dark and depressing times for Yvonne. She had no steady source of income and struggled to put food on the table for her young children. What's more, she was ostracised by the local community, despised because her husband was a traitor to his country. Fortunately (or perhaps unfortunately) Andrew wasn't in prison for very long. But the stigma of being a German sympathiser would stay with him, and so her husband had struggled to find employment during the post war period.

The job in the Palestine Police had been a godsend. Andrew's older brother John had gotten him that job. John was such a good man, so different from his younger sibling. The pay in the colonial police had been good, and her husband sent a decent allowance back to support his family. But Andrew had been home for over six months now, and there weren't many jobs going in depression stricken Britain.

Yvonne was almost afraid to ask the question, lest she provoke an angry response from her ill-tempered husband.

"So, how did you get on today, love?" she enquired sheepishly, having first waited for her husband to extinguish his cigarette. "I heard they were looking for men down at the docks?"

"Huh," Andrew spat back dismissively, without bothering to look up from his newspaper. "A bloody waste of time, just like I knew it would be. The unions control the whole place, and they only give jobs to their own lot. They're all bloody Communists too...I'll tell you, woman...This country has gone to the bloody dogs!"

Yvonne shook her head. It was always the same with Andrew. He always blamed someone else for all of his problems...the government, the communists, the Jews...it was never Andrew Preston's fault. He never took personal responsibility.

Yvonne was feeling frustrated and angry. It seemed to her that Andrew was making no effort to find work or to support his family. She had promised not to provoke her husband's anger tonight, but she just couldn't help herself.

"Well love," she began, as the defiance in her voice became more evident, "you know my father is hiring new staff for his factory. I'm sure, if I put in a good word, he could find something for you…"

She knew how Andrew would react to this suggestion. It was a blow to his pride to suggest that he would even consider taking an entry level job in a garments factory let alone work for his hated father-in-law. Predictably, her husband reacted with fury to the proposal. He threw down his newspaper and looked her straight in the eye, before shouting, "What? Was that meant to be some sort of joke? Because I'm not bleeding laughing!"

"It was just an idea," Yvonne replied defensively. "My father could help us. And, you haven't had much luck looking for work, these past couple of months."

"Oh, I see!" Andrew sneered. "So you think I can't get a job myself? That I have to accept charity from your bleeding father?"

"I didn't say that, Andrew," said Yvonne, in a more conciliatory tone. "Please calm down."

But she knew that it was too late to calm him. Andrew's blood was up, and there was no reining him in now. He got up from his chair and stood over her. He pointed his finger right in her face in an attempt to intimidate her. Yvonne flinched but she met her husband's eye. She would not show him her fear, not this time.

"You would like that, wouldn't you?" he screamed. Yvonne felt his spittle hitting her face. "You want to see me working as damn skivvy for your bastard father, to see me humiliated!"

Yvonne did not answer. There was no point. She just sat forward and took her husband's verbal abuse, hoping against hope that the argument won't turn physical. His next action surprised her, because he laughed aloud…a mocking and cruel bellow which filled up the small kitchen. His laughter lasted for some time, and Yvonne felt increasingly uncomfortable.

"What's so bloody funny?" she eventually asked.

"You know," he eventually replied, after he recovered from his hilarity, "my darling wife, I wasn't going to tell you this tonight. I was going to wait until my brother and the children were here…but, you know what, you bloody bitch? I just can't wait to share the good news with you…my so called 'loyal and faithful' wife! I can't wait to see the look on your face, you bloody stupid woman!"

Yvonne was scared now. She saw the devious look in his eyes and knew the bastard was about to spring some fresh misery upon her. Andrew enjoyed torturing her; he got a sick kick out of it.

"Tell me what?" she asked anxiously. Half of her didn't want to know the answer.

Her husband smiled sadistically, as he relished the opportunity to cause his wife further pain. Yvonne felt a surge of sickening fear rising from the pit of her stomach. She didn't know what was coming, but she knew it was going to be bad.

"We're leaving this dump," said Andrew, as his smile broadened. "We're leaving forever."

"Leaving where?" Yvonne asked, in confusion. "This house, do you mean?"

Moving home would be good news as far as Yvonne was concerned, but she doubted this was what he meant.

"Yes," replied Andrew, sarcastically. "We're leaving this house, leaving this bloody city and getting out of this God forsaken country!"

"What the hell are you talking about?" demanded Yvonne. She was getting angry, and was sick of Andrew's childish games. "Are you having me on?"

Her husband nodded his head with vigour. He was no longer angry. Now, he was deadly serious and he looked his wife directly in the eye, as he spoke.

"We're leaving England for good. All the arrangements have been made. I've been visiting the German embassy in Westminster, going down there every week for meetings with top officials." He paused briefly to let the implications sink in. Yvonne felt a cold chill of fear rising up her spine.

"They accepted me, Yvonne," Andrew said, as his face beamed with pride. "They did all their tests, a full physical, blood test; the whole lot…At the end of it all they said I am a steady Grade 2 Aryan, which is the highest racial grouping any non-German can rise to…"

Yvonne had little to no idea what her husband was talking about. She noted how Andrew looked and acted like a little boy returning home with his school report, seeking approval from his mother. Yvonne had no intention of humouring him.

"What is all this rubbish?" she asked, scathingly. "Do you think I know what in God's name you're talking about?"

Once again, Andrew's face screwed up in anger. He spoke his next words through clenched teeth.

"I wouldn't expect you to understand, my dear wife. But the Germans can see the true measure of a man. They know strength of character when they see it…that, and pure breeding. They took one look at me and they knew I was one of them, a true Aryan of the best stock…"

Yvonne could almost have laughed aloud. She had to fight hard to control herself. Her husband was talking about himself as if he was some kind of thoroughbred horse. But Yvonne was very worried. She just knew that Andrew had done something stupid. She stayed silent and listened, as she felt a sense of impending doom.

"…The Germans want me and my family," he continued. "The National Socialists are destined to colonise the rich lands of Eastern Europe, the newest provinces of the Reich, conquered from the vile Slavs and the Jewish-Bolshevik swine. And the Fuhrer needs men like me. There's a place for us on this new frontier, a homestead and a plantation out in the black earth territories of Ostland. This is my destiny…to settle my family in this utopia, far from this rotten, worthless country…"

Yvonne couldn't believe what she was hearing. These words weren't Andrew's own. She was sure of that. The language was too articulate. Someone had taught him this little speech, probably the Nazis he was meeting up with. It was all completely ludicrous. Andrew spoke about the Nazis as if they were superhumans and Hitler as if he was a God. This 'Ostland' was a country Andrew had never been to, and probably couldn't even find on a map...but, nevertheless, he believed this far-off land was some sort of paradise. He talked of a plantation, but Andrew was East End born and bred, and he knew nothing of farming. Yvonne had heard stories of German agents and recruiters operating in London and other parts of England. They wanted to recruit Englishmen and English families for their damn colonies in the East; to trick the gullible and foolhardy into defecting to their evil regime. The whole thing was absurd and sick. Yvonne just hoped this was another of her husband's childish fantasises, but she already feared the worst.

"Please tell me...," she pleaded, "please tell me, Andrew...tell me you haven't done something stupid! What have these damn Nazis talked you into?"

"It's a done deal, woman," he said sternly. "I've signed the documents and pledged my allegiance to the Fuhrer. We leave in two weeks. That should be plenty of time for me to put our affairs in order, and for you to pack up our possessions and prepare the children for our trip."

Yvonne suddenly felt a profound change occurring inside her. For the first time in years, she wasn't afraid of her husband. Instead, she was consumed by an overwhelming rage. Andrew's latest stunt had pushed her over the edge.

In that instant, Yvonne was no longer a put-upon, submissive housewife who would cave in to her husband's every demand. In that moment, she saw red.

Yvonne jumped up so quickly that she threw her chair down to the stone floor and furiously bolted around the kitchen table. She banged her thigh against the side of the bench, hardly even noticing the pain, as she flung herself towards her perplexed husband, who appeared to be frozen to the spot, such was his total surprise at witnessing her violent reaction. She charged towards him, bringing her clenched fists down against his exposed body. Andrew's instincts took over, and he raised his hands to shield his head from the blows.

"You bastard!" she screamed. "You rotten bastard! How dare you! What the hell have you done to us?"

Predictably, her husband's inaction didn't last long. He soon regained control and grabbed her left hand in a painfully tight grip before clenching his right hand into a hard fist, and striking out.

Yvonne felt a stinging pain as the closed fist impacted with her jaw. She felt her eyes roll up inside her skull, and then she was falling. She hit the hard floor with a bang and screamed out in pain and fear.

Andrew stood over her. He was dominant once again, and his violent rage had not yet subsided. Yvonne watched on helplessly as the brute raised his right leg, showing his heavy workman's boot. She cried out for mercy, but knew she would receive none.

He kicked her hard in her ribs. She cried out as she reeled in agony. He raised his boot again, and kicked her a second time. Yvonne bit her tongue as tears welled up in her eyes. Just seconds ago, she had been fighting back, for the first time in her life…but now she was defeated, broken and scared. Her monstrous husband had reminded Yvonne of her place.

She braced herself for yet another kick but, to her great relief, Andrew had vented the worst of his anger and the abuse turned verbal.

"You stupid bitch!" he exclaimed. "Have you gone bloody crazy?"

Yvonne could have laughed in spite of her pain and her fear. He was calling *her* crazy?

She had taken a beating from her thug of a husband and he'd left her bleeding on the kitchen floor. Nevertheless, Yvonne still felt defiant. Now she was fighting for Edward and Julie. Andrew intended to put her children in harm's way, to bring them right through the Gates of Hell. Yvonne would not allow this. She would not give in.

"I won't go…" she whimpered. "You can go over there with your Nazi friends. We're staying here…"

"Hah!" Andrew sneered. "That's what you think, woman. You're coming alright, mark my words!"

"I'll leave you," Yvonne continued, as she became increasingly more desperate. "I'll divorce you…I'll run away."

Andrew laughed once again, as he continued to cruelly mock his battered wife.

"A woman's place is by her husband's side. The courts will never give you a divorce. And, if you run away, I'll find you and I will kill you. And, no matter what happens to you, my beloved, my son and my daughter will come with me...." He paused briefly to point poignantly towards the kitchen window. "My boy's future is out there...out on the great Aryan frontier. This is where his destiny lies. In the East, he will become a man."

And, at that moment, as she looked into her psychotic husband's fiery eyes, Yvonne knew she was beaten. Andrew really didn't care about her anymore. He didn't love her...maybe he never had. If it came to it, he would leave her behind or even kill her, and he would take Edward and Julie to Germany. And what could she do to stop him? In the end, she only had one course of action open to her. As a mother, she would continue to protect her children as best as she could. Yvonne would do whatever was necessary to shield Edward and Julie from their monstrous father, and from whatever horrors they would face out in Nazi-occupied Europe. She could do no more.

Yvonne slowly and painfully got to her feet. She felt the terrible pain in her side and hoped that Andrew's savage kicks hadn't broken her ribs. Her right cheek was stinging from the pain of the initial punch. This would surely come out in a bruise, she realised. And, once again, Yvonne would have to find a way to disguise her injuries from the rest of the world. This was her hidden shame.

Andrew backed off and looked away. He apparently didn't want to see his own foul handiwork, and he certainly wasn't going to offer his bruised wife a helping hand. Yvonne could smell her stew cooking in the hot oven. The evening meal would be ready in a matter of minutes. The violence which had occurred wouldn't matter one bit to Andrew. He would still expect to be served his dinner. And, if Yvonne failed to deliver her husband's meal, she was likely to receive another beating.

She ignored the piercing pain in her ribs and struggled across the kitchen floor to the oven. She used gloves to remove the pot and a wooden spoon to dish out a portion of beef stew into a bowl. Next, she carefully carried the bowl across to the table and placed it in front of her husband, who was waiting in silence, poised with his knife and fork at the ready. She poured him a cup of tap water to wash it down. Andrew had a surprisingly simple taste in food and prided himself on the fact that he never drank alcohol. The man didn't even have the excuse of being a violent drunk…he was simply a brute.

Yvonne stood and watched as he tucked into the stew, piling forkful after forkful into his mouth. He had next to no table manners; he ate like a machine, seemingly without enjoyment. He was barely bothering to chew his food before swallowing and Yvonne quietly indulged in a twisted revenge fantasy as she watched him do so.

She imagined a hard piece of meat becoming trapped in his throat. In her mind, she saw him choking, gasping for air as he tore at his throat. His face would turn red, and he would look to his wife for help. But she would do nothing. He would fall to the hard stone floor, as his windpipe closed and his brain was deprived of oxygen. And Yvonne would watch him die. No one would ever know what had happened. It would be Yvonne's secret, and she'd finally be free from the bastard.

But Andrew didn't choke. He just kept on eating until his bowl was clean. And then he demanded more.

Yvonne obeyed her husband's command and refilled his bowl. She could not bear to watch him gorge himself any longer. It made her feel sick. She could not eat anything herself. Yvonne was hurt and she was scared. Her stomach was in knots. She just wanted to get away from this animal; to escape for even a brief respite from this living hell, and she soon got what she wanted.

"You need to go upstairs now," Andrew said, between forkfuls. "My brother's coming around in a bit. I don't want him seeing you."

Yvonne immediately understood why her husband was sending her away. He didn't want his older brother John to see her bruises. John was a gentleman through and through, nothing like his thuggish younger sibling. He wouldn't approve of Andrew hitting her and would surely confront his brother on the matter. Yvonne liked the idea of John Preston being her knight in shining armour. She had fantasies of the honourable brother coming to her rescue, saving her from this vile brute. But she knew this was nothing more than a deluded dream. She didn't want to see John or anyone else right now. She simply wanted to hide away, out of sight, out of mind.

She went to leave the kitchen and ascend the staircase. But, before she left the room, her curiosity got the better of her. She halted in the doorway and turned her head ever so slightly.

"Why is John coming around?" Yvonne asked. Her voice was soft and cautious. She did not wish to provoke her husband's anger once again.

"We've got plans to discuss," Andrew answered, without looking up from his bowl.

"Plans?" she enquired. "What plans?"

"For God's sake, woman!" snapped Andrew.

Yvonne feared that she had gone too far, but she soon got her answer.

"The plans for the trip, that's what we need to discuss. My brother is coming with us. Now, get out of here, you stupid woman, unless you want to feel the back of my hand again?"

Yvonne didn't need to be told twice. She promptly left the kitchen and ascended the stairs, all the time trying to contain her feelings at hearing this latest news; a mix of confusion, hope, anger and bewilderment.

Yvonne reached her marital bedroom and slammed the door shut behind her. She collapsed onto the mattress. She was physically and emotionally exhausted, and her bruises were hurting badly.

This was a familiar routine for her, but it never seemed to get any easier. Her tired brain was swimming with questions. What would happen to her and the children? How would she protect her family? And why would John agree to go along with his brother's ridiculous and highly dangerous scheme?

Yvonne hadn't known Andrew's brother when they first got married. He was away in the Army during the war, and then the brothers were estranged for many years. It was late 1944 by the time Andrew and John reconciled. After the reunion, John had started to come and visit their family regularly. Yvonne got to know him better, and she came to adore him.

Yvonne wished she had met John before his brother. Maybe she could have married him instead, and fathered his children. John would make the perfect husband. He was polite, even-tempered, kind and intelligent…everything that his brother was not…

She lay on the bed for about five minutes before she heard the knock on the door. Then she heard male voices in the hall. Andrew would be telling his brother some story or another. 'Yvonne is sick, she's retired to bed.' Would John believe him? Probably not, but he would be too polite to say anything.

Yvonne briefly considered marching down the stairs and confronting both men. She could show John her bruises and tell him what his beloved brother had done to his wife. But she quickly dismissed the idea. Such a reckless action would not do anyone any good.

Why, she asked herself, why in God's name would John agree to defect to the Nazis? He was an ex-British soldier, for crying out loud!

Yvonne didn't understand it. But, then again, John hadn't been quite the same since he returned from Palestine. Since they came home, Andrew seemed to have more influence over his older brother, as if something monumental had occurred which had changed the entire dynamic of their sibling relationship. She didn't know what had happened out in the Holy Lands. Neither man ever talked about it. She had asked her husband about Palestine a couple of times, but on each occasion he had fobbed her off saying, 'It's war. A woman would not understand.'

She could have laughed when she heard this. The men had their war, and women like Yvonne had theirs. Hers was a constant fight for survival and the enemy lived inside her own home. There was no prospect of final victory, no hope for a glorious triumph. Hers was an endless war of attrition, forever wearing her down.

All she could do was absorb his physical and emotional abuse. Her children were all that mattered now. And so she would go out to 'Ostland' with John and Andrew. She would go to Hell and back for her children, and she would protect her son and daughter until her dying breath.

# 2/ 'Leaving Blighty'

EDWARD PRESTON HAD ONLY just turned sixteen when his family left the United Kingdom, apparently for good. It was a boiling hot summer's day in the South East of England. Edward would always remember the weather on that particular day. His family had awoken early in the morning to travel by tube across East London and over to Victoria Station. From there, they negotiated their way down a busy platform and boarded the train to Dover, the Channel port located in Southern Kent.

All their family possessions - clothes, furniture, books, trinkets and ornaments - everything had been packed up into boxes over the last couple of weeks and sent ahead to Dover. His parents had spent a small fortune paying for the removal and transportation of their belongings. Edward's father had complained bitterly about the added expense. He said that the German Embassy should have paid for all of this. His mother had said nothing.

Edward's Uncle John had met them at the station. He wore a dark suit and long coat, and carried only a single, small suitcase. Edward liked his uncle. He was warm and had a good sense of humour, and would always keep him and his sister Julie entertained during his visits.

What's more, Uncle John always had the best stories to tell about his time in the Army. He had been all over the world with his regiment; the West Indies, Newfoundland, Egypt, Arabia, India and Malaya, to name but a few. John would convey many tales of exotic locales and colourful characters whom he met on his travels. There were only two periods of his service which Uncle John refused to talk about; the first was the Battle of Dunkirk, and the second was his stint with Edward's father in the Palestine Police. Edward didn't know why, but his uncle always clammed up whenever he was asked about either of these two periods of his life.

Uncle John didn't seem himself on the morning of their trip. He had coolly greeted his brother and had barely acknowledged Edward or his younger sister, or even their mother. Something definitely wasn't right with his uncle, but Edward couldn't figure out what.

The family boarded a second class carriage on the Kent bound train. They each carried with them a small suitcase containing changes of clothes, identification papers, toiletries and other essential items required for their trip. Everything else had been sent ahead. There was little talk during the lengthy train journey. His mother had hardly said a word all morning. She looked very sad and spent most of the trip staring vacantly out of the carriage window. It upset Edward to see her like this. Uncle John was also silent. He seemed to be lost in a world of his own, caught up within his own inner thoughts. His sister Julie had barely shut up over the last two weeks. She had complained constantly over their trip to Germany, whinging about leaving her friends and her school behind. Edward had had several blazing rows with his sister over the last couple of days. He didn't understand why she had to be so difficult about everything. Why couldn't she understand that their father knew best? Edward supposed his sister was just a typical 14 year old girl. Thankfully, Julie now seemed to have resigned herself to her fate, and she had taken to sulking quietly.

Edward himself felt a conflicting mixture of emotions about their journey. He would miss his school chums, of course, and his family. Edward was particularly sorry to leave his beloved grandparents behind, but he still hoped against hope that he'd see them again, some day. He was also a bit frightened, of course. His family were travelling into the unknown, going to live in a faraway land which had until recently been a warzone, and was now governed by Britain's wartime enemy. Edward didn't know what awaited him and his family out there in Eastern Europe. But the uncertainty was also what made this expedition so exciting. It all reminded Edward of one of his Boy's Own Adventure Magazines, of brave young men and their daring exploits; flying planes, fighting in battles, winning car races, travelling through unexplored jungles and confronting cannibal tribes and dangerous wild animals.

The Germans produced their own version of Boy's Own. They called it *Der Arische Junge*, or 'The Aryan Boy'. The Nazis published an English language version of the magazine which they exported to the British Empire. Many of the newsagents and shops in London refused to sell 'Aryan Boy' because they considered the magazine unpatriotic. However, Edward's father always managed to get the latest editions for him. The basic storylines of 'Aryan Boy' were broadly similar to its equivalent English publications. The tale would usually consist of a blond haired German boy moving out to the new colonies of Ostland, Ukraine or Muscovy. The lead character would thrive out on the frontier, finding fulfilment in rural life and farming. Then, at some point, the boy would uncover a sinister conspiracy by hidden Zionists, or an assassination attempt by a Red partisan. The hero would foil the devious plot by the end of the story, and the magazine would finish with some words of wisdom by Adolf Hitler, meant to inspire the reader to follow in the fictional hero's footsteps.

If truth be told, the Nazi comics often left Edward more bewildered than inspired. But he continued to read them, mainly to keep his father happy. His dad had always been a great admirer of the Fuhrer. But, Edward was getting too old for these childish fantasies. That's what his father had been telling him recently.

Up to this point in his life, Edward had only read about other people's heroic exploits in books and magazines. But now, he was about to live through his own adventure. As his dad had told him, Edward was no longer a boy, and this journey would turn him into a man.

The uncomfortable silence in their carriage made the train journey hard to bear. Edward's father was the only one who spoke.

He talked endlessly about the magnificent sights they would see on their trip through Europe, and how much better their lives would be, once they reached their new home. Edward loved and respected his father, and he knew his dad had their best interests at heart. Nevertheless, even Edward grew sick of his father's rants and endless jibber jabbing. Everyone was relieved when the train pulled into Dover station.

The family quickly gathered together their cases and pushed through the scrum of other passengers in the corridor. They ascended onto the platform and made their way through the ticket gates. Edward was very much aware of the suspicious, unfriendly and often hostile looks the family received from other passengers, and also from the railway staff. It was as if they all knew exactly who the Preston's were, and apparently they did not like Edward's family one bit. This made him feel very uncomfortable. He became paranoid, fearing for the safety of himself and his family. He just wanted to get away from these hateful eyes as soon as possible.

The family was rushed through the station and bundled into a dilapidated old taxi which was waiting for them out on the street, just beside the exit. The entire family was forced to cram into the small vehicle for the short trip to the docks. Edward and his sister were squeezed in so tight that they could hardly breathe. Edward's dad sat in the front seat beside the driver. He continued to boast about his connections to the German government throughout the short drive.

"All of our travel arrangements are paid for by the Embassy," he said proudly. "And they've provided ample Reichmarks as spending money during our stop offs. There's been no expense spared by the Fuhrer's government. It just goes to show how much they value our family."

His father looked at Edward as he spoke the words. He was looking for approval. Edward obliged his dad by smiling and nodding his head. It did strike Edward as odd that his father was praising the Germans today, when just yesterday he had been complaining about having to pay himself for the removal truck.

Edward had never been to Dover before, but he would have little opportunity to see the town today, as the taxi tore through the streets. The family had holidayed in Ramsgate a couple of times when Edward and Julie were young. He had fond memories of that seaside town, but it seemed Dover was a commercial port, not a holiday resort.

The car soon arrived at the docks. Dover port was quite large, but Edward reckoned it wasn't as grand as the docks of the East End. It consisted of several piers equipped for big boats, both merchant ships and passenger liners. Edward looked up in awe at the towering cranes above and across to the huge boats docked at the elongated concrete piers.

The taxi finally arrived at their assigned pier on the western side of the harbour. Edward was relieved to exit the crammed vehicle and to get out into the afternoon sun. The waiting boat was unimpressive, as far as Edward was concerned. It was a small and run-down passenger ferry which looked like it had seen better days. The way his father had described it, Edward had half expected to be sailing on one of the Kreigsmarine's new E-boats. In contrast, this ferry was little better than an old rust bucket. This was disappointing.

Edward and the others started to unpack the family's cases from the rear of the taxi. Meanwhile, his father was in the middle of an argument with the driver. Apparently he didn't want to carry his family's cases onto the boat, and he expected the taxi man to do so. The verbal quarrel grew more heated, until eventually the cab driver told his father to 'sod off' before he slammed the car door shut and drove up the pier and away from the docks.

Andrew Preston stomped away, with a furious look etched on his face. Edward didn't understand why his father got so angry about such small things.

His father continued to rant and rave for several more minutes. In the meantime, Uncle John took control and carried the family's cases to the pier side. There they stood and waited, while the ship's crew prepared to lower the gangway. During this interlude, Edward observed a scene occurring on the adjacent pier, perhaps a couple of hundred yards from where they now stood. There was another ferry docked, which looked similar to the one his family was about to board. Edward watched as a group of passengers descended from the boat and walked down to the pier. There were about four dozen people in total; seven or eight families and a few lone travellers. The group's members all had one thing in common. They were all haggard looking, dressed in filthy, torn, old clothes. Their faces were thin and pale. Every one of their number looked tired, hungry, desperate…and frightened.

Edward watched on in shocked horror as the bedraggled group spilled out onto the concrete and assembled under the hot summer's sun. The party was causing quite a ruckus; children cried out and babies screamed, women nattered and men shouted in a language Edward did not recognise.

Edward saw a smaller detachment of uniformed men approaching the newly arrived group. These men wore peaked caps and smart black uniforms with white collars. Their buttons shone in the sunlight. He saw four men in total, and he guessed they were all customs officials. Presumably they were here to deal with and question the newcomers.

The tidy dress of the government agents was in stark contrast to the bedraggled appearance of the foreigners. Edward watched as the customs men herded the crowd into a line. The migrants looked intimidated, frightened even. Their children cried as their mothers clutched them tightly. The fathers took responsibility to step forward and speak with the officials. Their body language was tense and uneasy. Edward guessed that these people held a bad impression of government representatives.

The officers started speaking with the male members of the group. Edward couldn't hear what was being said, but it was obvious that the two parties were experiencing difficulties in communicating with each other.

The customs men shouted instructions and ticked off clip boards. The male refugees were becoming more and more agitated. They were clearly unhappy at this line of questioning. Edward heard raised voices, and he saw the ragged foreigners waving their hands in frustration, as they passionately argued with the British officials.

The whole situation was becoming more and more tense, and Edward was getting worried.

At that very moment, Edward's attention was drawn towards a small building at the far end of the pier. He guessed that the structure was either a custom office or a guard's post. The door opened and two men emerged, young lads in dark green uniforms. They were soldiers, and both looked ready for battle. The troops wore tin helmets and carried long rifles in both hands. They strode determinedly towards the customs men and soon confronted the group of refugees. It was obvious to Edward why the soldiers were here. Their purpose was to intimidate the newcomers, and the Tommies did their job well.

The head of the customs team clearly felt more confident with the armed soldiers there to back them up. He shouted out so loud that his bellow drowned out all other voices.

"Look here, you foreign bastards! The lot of you better shut up and start playing ball, otherwise we're going to put you on the next boat back across the Channel! Would you rather take your chances with the bloody Krauts?"

The threat clearly had the desired effect. The male refugees backed off and said no more. The women looked terrified, and the children cried even louder. Edward felt sorry for these poor people. He wondered who they were, where they were from, and how they had come to be in Dover. His father soon provided the answers to all of his questions.

"Bloody lowlifes...so called 'refugees'!" said Andrew Preston. "They flock to this country in their thousands, swamping our Southern ports...Jews, Gypsies, Communists, criminals and partisans...all are the enemies of National Socialism. They come across the Channel in boats, some like that ferry there." He pointed towards the small ship from which the refugees had just descended. "But others sail across the water using fishing boats, old yachts, row boats or even bleeding rafts, roped together with pieces of drift wood! A few go down in rough seas, and others get sunk by the Kriegsmarine...blown out of the bloody water!"

His father laughed cruelly when he spoke those words. Edward was unable to disguise his utter dismay and shock at his dad's callous description of the refugees' plight. He couldn't believe his own parent could hold such a total lack of humanity towards these poor people. Andrew Preston must have sensed his son's discomfort. He grabbed hold of Edward's arm and pulled him close, forcing his son to face him eye to eye.

"Don't feel sorry for them, Edward...don't you dare! You have a kind heart, that's your weakness. But these animals, they are the enemy! They swamp this country, corrupting our national identity...and yet the government takes them in, gives them shelter and spends a fortune on supporting them. And, how do these bastards thank their saviours? They bite the hand that feeds them, that's how! This country is weak, son...that's why we have to leave. Do you understand?"

His father's intense eyes cut through him. Edward was in awe of his parent; he both feared and respected the man, and he lacked the courage to stand up to him. He nodded his head meekly and looked down at his feet. His father seemed satisfied and released his grip. And, Edward thought, perhaps his dad was right after all. Maybe, he was weak and over sensitive. He needed to toughen up...to become a man.

It was an uncomfortable moment, but Edward's mother broke the silence, as she spoke for the first time in several hours.

"Isn't it funny," she said, in a piercing and defiant voice. "It's odd, to see so many people trying to get in to England, and we're the only bloody fools trying to get out."

"That is funny, mother," Julie said with a smile, as she backed up her mum's facetious comment.

Andrew Preston immediately forgot about his son and instead shot his wife a furious look. Edward was frightened to witness his father's body language, as the man clenched up and scowled at their mother. Only a stern look from their uncle made him back down.

Their father did answer his wife, however. He spoke in a scathing, cutting tone, saying, "The Reich is home to the strong and the pure. It's where we belong."

His mother scoffed in contempt at her husband's comment, and Julie sniggered. Edward was annoyed at both of them. His sister was a cheeky so-and-so with a big gob, but Edward didn't understand why his mother always said things which she knew would annoy his father. He had a bad temper. His mum knew this - so why did she provoke him? Still, her words made Edward think, and he was beginning to worry about what they would find on the other side of the Channel. But he had to trust his father. The man knew what was best for his family, and surely he would never put any of them in danger.

The whole family watched on in silence as the group of frightened refugees was hustled away by the custom officials and armed troops. They were marched up to the pier towards a pair of waiting trucks. In spite of his father's stern warning, Edward couldn't help but wonder what would become of these poor sods.

By now the crew of their boat had completed their preparations and had lowered the gangway. Edward was relieved that his family could finally leave this damn port, but, before they could ascend, the Preston's were in for yet another unpleasant surprise. At that moment, a black saloon car tore down the pier at speed, heading directly towards their boat. The whole family turned in that direction and watched as the vehicle suddenly halted just yards from where they stood. Edward looked on with curiosity and more than a bit of anxiety, as both of the car's doors swung open, and two men jumped out from either side.

The man who emerged from the driver's seat was middle aged and stood at about six foot tall. He had a receding hairline and a weathered, hardened face. The man wore a long beige trench coat with a grey suit underneath. He didn't seem to be bothered by the heat of the summer's afternoon. At second glance, Edward realised that he recognised this individual, but it took him a second to place the man.

Quite suddenly, he remembered who this newcomer was and where he'd seen him before. At that moment, a chill of cold fear shot up Edward's spine. He found himself frozen to the spot, unable to move or to divert his eyes from this sinister interloper. The man in the trench coat was a policeman, a detective from Scotland Yard's Special Branch. Edward didn't know the fellow's name. They had never been introduced. However, he did recognise his face from another context. The detective had been a regular visitor to the Preston's' home street over the last couple of years, and he'd been an uninvited guest in their family home on more than a few occasions.

The Special Branch officer was assigned to the Dangerous Subversives Division of the force. Edward's father had told him as much. Andrew Preston sneered with contempt when he spoke about the Metropolitan Police. He called them the Cheka, after the Russian Secret Police. His father said that the Special Branch spent all their time harassing patriots like him, and they did nothing to counter the rise of the Communist Party. Edward didn't know how true his father's words were. However, he did know how much his dad hated the police.

Instinctively, Edward feared an ugly confrontation between his father and the policeman. Even worse, he suspected that the Special Branch detective had come here to stop the family boarding the ferry and perhaps to arrest his father.

The policeman stood stationary beside the open door of the car. He did not advance towards the Preston family but instead he simply stared at them, without speaking even a word.

Edward turned to look at his father and, to his immense surprise, he saw the man was smiling. Andrew Preston shouted out towards his assailant. He openly mocked the Special Branch policeman with no apparent fear of arrest.

"Cheerio, you roozer bastard!" he cried. "Enjoy your bloody Marxist utopia!"

He laughed aloud at his own supposed wit. The policeman didn't reply. He just stared blankly towards his enemy, meeting him eye to eye.

It was then that Edward realised why the policeman was here. The detective hadn't come to the pier side to arrest the Preston family or even to stop them from boarding the ship. Instead, he'd come out simply to see off an old adversary. Perhaps he wanted to make sure the family were really leaving. Either way, the detective would give them no more trouble. Edward felt a great relief.

Edward had been so focussed on the policeman that he'd hardly noticed the second man, who stood by the passenger's side of the saloon car. This individual was older, grey haired and moustached. He wore a neat green dress uniform, including a buttoned jacket and a peaked cap. Edward soon realised that the uniform marked him out as an officer in the British Army. What was this fellow doing here? Edward wondered. He soon got his answer.

His uncle John stepped forward. Edward noticed a look of profound shock on his uncle's face. It was obvious that he knew this military man, and clearly John hadn't expected to see the fellow this afternoon. The officer was glaring angrily towards Uncle John. There was hatred in the military man's eyes. He continued to stare for several moments, and then he opened his mouth, and he spoke his scathing rebuttal in an upper class English accent.

"You should be bloody ashamed of yourself, Sergeant Preston! Bloody ashamed!"

Edward turned to look upon his uncle and was distressed to see the pained look upon John's face. It was as if the officer's words had physically hurt him.

Edward wondered what the relationship was between his uncle and the grey haired military man. He knew John had been a sergeant during the war, and so perhaps this older fellow had been his commanding officer. Edward couldn't be sure, but it was obvious that the officer's opinion had a profound effect on his uncle.

John did not answer his accuser. Instead, he promptly put his head down in shame and proceeded up the gangway with his cases. The rest of the family soon followed him, as they left the ugly scenes at the pier behind them. It was only in that moment when Edward realised how difficult it was for his uncle John to leave England behind, because he felt he was betraying his country.

It was a calm day to cross the English Channel. The wind was virtually non-existent and the waves were small and low. The Preston family put their cases into storage and ascended to the top deck shortly after the ferry set sail. They watched the shoreline as the boat pulled away from the harbour, and, soon afterwards, a most iconic sight came into view. The famous White Cliffs of Dover.

Edward had never seen the cliffs before, and he supposed he might never get the chance to again. The whole family stood on the deck and watched as the majestic chalk cliffs came into view. They must be hundreds of feet high, Edward reckoned. The natural formation really was as impressive as he had heard. This was truly an iconic scene, an immortal piece of merry old England. And only then did it hit the boy. They were really leaving, departing their home, perhaps forever.

In spite of himself, Edward did feel sad in that moment. He looked to his family members and, from what he saw in their eyes, he reckoned they shared his feeling. All of them, except for his father. Andrew Preston didn't look sorrowful in the slightest. In fact, he was grinning like a Cheshire cat. Clearly, their father was exceptionally happy to be leaving, and he was having no second thoughts. And then their father opened his mouth and spoke, saying; "So Long, Old Blighty!"

Andrew Preston turned his back on the scene and causally walked away, as he left the remaining four Preston's to grieve for their former country.

# 3/ 'Submission'

JOHN PRESTON HAD EXPERIENCED three truly horrific days during his life thus far. The first occurred on the 3rd June 1940, when he'd been wounded and then captured by the Wehrmacht, during the final days of the Battle for Dunkirk. The second was the day Elaine died, out on that dusty street in Jerusalem, when the Zionist bomb tore apart the King David's Hotel, burying his beloved under so many tonnes of rubble.

The third horrendous event in his life occurred on the day when he left England in order to defect to Nazi Germany, for this was the moment when he was made to feel utterly ashamed of betraying his country.

The officer who had confronted John Preston on the pier side was none other than Colonel Augustus Wilson of the British Army. The Colonel had commanded John's battalion during the war. He was a decent commanding officer; tough but fair.

The men held a grudging respect for Wilson, and John had always looked up to him. He hadn't seen the old Colonel for many years, but still John had recognised him almost straight away. The man's distinguishing features and his air of aristocratic superiority was unmistakable.

How did the old officer know? How did he know John was defecting to Germany? How did he know the Preston family were leaving from that pier on that day? John would probably never find out the answers to these questions.

In the end, it didn't really matter how the Colonel had found out. It was Wilson's words which made the impact. *You should be ashamed, Sergeant Preston. Bloody ashamed!* Those words had cut through John like a knife; they had scarred his very soul. He would remember the Colonel's accusations to the end of his days.

His decision to defect hadn't been an easy one. It had been his younger brother Andrew who had persuaded him, but this didn't happen overnight. The loss of Elaine had hit him hard. His grief had almost overwhelmed him. The life of a wonderful and beautiful young lady had been snuffed out, and all of John's future plans had been smashed to oblivion. Nevertheless, John hadn't given up after Elaine's death. He'd still hoped to salvage something out of the whole bloody mess. He'd tried to rebuild his life after returning to England, but it was hopeless. It felt like de-ja-vu. Just like in 1940, John was returning home after fighting a bloody foreign war for his country, and, once again, the government and the people couldn't care less about him or his comrades. In 1940, the people had yearned for peace at any cost, and so the government had sold out the soldiers on the battlefield by submitting to a shameful surrender.

Giving up Gibraltar, Malta and Suez and paying repatriations to the Germans must have seemed like a good deal for Halifax and his fellow appeasers, no mind the brave men who had laid down their lives fighting the Hun juggernaut. But the country had lost much of her power and prestige following that humiliating peace, and by 1948, the British population were poor and hungry.

The focus was on domestic politics, and no one cared about the dirty little colonial wars fought in all four corners of the Empire. The conflict in Palestine was quickly forgotten, as the Colonial Office negotiated a settlement which gave the Zionist terrorists a role in government...such, it seemed, was the reward for cold-blooded murder.

Other shameful surrenders would soon follow. India had been granted full independence during the summer of 1947, just as Andrew had predicted. The Empire was crumbling.

What's more, the treatment of veterans in post-war Britain was truly shocking. Unemployment was high all across the nation, but no provision was made for those men who had risked their lives for their country. In 1918, Lloyd George had promised 'A Land fit for Heroes,' but successive governments had failed to deliver on this pledge. John and Andrew's own father had been one of the Great War veterans let down by his country. The 1940 generation had been different, of course. John's Army were routed in battle, and so the people blamed them for the humiliation of Britain's defeat at the hands of Hitler's Germany. The 'Cowards of Dunkirk' is what some of the right wing newspapers had deemed to christen the 1940 veterans. Such an accusation was grossly unfair, given that Lord Halifax's cabinet had failed to co-ordinate a coherent battle plan to counter Hitler's Blitzkrieg tactics. Likewise, the War Office had botched the planned evacuation from Dunkirk harbour, and Halifax had appeased Hitler and signed a peace treaty which had effectively ended Britain's status as a great power. And yet, in spite of all this evidence to the contrary, the dishonest and slimy politicians had rewritten history to place the blame for defeat with the British fighting men. John Preston had suffered through years of this rubbish, and he'd had enough of it.

German agents and recruiters had been operating in the United Kingdom and in other parts of the British Empire for some years. Westminster was opposed to their activities, but they couldn't expel the German diplomats without causing a major diplomatic incident. And the UK government did not want to risk another war with Germany, especially now, when the Germans were so far ahead of Britain in both economic and military power.

The Nazi recruiters were primarily interested in encouraging Englishmen and their families to move to Eastern Europe, and to settle in the newly established Nazi colonies located throughout the conquered territories. Naturally, John's younger brother Andrew was keen to accept the German offer. Andrew Preston had been a long-standing supporter of Fascism and remained an ardent admirer of Adolf Hitler. For whatever reason, Andrew had been determined for John to accompany him and his family in their defection.

Naturally, John had been reluctant to follow his brother. He was a soldier who felt betrayed by his country, but it was quite another thing to defect to the enemy. But Andrew had been so persistent. He just wouldn't take no for an answer. And some of his arguments had been very compelling. It seemed that Hitler knew how to treat war veterans. There were no unemployed ex-soldiers in Germany, no Army wives queuing up for bread rations. Instead, ex-Wehrmacht men were granted vast land concessions in the former Soviet territories.

The Germans were richly rewarded for their victories in battle. Andrew frequently spoke of blonde haired young Fraus, resilient and pure German maidens seeking husbands and eager to mother many children. Perhaps this was nothing more than a fantasy, but John was still attracted by the utopian vision. In spite of Elaine's death, he still harboured a deep desire to marry and to start a family.

There were many arguments against the defection, but, in the end, the only reason which mattered was family.

John was very fond of his sister-in-law, and he adored his niece and nephew. And, in spite of everything Andrew had done over the years, John was still loyal to his brother. Nevertheless, he knew his brother was unstable and unpredictable at the best of times. There was no telling what Andrew would do out there in Eastern Europe, or wherever in hell they would end up. John reckoned it was better to stick with his brother's family, to try to protect them, rather than staying in England, where he'd be alone and no use to anyone.

And now John Preston sat on board of an old ferry crossing the English Channel, and all he could think about was the scathing final words of Colonel Wilson. He was only on the first leg of a long journey, but already he couldn't help feeling that he'd made a terrible mistake.

For John, the short boat journey across the Channel passed by in a blur. He had spent the bulk of the trip up on the deck, staring aimlessly out to sea, as he was lost in his thoughts…a prisoner of his memories. Before he knew it, they had arrived at their destination.

The ferry docked at the Port of Calais, having completed the shortest sea journey between England and the continent. A mere twenty miles, this was all that separated 'free' Britain from subjugated France. This small stretch of water had saved England from invasion during the dark summer of 1940, but it had also doomed the British Expeditionary Force to death and capture during the final battle.

The boat's crew fixed the moorings before they lowered the gangway. There were only a handful of passengers other than the Preston's. The family, all five of them, stood on the pier-side as they waited for their cases to be unloaded and their transportation to arrive. John glanced across to his brother's family - Yvonne and her children, Edward and Julie. All three looked bewildered and weary. Their physical appearance reminded him of the refugees they had encountered in Dover. He supposed they were the foreigners here, strangers in an alien land. He looked up to the blue sky above, and sighed loudly.

Andrew took note and sought to raise the spirits of his older brother, saying, "Cheer up, John mate. This is the beginning of your new life."

John looked across at his brother. He saw the smug grin on Andrew's face and he had to fight a strong urge to punch him. He turned away, muttering, "I just didn't expect to see the Colonel there, on the pier-side. It really hit me for six."

"Forget about that old fart," Andrew replied sharply. "It's because of idiots like him that Britain lost the bloody war! The man's just bitter…that's his bleeding problem!"

John nodded his head. Andrew didn't know what he was talking about. He didn't know the Colonel. But he was right on one point - John did need to forget about the ugly incident in Dover. He needed to focus on the future now. He decided to steer the conversation back to the specific details of their journey.

"Well, I suppose we'll be back on the tracks soon enough," said John. "Will we be catching the train from here, or do we need to make a transfer?"

The smile disappeared from Andrew's face. Suddenly the man looked overcome by embarrassment. He might even be feeling guilty. "No," Andrew eventually muttered, after a prolonged and awkward pause. "...No, we're not travelling to Germany straight away. The Embassy wants us to make a stop off first. There's some sort of press conference they want us to attend..."

"Press conference?" said an incredulous John. He didn't like the sound of this one bit. "What the bleeding hell are you on about? Where are the Germans taking us?"

Andrew was unable to meet his brother's eye as he muttered his answer, "Dunkirk. We're going to Dunkirk."

John Preston felt a cold chill at the very mention of the infamous Channel port. In his mind, the French harbour town was associated with so many horrific memories...the bloody battle, the humiliating defeat, and John's own injury, inflicted upon him during the course of the fight. He felt a painful twinge in his upper thigh. It was almost as if his own body was reacting to the memory of the trauma experienced on that fateful day. John was so shocked that it took him a moment to realise the significance of his brother's sudden announcement. But, after his shock had subsided, John was able to think more clearly, and it became obvious to him why the Germans wished to hold a 'press conference' in Dunkirk.

Suddenly, John Preston's fear was replaced by anger. He turned on his younger brother and unleashed a fierce verbal tirade which took Andrew off guard.

"You knew about this, didn't you?" John snapped. "You bloody well knew this is what the Krauts had planned! And you said nothing...you lied to me, you bastard! You lied to your own flesh and blood!"

Andrew glanced up and down the pier in sheer panic. He appeared to be checking if anyone had overheard John's outburst. Luckily, the pier was currently empty. The only people listening to the brothers' heated conversation were Andrew's own family. Edward and Julie both appeared to be shocked and more than a little frightened.

In contrast, Yvonne was watching the argument with an intense interest, a morbid curiosity, if you will. Andrew was still in a state of alarm. He held his hands up defensively and whispered a panicked reply into John's ear.

"Shhh! Keep it down, for God's sake. This isn't England. You can't say words like 'Krauts' over here! They'll throw us all into a bloody concentration camp, for crying out loud!"

John realised his brother was right. This wasn't the time or the place for a full blown argument. But he was still furious with Andrew, and he wanted some answers.

"You did know about this, didn't you?" he repeated. "You kept this from me…kept it a secret." John clenched his teeth, as his anger came back to the fore. "I ought to punch your bleeding teeth out!"

"Look," Andrew replied frantically, "look John, I'm bloody sorry. Is that what you want to hear? I was afraid you'd refuse to come, if I told you about this part. We'll only be in the port for a couple of hours…a couple of speeches by the Germans, a few photos by the press, and then we'll be on our way…it's a piece of cake."

John was far from convinced. He shot his brother yet another angry look.

"I know how you feel about Dunkirk," Andrew said, in a more conciliatory tone.

"You don't know a bloody thing," John shot back. "You didn't fight for your country, like I did."

This last comment seemed to get under Andrew's skin. The younger sibling looked down at his feet in apparent shame. This was a rare emotion for Andrew Preston to feel. John felt a perverse sense of satisfaction, as he knew he'd got to his brother. He'd had the last word in the argument, but this had changed little. John Preston was still in Fascist France and he would still have to go back to Dunkirk, whether he liked it or not. He was destined to revisit the scene of his nightmare.

A moment later, John's attention was drawn by movement on his right hand side. He watched on anxiously as a black Mercedes-Benz sedan sped down the pier, heading towards their docked boat. A small flag was clearly visible upon the bonnet of the car; it was the emblem of Nazi Germany, the dark swastika set against the red and white backdrop. The car looked brand new, as its surfaces gleamed in the afternoon sunshine. Vehicles like this were a rarity back in recession-struck Britain. The black sedan was soon followed by a second vehicle. Car number two was a camouflaged truck of military origin. John was an ex-military man so he recognised the truck as being a L3000 model, an all-terrain vehicle used extensively by the Wehrmacht during the war. He assumed this second vehicle would be the Preston's' lift. Not exactly travelling in style, John thought.

Now the whole family was looking in the direction of the approaching vehicles. Andrew was the only one of the five who knew anything about the plans for today, but even he seemed perplexed and agitated in this uncertain moment.

The dark sedan halted close to where the family stood. John had a disturbing feeling of de-ja-vu. The whole scene was very reminiscent of the ugly encounter on the Dover pier, only a couple of hours ago. He watched on warily as the back doors of the vehicle were flung open simultaneously. Two men emerged from the back seat. The similarities to the Dover encounter were both eerie and unsettling, because two men stepped across the concrete pier and walked determinedly towards the Preston family; one was a military officer in full uniform, and the second was surely a policeman, given his dress sense and general demeanour.

John stood motionless and wondered what the hell was going on. Even his brother looked confused and uneasy.

The two individuals continued their short march towards the Preston family. They were both Germans. This much was obvious to John. The military man wore the distinctive uniform of the Wehrmacht, and his insignia marked him out as a captain in the German Army. John estimated the man's age as late 30's or early 40's, but he looked older than his years.

As the captain came closer John noted the scar visible on the German's right cheek. A war wound, John assumed. The Wehrmacht officer had the look of a veteran, what with his hard face and his world weary eyes, long since devoid of innocence. John knew that look alright. Surprisingly though, the captain seemed fairly friendly, at least for a German. He smiled faintly as he held out his right hand, shaking with John first and then with Andrew.

"My name is Captain Henrich Muller. It is a pleasure to meet you both," he said by the way of introduction. John noted that the man spoke in word perfect English with only a slight accent. Presumably this is why the Nazis had assigned him to meet with the Preston family.

John introduced himself, as did his brother. He could tell Andrew was somewhat miffed, presumably because Muller had shaken hands with John before him. Andrew could be petty about things like that. John was impressed to witness Muller shaking hands with each member of the family in turn. The German captain had the manners of a true gentleman. He did not kiss Yvonne on the hand or the cheeks. This was the French tradition but was far too personal for a German officer. Muller spoke with both Edward and Julie, and he seemed to be attempting to put both of the teenagers at ease.

"Welcome to France," said Muller, after the initial introductions were completed. "I trust your journey was comfortable?"

"Very much so, captain," Andrew answered eagerly.

John didn't respond. His attentions were drawn to the second figure that had climbed out of the Mercedes-Benz sedan. This individual wore a dark brown leather trench coat and a black fedora hat. In contrast to Muller, this second German was far from friendly. He held back from the group and did not speak a word to any of the Preston's. Instead, he simply glared at the family with hostile and suspicious eyes. John was sure this man was not a soldier. His initial suspicion was police officer, but this German was no normal rozzer. John had heard the chilling stories of the Gestapo, and he assumed this individual was a member of that sinister organisation. He just wondered what the hell this bastard was doing here on the dockside.

Muller appeared to notice John's distraction. The captain turned his head and nodded towards the Gestapo man.

"And this is my colleague, Herr Hoffman," said Muller. "He is here to ensure our protection during the trip. Alas, my comrade speaks little English, so you must excuse his lack of words."

71

Andrew appeared satisfied by the explanation, and he was probably impressed by the fact that his family had been allocated 'police protection' for their journey eastwards. John himself was not so easily fooled.

He knew the Nazis better than his brother did, and he reckoned the real reason for Herr Hoffman's presence was to ensure the Preston family only spoke to the correct people, saw the correct sights, and didn't do or say anything that was verboten.

Muller seemed to sense the awkwardness in the group, so he elected to break the silence.

"Well, my English friends," he began, "we must 'make moves', as you say." He pointed towards the military truck parked behind the Mercedes-Benz. "Your chariot awaits."

"Don't tell me we're travelling in that old heap!" interjected Julie.

Andrew shot his daughter an angry look, but Muller merely laughed at the girl's outspoken audacity.

"I'm afraid so, young lady," answered the captain, after his laughter had subsided. "I apologise that your transportation is not more luxurious, but this 'old heap' is the best the Wehrmacht could manage. Thankfully, your journey will be relatively short."

Julie tutted. Her older brother gently punched her in the arm, as he told his sister to 'shut up'. The rest of the family, including John, picked up the family's suitcases and bags and dragged their possessions over to the waiting German vehicle.

The truck left the port with the Preston family and their meagre possessions piled into the back. John was largely silent during the drive, as he considered what humiliations would await him in Dunkirk.

He was only vaguely listening to the ongoing conversation between Captain Muller and Yvonne, who sat side-by-side on the hard bench in the rear of the van.

"Your English is excellent, Captain Muller," she commented.

"Thank you, Mrs Preston," Muller replied. "You are too kind. I did in fact study Law and English at the University of

Munich, many years ago now. As a part of my studies I spent a year visiting at Cambridge. This was before the war, of course…"

"My word," Yvonne replied. There was a smile on her face and a twinkle in her eye. "You are a most remarkable man. Tell me more, captain…"

Yvonne was blatantly ignoring the hard looks she received from her husband. Andrew was clearly jealous and annoyed by his wife's flirtation with the German officer. If John didn't know better, he could have sworn Yvonne was doing this on purpose to wind up her husband. He had no idea how in hell their marriage was going to survive the stresses and traumas of the coming journey.

He observed little of the French countryside during the road trip. Whatever he did see was through the glass portals on the side of the truck. The country appeared to be affluent. The fields were green, the livestock were plump and the farmhouses were large and well maintained. The villages they passed through appeared to be prosperous and vibrant. It seemed that this part of France had recovered well during the post-war years. Then again, appearances could be deceptive.

John doubted that everyone had prospered under the collaborating Vichy regime - and, of course, the Nazis would only let their visitors see the positives. As if to emphasise this point, John could clearly see the Mercedes-Benz sedan trailing just behind their truck. A chauffeur drove the following car, but Herr Hoffman, the sinister Gestapo man, was sitting in the back seat. And Hoffman was watching everything.

It took the two vehicle convoy less than an hour to drive the country roads between Calais and Dunkirk. John felt a cold chill whenever their vehicle approached the port town, as all of the horrible memories suddenly came back to him. Nevertheless, he experienced a morbid curiosity which prompted him to look out the portal windows, to observe the suburbs of Dunkirk as they sped by. John's initial reaction was surprise, as he couldn't quite believe how much the town had changed in eight short years. However, on second thought, this wasn't so surprising. The old town had been largely destroyed during the fierce fighting of late May and early June 1940. The Wehrmacht artillery and Luftwaffe bombers had obliterated so many of the buildings, and most of the rest had been blown up by the retreating British Army sappers. John knew there were towns and cities all across Europe which had suffered the same fate.

Britain had been lucky, since Halifax signed the peace treaty with Hitler before the Luftwaffe could commence aerial bombing of English cities. In fact, the fear of German bombs had been a major factor in frightening the British public into accepting the humiliating peace.

During the summer of 1940, London was rife with talk of the one million cardboard coffins which Chamberlain had supposedly ordered before the war.

Naturally, the French had rebuilt the port town during the interceding eight years. As they drove through the suburbs and then the town centre, John observed many new build houses, business premises and public buildings. There were barely any signs of the brutal battle which had occurred here in 1940. It was almost as if it had never happened. Nevertheless, John was not impressed with the new Dunkirk. The freshly built structures were grand but unimaginative in their design. John saw so many austere, symmetrical and ugly buildings spread throughout the town; all of which bore the depressing and oppressive hallmarks of Fascist architecture.

They reached their final destination after a few more minutes. John still remembered the rough layout of the town so he quickly realised that they were close to the harbour. This was the third port they had visited in just one day.

John briefly contemplated slipping away from the group and making his way to the piers. From there, he could attempt to board a ship bound for England. He could return to London, apologise for his catastrophic mistake and get on with the rest of his life.

He quickly dismissed this half-baked idea. There was no way Muller and Hoffman would let him get away. Not now. And besides, fleeing was the coward's way. John Preston had never run from a challenge or a danger in his whole life. And, even if he could escape, he would still be condemning his brother's family to an unknown fate. He dreaded what was to come, but John would see it through. He had no other choice but to do so.

The entire family disembarked from the back of the truck and stepped out onto the concrete paved street. Muller instructed them to leave their bags and possessions on the vehicle, because they would not be staying in Dunkirk for long. Hoffman was there too, of course. His invasive eyes were always on the Preston family. He observed them as closely as a hawk would watch its prey. The Gestapo man was soon joined by two local gendarmerie, paramilitary French policemen, dressed in their distinctive dark blue uniforms, tall hats and blue capes. Both men carried bolt-loaded carbines, slung across their shoulders, and revolvers held in holsters around their respective waists. In spite of their weapons both of the Frenchmen looked noticeably uneasy. John noted their defensive body language and guessed that the gendarmeries were frightened by their German counterpart. It was clear who still held the real power in this supposedly 'independent' France.

The family were ushered away from the vehicles by the French police officers. Next, they walked down the street and came face to face with a packed promenade set on a waterside jetty. John didn't remember this from 1940, but he didn't dwell on the structural changes to the harbour district. Instead he focussed on the almost absurd scenes occurring on the promenade.

A number of people, perhaps a couple of hundred or more, were seated in neat rows of chairs which were set along the street, facing forward, towards the sea. John saw many well-dressed men and also a few women, all seated and awaiting the start of proceedings. A low murmur could be heard from up the street, as dozens of delegates carried out hushed conversations amongst themselves. Some spoke in French, others in German. But John looked over the heads of the seated audience and to the stage in front of them.

The elevated platform was relatively small, only about twenty odd yards in length from the left to right hand side. There was a simple podium at the centre of the stage, with a microphone linked up to speakers set on either side of the platform. Behind the podium were a total of a dozen chairs, six on each side. All were

75

currently empty. But what really drew his eye were the decorations attached to the stand directly behind the stage. There were a total of three flags hanging from the stand.

In the centre was the Swastika, the infamous symbol of Nazism, the very sight of which prompted feelings of intense anger and terror. The Nazi banner was easily three times the size of the other two flags which adorned the stage. This was clearly a ploy in psychological symbolism, a demonstration that Germany was the leading nation, and all other countries were subservient to their rule. The flag on the left hand side was the Tricolour of conquered France, and to the right was the Union Jack of John Preston's own country. And now he knew why the Germans had brought him here. His heart sunk and his stomach churned. John felt as if he was going to be physically sick.

He diverted his eyes away from the ominous stage. It was only then that John saw the final piece of this farcical scene. To the right of the stage he could see a group of musicians setting up their instruments. It was a small brass band, consisting of just five members dressed in full tuxedo suits and equipped with a variety of polished wind instruments. John could only imagine what role these musicians would play in this ridiculous spectacle. He shook his head in disbelief and fought the urge to burst out in hysterics. Somehow, he didn't think Herr Hoffman of the Gestapo would take too kindly to such a display.

At that moment, John felt a firm hand on his shoulder. He turned around and came face to face with Captain Henrich Muller. The German officer looked deadly serious, although John detected a hint of sympathy in the man's eyes.

"Come on, Sergeant Preston," said Muller. "The time has arrived…"

"What the hell do they want me to do?" asked an incredulous John.

Muller came in close, whispering in John's ear. Clearly he did not want to be overheard. "General Hans von Koch is the speaker this afternoon. He is the commander of the German garrison in Northern France. Von Koch will take the podium and will give his speech. All you have to do is stand beside the General and pretend to be interested…don't worry, my English friend…it will all be over soon enough."

The captain grabbed John's arm and ushered him towards the steps leading up to the elevated stage. At the same time, a number of other delegates ascended onto the platform from the other side. Half a dozen men clambered up onto the stage and took their respective seats. They were all Germans, and mostly uniformed officers of the Wehrmacht, Luftwaffe and Kriegsmarine. These men represented just a tiny fraction of Hitler's vast war machine, the mighty army which had conquered virtually all of Europe. The German soldiers had been his enemy once, but now John Preston shared a stage with these men. The old animosities had apparently been put aside, but John would soon discover what the Nazis thought of him, the defeated ex-British soldier.

General von Koch was the last man to ascend to the platform. He marched up the steps with all the arrogant confidence one would expect from a Prussian aristocrat. His uniform was immaculate. Many shining medals adorned his grey jacket, including the Iron Cross, the most prestigious award open to the Wehrmacht. His facial features were distinguished and his moustache prominent. The general was probably in his 60's, but he looked to be in good physical shape. John had a mental image of what a German general should look like, and von Koch appeared to meet that stereotype, almost down to every last detail.

The general marched up to the podium, and every man and woman in the small audience stood up to acknowledge his entrance. Von Koch's entrance was met with a polite and prolonged applause from the assembled delegates. John looked to the faces in the crowd. He saw their sycophantic adoration of the German general. It was evident in their eyes. Some of the crowd were Wehrmacht officers, and no doubt they were obligated to show reverence to their commander. A few others were pressmen, clutching hold of their cameras and impatiently awaiting their opportunity to snap a winning photograph. However, the majority of those present were well-dressed civilians, not Germans but local Frenchmen. Collaborators, that's what they were. These were people who had benefitted from the German occupation. They had betrayed their country in exchange for money and prestigious positions. It made John feel sick, but then he realised that he and his brother were no different from them. The Preston's were traitors too.

Andrew sat a couple of rows from the front, his face beaming with pride and an almost child-like excitement. Yvonne and the two children sat by his side. Only Edward looked vaguely impressed by the proceedings. Yvonne and Julie both looked thoroughly bemused by the whole spectacle.

The general raised a single hand to summon silence. Von Koch was used to being obeyed without question. The applause stopped in an instant, and every delegate took their seat. John was standing to the side of the podium. He felt like a fish out of water, a curiosity on display like some sort of captured animal in a zoo. The general didn't even bother acknowledging his English visitor. Instead von Koch looked down to his written notes, and he began to speak out in a well-chipped Prussian accent.

His voice was authoritative and piercing, and the whole crowd listened intently to von Koch's words. There was nothing for John Preston to do but stand up on the stage and, as Muller had instructed, 'pretend to look interested'. He would need to wait until such time as von Koch summoned him to play his own small role in this farce.

The crowd was apparently mesmerised by the general's speech. John Preston was not. He understood some German, having picked up bits and pieces of the language during his time as a POW. He didn't understand every word the general said, but he did follow the overall gist of von Koch's speech.

The Prussian spoke of German military victories, of the triumph of National Socialism, the genius of the Fuhrer and the self-evident superiority of the Aryan race. It was all very predictable and tediously unoriginal. For all of his supposed greatness, General von Koch might as well have been reading out a standard release written by one of the clerks in Joseph Goebbels' Propaganda Ministry. Next, the Prussian officer spoke at length about the evils of Communism, and the need for continued vigilance, especially in the Eastern territories conquered from the former Soviet Union.

It was only during the final section of his talk that the pompous von Koch saw fit to acknowledge John's presence. He briefly looked across at John or rather he glared at him whilst barely suppressing his contempt for a defeated enemy. The general half-heartedly talked of a new era of peace between the German and British Empires.

John could see the German was struggling with the words, as presumably he didn't regard the British as his equals. Clearly von Koch himself was under orders to welcome the Preston family, although his welcome would be a cool one.

Finally, the tedious propaganda speech came to an end and John almost felt relieved, except he had a bad feeling that the worst part was still to come.

The German general turned to face John, and he introduced him as a former British soldier and veteran of the war. Von Koch didn't insult his English 'guest' in direct terms, but he made sure to stress that John had been a mere sergeant in the British Army, and he emphasised the fact that John Preston had been captured and made a prisoner during the German victory at Dunkirk.

John had to hold his tongue and fight back his rage. In his mind he fantasised about lunging for von Koch, grabbing his throat and throttling him right there in the middle of the stage. He wondered how far he would get before the Gestapo and Gendarmeries would stop him. In all probability, he'd be shot down on the spot.

The Nazi von Koch was now facing him straight on. The Prussian's cold, pitiless eyes glared right through his English adversary. John could tell this was the moment, the point where Hitler's man would demonstrate his absolute supremacy. And, sure enough, his worst fears came to pass. The German general quite suddenly lifted up his right foot, before slamming it down hard against the platform. The sound of his heavy boot impacting reverberated across the stage, as the entire audience fell deadly silent. In the next instance, von Koch raised his right arm high in the air in a sinister and monstrous salute, and he cried out two words in a booming and piercing voice;

"Heil Hitler!" shouted von Koch.

John stood perfectly still, as if he was frozen to the spot. He opened his mouth to speak, but could not find the words. Simply put, he was gobsmacked. The uncomfortable interlude could only have lasted a matter of seconds, but it was long enough to cause embarrassment and anxiety amongst the crowd. John suddenly had the inclination to glance across to his right hand side, to where his younger brother was seated. Andrew was sitting forward in his chair, looking directly at him. His eyes were full of an intense anxiety. It was almost as if Andrew was attempting to use some form of sibling telepathy. He was silently urging, pleading, with his brother to say those words.

Next, John looked back to the general. The Prussian von Koch was struggling to control himself. The German officer was used to being obeyed. He would not tolerate any form of insubordination or defiance. His face was filled up with a barely repressed fury as he stood with his right arm still aloft. Nevertheless, General von Koch could not lose his temper on this occasion. If he did, a serious diplomatic incident would surely ensue. John Preston did not want to comply. It was against everything he stood for to salute this Nazi swine...but he had to accept his situation. John wasn't in England anymore. He had made his decision and had voluntarily come to this Fascist nest of vipers. He could defy the Germans even now, but, if he did, the entire Preston family would surely end up in a concentration camp. It was this thought which swung it. John could not condemn his family to such a terrible fate. Their safety was worth more than his pride.

After a couple of more seconds delay, he met von Koch's eye, stamped his foot, and raised his right arm upwards to mimic the Prussian's Nazi salute. Next, he uttered the words in a barely audible voice;

"Heil Hitler..." said John.

His humiliating submission was complete.

John was almost blinded by the flashes of so many cameras clicking simultaneously. The photographers had captured his moment of capitulation, forever immortalising his shameful act.

Von Koch was not entirely satisfied. Clearly, he was still angry at the delay in John's salute, not to mention his half-hearted compliance. Nevertheless, the German accepted Sergeant Preston's surrender for what it was. The goal of this afternoon's farcical meeting had been achieved. The general turned back to the podium and uttered a few more words in conclusion. A moment later the audience rose as one and applauded. John saw his brother was amongst their number. Andrew clapped and cheered as loudly as anyone else present on that afternoon.

When the standing ovation died down, the band began to play. They strung out one verse of 'God Save the King' before moving on to the familiar German anthems of 'Deutschlandlied' and 'Horst Wessel'.

The musical accompaniment continued the central theme of today's event; that is the post-war hierarchy, setting the mighty German Empire above the weak and crumbling United Kingdom. This was Hitler's New World Order, his twisted vision of a National Socialist and German future. And John Preston had unwittingly played a central role in this vile propaganda. He had humiliated himself and betrayed his country.

There was no way back now...surely he could never return to England after today.

# 4/ 'The Ghosts of Dunkirk'

THE BAND FINALLY FINISHED their performance after another agonising few minutes. Right after this, General von Koch left the event without neither a bye nor leave. He descended from the stage uttering not another word to John, or to anyone else for that matter.

The other Nazis on stage rose from their seats and descended from the platform to mingle with the French Fascists in the audience. Glasses of champagne and plates of hors d'oeuvres were carried out by uniformed waiters and distributed amongst the crowd.

No one paid any attention to John. He assumed that his part in today's event was complete, so the Nazis no longer had any use for him. John had no desire to celebrate this afternoon's sick farce and took his opportunity to wander off.

Ten minutes later, John Preston was walking alone across the harbour and down the adjacent pier. He realised that Hoffman or one of his lackeys would inevitably follow him, but he didn't care. He just wanted to be alone, if only for a few short minutes. The ex-sergeant tried to swallow his anger and forget about the nauseating incident that had just occurred, but this proved to be impossible.

For John Preston, Dunkirk was a town full of ghosts. The port had changed much since 1940, but Dunkirk harbour was still filled with grim reminders of the terrible battle which had occurred here during the last war. Dark clouds were gathering in the sky above, and soon the sun disappeared from sight. He could see the whole harbour stretched out before him. The two massive concrete breakwaters were clearly visible in the foreground. He remembered the two elongated piers, which were known as East Mole and West Mole. Both had been heavily bombed by the Luftwaffe during the last days of May 1940, so much so that they became unusable to British shipping. The destruction of the twin moles was closely followed by the sinking of HMS Ivanhoe, the wreck of which partly blocked off access to the harbour.

These twin catastrophes were confounded by the continued aerial bombardment and the reluctance of Royal Navy commanders to risk further ships in the harbour. Therefore, the evacuation effort was shifted to the beaches, where men had to wade out into the tide to board small boats and civilian craft. This strategy was painfully slow, and only a couple of thousand soldiers could be evacuated per day. And all the time, the Wehrmacht panzers and storm troopers fought their way closer and closer to the harbour, as John and his comrades fought on fiercely in a vain attempt to hold them back.

John spent several minutes looking out over the harbour, as if he was mesmerised by the tide and the waves. He didn't even notice the second man approaching from his rear. The interloper interrupted John's quiet solitude, much to his annoyance. He turned around and came face to face with his English-speaking German escort, Captain Henrich Muller.

"A changeable day," stated Muller in an apparent attempt to start a conversation.

"Yes," answered John, with an intentional lack of enthusiasm. There was a slight pause before he spoke again. "I suppose you're worried I'm about to do a runner," said John, in a sarcastic tone of voice. "Maybe your friend Hoffman thinks I'll swim back across the Channel."

John regretted the words as soon as he had said them. He was worried that the factitious comment would provoke Muller's anger. Instead, he was surprised to see the captain smiling, ever so slightly.

"I am not unsympathetic to your plight, Herr Preston. If I

had been in your position today…well, it was difficult for you, I am sure."

John nodded his head but did not speak. The Wehrmacht officer appeared to be friendly, but John still did not trust him. He suspected that Muller was trying to trick him into saying something out of turn. With no reply from John forthcoming, Muller continued his solo discourse.

"You fought at Dunkirk," said Muller, as a matter of fact rather than a question. "With the British Expeditionary Force. I myself fought in the same battle as a lieutenant in the 1st Panzer Division. Perhaps we met each other on the battlefield? Maybe we traded shots during the melee?"

John looked to his adversary with some level of curiosity. He really didn't know what the German captain was getting at. Was he really trying to establish some common ground? And, if so, for what purpose?

"You know," Muller continued, as apparently he was undeterred by John's continued silence. "My opinion is that the British fought well during the campaign. The common soldiery put up a brave fight. The fault for the BEF's defeat surely lies with your weak politicians and incompetent commanders."

John was greatly surprised by Muller's admission. He had never before known a German to be gracious in victory. Today had been one of the worst of John Preston's life, but Muller's words had restored just a small part of his pride. For this he was grateful.

"Isn't this always the way in war?" John finally answered.

"The battle could have turned out differently," Muller added.

John shook his head. "We were already done by the time you pushed us back to the coast. Our only hope was a successful seaborne evacuation, but that operation was poorly planned and badly botched…"

Captain Muller looked back over his shoulder before he spoke his next words. Clearly he was checking that the men's conversation was not being overheard. John assumed that such paranoia was second nature in Hitler's Reich.

"I have a friend who worked for the OKH in Berlin, during

the war," said Henrich. "He told me the Fuhrer originally issued a Halt Order to our forces as we advanced on Dunkirk. He changed his mind for some reason, and we were ordered to continue the attack. We were all exhausted at that point of the battle, having advanced so far so quickly...but our end goal was in sight, and so we fought on. Perhaps, if our divisions had been diverted, your evacuation could have succeeded, and Britain could have fought on..."

The captain was being overly generous, and John realised his analysis was flawed.

"Perhaps," he answered. "But I suspect we would have sued for peace regardless. Halifax never wanted to continue the war. Now, if Churchill had become Prime Minister...that might have been a different story. Winston was a real fighter, not an appeaser..."

Muller smiled once again, before he responded.

"Maybe so, my English friend, maybe so. But this is all history. We are two old soldiers, with little left except for our memories..."

John couldn't have put it better himself. The two men continued to stand by the harbour and gaze out to sea, as all of the past horrors of war came flooding back...

*The 3rd of June 1940, the Port of Dunkirk*
At dusk, the bombing finally ceased. The Germans had been giving them hell for hours. John had thought it would never end. The Wehrmacht artillery bombardment had been relentless, a rain of death and destruction falling upon the defenceless French town.

Sergeant Preston and his comrades-in-arms had sheltered beneath ground during the intense shelling. This kept the platoon relatively safe and sound, but the attack had still been utterly terrifying. The men had cowered in the cellar of the small abandoned hotel, listening to the continuous bolts of lightning striking above and around them. John prayed that the building wouldn't suffer a direct hit, otherwise they would surely be burnt or buried alive. If he was going to die in this battle, John hoped he would get a bullet to the head...quick and painless. His worst fear was getting cut up or maimed by shrapnel or a land mine. Being a cripple…this was John Preston's worst nightmare.

He didn't know how long the Germans had been bombing their positions. The Luftwaffe had hit them first, and the artillery had soon followed. This was the Kraut's infamous Blitzkrieg tactic, tried and tested first on the plains of Poland, and now in the fields and lowlands of North West Europe. John had to hand it to the Hun…they had perfected the art of modern warfare, combining infantry, artillery, tanks and aircraft to produce an overwhelming and devastating attacking force.

The Germans had given the French and British a bloody good pasting during this fierce but rapid campaign. In just a few short weeks, the BEF had been pushed right back to the English Channel. And here they made their final stand, in the unassuming port town of Dunkirk.

The Germans had been bombing all day…but now, all was eerily silent. John wondered what was left of the town above their heads. The battle had been raging for five days and nights, and poor Dunkirk had taken one hell of a pounding. The sergeant thought there could hardly be a building left standing after the latest bombardment. He felt sorry for the remaining residents of this town, but this was a war, and there was no time for sentimentality.

The bombardment had ceased. In a way, this was a great relief. The psychological impact of being shelled was impossible to imagine unless you had lived through it. John remembered his father speaking of such things, on the rare occasions when he reminisced about the horrors he'd experienced during the Great War. He'd never really believed his old man, not until now.

John glanced around the room, looking into the faces of his comrades, sixteen men, all huddled inside of this cramped and damp cellar. Sixteen British soldiers….all that was left of the infantry platoon which had fought nearly non-stop for the last five days. Many had already been lost, either dead or wounded. Divisional command hadn't sent any replacements, nor would they. John knew these soldiers so well. They had slept, ate and fought together for so long. These men were John Preston's brothers in arms. He knew they were all tired, strung out and increasingly desperate. John could smell the stench of unwashed bodies, he could see the dirt on his men's faces, and he saw the fear in their eyes.

They all knew what was going to happen next. If the German guns had stopped this could only mean one thing - the Huns were getting ready to attack.

The boys needed leadership right now. They were physically exhausted, demoralised and terrified following the intense shelling, but all present would need to get upstairs and fight, if they were to have any chance of surviving what was to come.

John Preston was a sergeant, an experienced NCO with authority over the enlisted men. It was his duty to lead the young boys by example, to enforce discipline upon them, but also to do everything in his power to protect them from the living hell the Krauts were about to unleash. It was a tough job, particularly given the desperate situation the platoon now found themselves in.

But John wasn't the CO of this depleted platoon, thank God. That duty fell to young Lieutenant Henry Fitzgerald. The junior officer rose up from his seated position and strode confidently into the middle of the cellar floor, as he prepared to address his troops. Fitzgerald was only 22 years old, straight out of Sandhurst and granted his first commission in the field.

France had been a real baptism of fire for the young lieutenant, but, fair enough, Fitzgerald had risen to the challenge. John had served under several appalling officers during his decade in service. In spite of the immense failings in command during the Great War, the British Army was still notoriously elitist, and the officer corps was filled up with so many incompetent, arrogant and sometimes cowardly sons of aristocrats…young men who had supposedly learned the art of war 'on the playing fields of Eton and Harrow'. Fitzgerald had more than a hint of arrogance about him…a typical upper class sense of entitlement. But, for the most part, Henry was a decent chap.

The young lieutenant had fought well during the campaign and he'd showed strength in leadership. But now it seemed clear to John that defeat was imminent and he doubted the lieutenant or anyone else could do anything to prevent the coming catastrophe.

Nevertheless, Fitzgerald carried a youthful exuberance and optimism which seemed impossible to diminish. He stood tall, looking each and every man in the eye, before he began to speak.

"Right men," barked Fitzgerald, in his well-clipped, upper class English accent. "The Hun have thrown everything they have at us. But we're still here, and now we're going to give those swine a damn good thrashing!"

Fitzgerald smiled and briefly paused. John assumed that the officer was expecting a round of enthusiastic cheers from the enlisted men. Instead, he was met with blank faces and stony silence.

Young Henry appeared slightly deterred by this under-reaction. He sensed the negative mood of the soldiers and so decided to change tact.

"Now look here, you chaps," he said, "I know we're in a tight spot. But we must fight on...we must prevail. The honour of the British Empire depends on it..."

John knew this wasn't going to be nearly enough to motivate the soldiers, so he promptly added his own comment.

"And the longer we fight, the more of our boys get picked up from the beaches."

"Aye," cried out Private Devlin, a cheeky young Irish lad from Kilburn. "And I heard the Navy only took two thousand men yesterday...two bloody thousand! And how many of us are still here, stuck in this here hellhole?"

There were grumbles of agreement from the other men. Preston knew he would have to act fast in order to avoid a mutiny. He shot Devlin a furious look and delivered a cutting rebuttal.

"That's enough out of you, private! Bloody defeatist talk, that's what you're at! Anymore lies like this and I'll have you on a bloody court-martial!"

Devlin gave in. He looked down at his boots and shut his mouth. Preston had re-imposed authority over the platoon, but the worst thing was, he knew what Devlin was saying was the truth.

Nevertheless, Fitzgerald seemed to be grateful for his sergeant's interjection. The lieutenant nodded to John before he barked out his orders to the men.

"Right," he said determinedly, "Sergeant Preston, take three men and establish positions on the top floor...Corporal Davies, take another three to the first floor. The rest of you men will be under my command. We will hold the ground floor and secure the building...when the Krauts come up the street, wait until you see the whites in their eyes before you open fire...now, get bloody moving!"

Most of the men didn't need to be told twice, and any who did got a swift kick up the backside from Sergeant Preston.

John took his detachment and quickly ascended the staircase. His men took up firing positions along the street-facing windows and all prepared themselves for battle.

John was crouched down beside the broken window on the third floor of the building. He had his .303 Lee Enfield rifle aimed outwards to the empty street below. There were three men by his side, all of whom were squatted down in similar positions, aiming their respective weapons, holding their positions and awaiting the inevitable arrival of their German foes.

There was Private Solomon, a young Jewish soldier who hailed from the same part of the world as John, namely Whitechapel in East London. Solomon was little more than 19 years old, and he looked even younger, with his skinny and ungainly body and the boyish whiskers on his upper lip. Solomon wasn't much to look at, but he was a decent soldier and held a particular hatred for the Nazis, given their treatment of his Jewish brethren in Germany and Poland. Further down the line stood Private Mitchell, a hard-as-nails 22 year-old Cockney lad, with his muscular arms adorned with regimental tattoos. Mitchell was the biggest man in this section, and so he was armed with the Bren machine gun. He leaned the frame of his large weapon against the window still and gazed intently down the gun sights.

The final man in this detachment was Private Andrews, a wiry and foul mouthed Scotsman, originally hailing from the tenements of working class Glasgow.

There were a total of four men on the upper floor, John included. Another four were stationed on the floor directly below.

The lieutenant and seven soldiers were guarding the ground level of the hotel, lest the German infantry attempt to storm the building. Lieutenant Fitzgerald had deployed his men well. They were ready to defend their position or to mount an ambush, depending on which way the Krauts came at them. John had fought alongside these men for weeks. He'd been to the depths of hell and back with them all and he knew they were tough and brave soldiers, loyal men who would hold the line for as long as humanly possible.

Nevertheless, Sergeant Preston knew their situation was dire. The men were exhausted and demoralised, the platoon was critically under-strength and, even more seriously, weaponry was in short supply. The platoon could hold off an infantry attack, for a time at least. They still had enough small arms ammunition to engage in a prolonged fire-fight. Their real problem was the lack of anti-tank weapons. The lieutenant had requested .55 Boys anti-tank rifles from the Regiment HQ, but no new weaponry was forthcoming. Instead, the men only had a handful of Mills hand grenades each. These could be used against lightly armoured vehicles, but would be all but useless against heavy duty Panzers.

Why are we still fighting? John asked himself. He wouldn't utter these words in front of the men. Such talk would be defeatist and would destroy what little morale remained. Still, he had to ask himself this difficult question. The Germans were winning this battle. In all likelihood, they would overwhelm the British defences within the next couple of days. And the evacuation was failing. That much was obvious. By all accounts, only a fraction of the BEF had been brought back across the Channel to safety in Southern England.

The implication was obvious. Unless something drastic was done, the bulk of British Army would be captured or killed on the godforsaken beaches of Dunkirk.

John tried not to think about it. He needed to focus on the job at hand. The sergeant surveyed the street below him through the sights of his rifle. The devastation caused by the German bombardment was severe. The row of houses on the other side of the street had been reduced to burning rubble. If any civilians had remained inside their homes, they surely could not have survived.

The hotel in which the British soldiers sheltered had miraculously avoided a direct hit, although almost all of the windows had been shattered by shrapnel. The hotel was not currently on fire, but the flames from adjacent buildings could well spread and consume them all. John wasn't too worried about this danger, as he expected the fight would be over long before the hotel burnt to the ground.

His attention was drawn by a sudden movement on his left hand side. John quickly swung his rifle around and pressed on the trigger. He relaxed slightly and released his grip whenever he saw the wretched family of French civilians; a husband and wife, both clutching hold of two young children. They frantically fled from the burning house and sprinted down the street in a blind panic. The children screamed so loudly that they could be heard all the way down the road. Their piercing and terrible cries brought a chill down John's spine.

What the hell was this family still doing here? he wondered. Who in their right mind would risk their children's lives so unnecessarily? But, of course, it was easy for John to think this way. These people lived in Dunkirk. It was their home. They hadn't asked for this war, but the savage battle had destroyed their houses and everything they owned. These were the true victims of this conflict, those who were caught in the crossfire of an unyielding, merciless industrial war machine.

The sergeant continued his careful scan of the rubble strewn street. He saw another victim of the bombardment, an elderly man who was clearly far beyond help. The French pensioner lay face down and motionless on the pavement. His blood spilled out onto the stone, emanating from an invisible but clearly fatal wound. Another life snuffed out. John watched the frozen corpse for several moments. He was temporarily fixated on this dead man and found himself imagining his story. Did he have a wife? Children? Grandchildren? Why was John so worried about this one old geezer, when he'd already seen so much death? Was it because he feared his own demise could soon follow?

A few minutes later a new actor entered the macabre stage. John looked on in bewilderment as the four legged animal came out from a side alley and limped along the street. The dog was thin, mangy and filthy. The animal looked wild and half starved. Its eyes were crazed and hungry. The mutt picked up the smell of fresh meat, and suddenly its head shot up. The dog romped across the pavement and made its way straight for the dead Frenchman. The old fellow might have been the dog's owner at one point in time, but now he was the mutt's next meal. John could only watch in horror and disgust as the animal tore at the dead man's jacket and bit into his flesh. He wasn't the only one watching.

After a moment, a single shot rang out. The bullet smashed into the brickwork just above the dog's head. This direct action had the desired effect. The dog was startled by the gunshot. He abandoned his meal and scurried down the street, fleeing for his very life. The shot had come from the floor directly below John's position. He guessed that one of the enlisted men had had enough of the macabre display. He didn't blame the lad.

The lieutenant wasn't best pleased. He shouted a harsh rebuke up the stairs, telling his men to hold their fire, and warning them that their position would be given away. John didn't think the gunshot would alert the Germans to their presence. In fact, there was shooting all around them; the sharp cracks of rifles punctuated by the rat-a-tat of machine gun fire. The low intensity gunfire was so constant that it barely even registered. Such was the background din of warfare. But John knew this was merely a prelude. The real fight was still to come.

It seemed like an eternity had passed, but in actual fact it had only been a matter of a few minutes. The delay was unbearable, and the heat from the many fires grew ever more intense. But John and his men didn't have to wait for much longer. He heard the mechanical din of the approaching vehicles, and then the thump of so many heavy boots.

The German force suddenly emerged on the horizon, slowly and cautiously marching down the abandoned street. He saw them on the right hand side and soon re-aimed his rifle, setting his sights on the lead elements of the detachment. All his men did the same.

John spoke to the boys in hushed tones, ordering them to hold their fire until the last possible moment. This was the lieutenant's command, and all the section chiefs would obey their officer. John sat back from the window frame. He didn't want to risk letting the Germans see him before the ambush was set.

He warily watched the enemy's advance, taking careful note of their number and weaponry. The German force was a full platoon of 30 odd infantry men dressed in identical dark grey uniforms and armed with a mixture of Mauser 98 rifles and Schmeisser MP40 sub-machine guns. The foot soldiers were supported by two half trucks, which John recognised as being Sd. Kfz. 221 light armoured cars. He was very thankful, because this detachment wasn't supported by a Panzer. Fitzgerald's platoon was outnumbered and outgunned, but, if they could take the Krauts by surprise, the boys still had a fighting chance.

Sergeant Preston pulled back the hammer of his .303, preparing the rifle to fire. He leaned the gun against the shattered window frame and put his left hand into his jacket pocket, pulling out a Mills grenade. He was as ready as he'd ever be. The first squad of Germans would be passing by the hotel in a matter of seconds. The time was now…what the hell was the lieutenant waiting for? Damn you, Fitzgerald….Give the bloody order!

The call to battle came quite suddenly, as Fitzgerald's war cry was heard by all.

"OPEN FIRE!" he screamed.

The Germans looked upwards, their faces frozen in shock and fear. They had been taken completely by surprise, and now it was too late to escape the lethal trap. Private Mitchell fired first. He opened up with the Bren gun, raining deadly automatic gunfire down on the hapless Germans below. The din of the machine gun was ear-splitting. Spent rounds dropped to the floor, and white fire spat from the barrel of the gun. The German infantry below screamed in abject terror, as men frantically ducked for cover or attempted to return fire. John saw a German cut to shreds by Mitchell's bullets. In an instant, the young soldier's uniform turned from grey to bright red, as round after round cut through his vulnerable body.

By now everyone was firing indiscriminately. Germans fell dead or wounded, their blood spraying across the street. Some fired back at the hotel, but with little effect. John had paused to observe the shooting spree, but he soon joined in the bloodbath. He aimed his .303 at a German soldier directly ahead. The enemy had raised his own rifle, aiming towards the upper floor of the building. He didn't get a chance to get off even a single shot. John aimed at the man's torso and pulled the trigger. The .303 round tore through the German's tunic. He cried out in agony as his chest exploded in a bloody display of viscera. The soldier fell down like a lifeless rag doll. He was clearly dead. John didn't dwell on it. He pulled back the hammer to load a new round in the chamber. Next, he re-aimed, identifying a new target. A soldier was attempting to flee from the scene of carnage. His back was turned to hotel, but he was still armed and dangerous. John took aim and fired. The bullet penetrated the German's back just below his shoulder blades. He screamed and fell face down on the cobble stones below.

Two men killed in a matter of seconds. John Preston couldn't think of them as human beings. He couldn't imagine his enemies as sons, husbands and fathers. If he did so, he'd never be able to pull the trigger. It was better to disassociate completely from the enemy, to consider them as nothing more than walking uniforms, as lethal machines which would kill him and his mates, unless he killed them first. This was the only way he could live with himself…to live with what he had done.

The firing all but ceased, although sporadic shots continued. The first German squad had been virtually wiped out. The street was covered with the dead and wounded. But the survivors had reacted quickly. Their remaining number had taken cover behind piles of rubble and burnt out vehicles. They peeked over the parapet and traded shots with the British soldiers above them. These men were pinned down and effectively neutralised, but the remainder of the platoon was continuing its advance down the street, supported by the two armoured cars.

John tensed up as he saw the duo of vehicles speeding down the road. He knew the armoured cars presented a much more serious threat to his men, as their reinforced shields would resist small arms fire, and their MG34 machine guns could rain deadly fire upon the British soldiers. The lead vehicle sped along the road and the gun turret swung around towards the hotel. A second later the MG34 opened fire, spraying automatic rounds towards the exposed building. John instinctively ducked back from the window and took cover. To his relief and shame, he soon realised he was safe, as the bullets had torn into the floor below him. He was horrified to hear the screams and shouts emanating from the lower level. His comrades had taken the brunt of the attack, and now they were dying in this godforsaken hellhole. Sergeant Preston felt a fury rising up inside him. He would not let his men's deaths go answered.

He turned to the three soldiers on his right hand side and shouted out his orders, speaking loudly to be heard over the gunfire and chaos of battle.

"ALRIGHT LADS!" he screamed, "USE YOUR GRENADES AND LET THOSE BASTARDS HAVE IT! AIM FOR THE HALF TRUCKS..."

Privates Mitchell, Solomon and Andrews obeyed the order in an instant, as they lowered their guns and prepped their grenades. John did likewise. He pulled the pin on his first Mills grenade and tossed the device out of the window. His bomb landed a couple of feet short from the first German vehicle. It exploded with a bang, and the blast blew off the front right wheel of the armoured car. His men followed up with their own grenades, at least one of which hit the vehicle head on. A second later the vehicle was in flames. The men to his right were cheering, but John knew there was no time to celebrate this small triumph. The second car was still active, and even now the vehicle's driver was swinging around its MG42 machine gun turret, re-aiming in order to fire upon the upper windows. John knew he would have to work fast, otherwise they were all dead meat. He quickly took a second grenade from his satchel and pulled the pin. John tossed the bomb, praying that his aim would be true. His throw was accurate. The grenade bounced against the bonnet of the car and rolled. It detonated a second later.

*BOOM!*

The blast had failed to destroy the vehicle. John could see as much straightaway. But, on second glance, he saw that the machine gun had been torn off its turret. With its primary weapon disabled, the half truck was no longer a threat. John breathed a sigh of relief, but there was no respite from the intensity of battle.

While Preston's section had been dealing with the armoured cars, Fitzgerald's men had been giving the Kraut foot soldiers a 'damn good thrashing'. The troops on the ground floor had fired mercilessly upon the exposed enemy, and the result had been deadly. John looked back up the street and saw the German infantry retreating in disarray. Many of their number had fallen, and the survivors had taken cover wherever they could find it. John felt like crying out in triumph. Against all the odds, the undermanned and under-armed British platoon had defeated a numerically superior enemy force. They had won this small engagement on a back street in Dunkirk. It didn't mean much in the grand scheme of things, but their victory was still something. The British soldiers enjoyed their brief moment of triumph but, inevitably, it did not last.

John heard the engine before he saw the vehicle. He listened to the ominous sound of tracks rolling against concrete, and straight away he feared the worst. A moment later the tank rounded the corner and slowly advanced up the rubble strewn street. Preston recognised the armoured vehicle in an instant. It was a Panzer II tank, pride of the German armoured divisions. He felt an impending sense of doom as the tank rolled farther down the road. This is what John and the others had feared the most. Their platoon had no anti-tank weapons and no chance of winning a fight against a heavily armoured Panzer. The hotel building in which Fitzgerald's platoon were sheltered was now well in range of the tank's Kampfwagenkanone autocannon. John and his men could only watch on impotently as the Panzer's turret turned, and the gun was aimed in their direction. The tank was well out of throwing range and, in any event, their Mills grenades would not pierce its strong armour. A few men ignored all logic and fired their rifles at the now stationary Panzer II. The effect was negligible, as the bullets simply bounced off the turret.

Time seemed to stand still, as John awaited his near inevitable death. He stared down the barrel of the cannon, as it fired.

*BOOM!*

He was temporarily blinded by the flash. There was an almighty explosion, and the ground shook beneath his feet. The cannon fired again.

*BOOM!*

Another hit. He heard terrible screams emanating from the floors below. The men to his right swore aloud and ducked for cover. It took John a moment to recompose himself, and to realise what had happened. The tank had fired two high explosive rounds into the ground floor, right into the hotel lobby occupied by Lieutenant Fitzgerald and seven other men. The screams and pained cries he heard surely confirmed that the German shells had found their intended targets.

"Poor bastards," John muttered, under his breath. "They probably didn't even see it coming."

John dreaded to imagine the carnage on the ground floor. It was a miracle that the whole building hadn't collapsed as a result of the powerful blasts. He knew it wouldn't take long for the Panzer to re-aim its primary weapon and to fire upon their effectively defenceless position. In that moment, he made a split second decision. The lieutenant was surely either dead or incapacitated, therefore, it was now his responsibility to command what remained of the platoon. To stay here would be suicide, and so, John would order his men to retreat, to flee through the back of the hotel and make their way to the harbour. At least he could give the three men in his section a sporting chance of survival.

He was about to shout the retreat order when his attention was suddenly drawn to the street below. He saw the enemy too late. By the time he had raised his rifle, the shooting had already commenced. There was a burst of heavy automatic gunfire. Bullets tore through the shattered window frames of the upper floor. There was a cry from his right hand side. He glanced across just in time to see Private Solomon's head exploding into a red mist of blood and gore.

The Jewish soldier fell down to the floor. He had been hit in the head by a round which had easily penetrated his tin helmet. In all probability, the poor boy had been killed instantly.

John reacted quickly. He aimed his rifle at the shooter, a MP40 wielding German soldier who had emerged from cover to kill Private Solomon. He fired but missed his target by about six inches. The German could have ducked back into cover, but he did not. Instead, the infantryman raised his sub-machine gun, aimed and fired. John felt a searing, excruciating pain in his right leg. He fell back, clutching at his thigh. Hot blood poured from his open bullet wound. The agony was worse than anything he had ever experienced. He felt he was about to pass out. He was only vaguely aware of events occurring on the floor.

Through his pain, he saw Private Mitchell return fire with his Bren gun, while Andrews ran to his aid. But it was all to no avail. There was a blinding light and a deafening explosion. The heat was so intense that it burnt his exposed skin. John's terror was so all encompassing that, for a moment, he forgot all about the bullet in his leg.

The room started collapsing around him, and then, the whole world turned black.

# Book Two

## The Lair of the Beast

# 5/ 'Welcome to Berlin'

IT HAD BEEN TWO days since the Preston family's unexpected stop off in Dunkirk. Forty eight hours since John's humiliating submission to the Hun. Yvonne felt bad for her brother-in-law. She could only imagine how degrading the whole experience had been for him. She was also furious with her husband, because he'd known about the whole thing beforehand, but had not thought to tell his older brother. Then again, John had made the conscious decision to defect into Nazi Germany. He'd had a choice, which was more than Yvonne had got.

There had been plenty of time to dwell on the damaging events of two days ago, but there'd been little or no opportunity to discuss it in private. The Germans were always there, always listening. Captain Muller seemed to be okay. He acted and spoke like a gentleman, and treated Yvonne and her children with respect. Yvonne had even seen fit to flirt with the Wehrmacht officer, although she had only done so to wind up her bastard of a husband. And sure, Muller seemed alright, but he was still a German, and Yvonne didn't fully trust him. And then there was that piece of work, Hoffman. The Gestapo man was a vile creature. Yvonne could tell this much from his demeanour and behaviour. His predatory eyes were always on her; eyeing her up as if she was nothing more than a piece of meat. Yvonne didn't want that animal anywhere near her children. It made her sick just to be in his presence.

The last two days had been spent in transit. Their party had travelled by car to Bruges and, after an overnight stop in a local hotel they had travelled by train across the Low Countries and into the heart of Germany. Their train had sped through beautiful countryside and idyllic German villages, but Yvonne didn't care. Andrew loved every minute of the journey, but Yvonne wasn't interested in the scenery. She didn't want to be here.

She dozed during the long trip and day dreamed about England; the green and pleasant land. She remembered the childhood holidays her family had taken in Ramsgate, so many years ago. Would she ever see her home again? And what about her parents? Yvonne wouldn't be able to visit them ever. Even writing would be difficult, as the postal services between Germany and England were infrequent, and all letters were subjected to heavy censoring. It made her feel like screaming out every time she thought about it. Damn you, Andrew, damn you to Hell!

The train journey had been difficult, to say the least. The entire family was piled into the same small carriage, along with their German escorts. Edward and Julie had been fighting nearly the whole time, John had been moping about in self-pity and Andrew was annoyingly upbeat, not to mention oblivious regarding his family's feelings.

By the end of the trip Yvonne was just about ready to kill somebody. She was almost relieved to reach their destination, although she despaired whenever she thought about the next leg of their journey.

Berlin, the mighty capital of the German Reich. Their train was stopping in the city overnight, and the Preston family's escorts had arranged a tour of the capital for them all. Yvonne had felt a growing sense of dread as their locomotive drove through the suburbs, passing by the huge factories and neat rows of workers' houses. She didn't particularly want to see Berlin. Why would she? The big city would only remind her of London, of all she had left behind. She would have rather stayed onboard the train, but somehow she doubted that Herr Hoffman would allow this.

Besides, Edward and Julie were going stir crazy, so they were both desperate to get out of the carriage and see the sights. Yvonne wouldn't let her children walk around this hellish place without her there to look after them. She was very anxious, as there was no telling what awaited them.

The train pulled into the platform at Zoologischer Garten, a huge and sprawling railway station which appeared to serve several different lines. It reminded Yvonne of Victoria Station in central London, from where they had started their journey.

The family struggled through the large crowds. Yvonne avoided the harsh looks of the locals, Berliners who glared at the obvious outsiders and whispered scathing comments in an incomprehensible tongue. She kept her head down and kept her children close.

Muller and Hoffman were met by a pair of uniformed men at the turnstile; two soldiers with handguns in holsters around their waists. Or perhaps they were policemen. Yvonne couldn't tell. She didn't think there was much difference between a soldier and a 'bobbie' here in Germany.

Hoffman stopped to speak with the two men. Judging by their submissive demeanour, Yvonne guessed that the pair of soldiers was subordinate to Herr Hoffman.

Both gave a Nazi salute to the Gestapo man before they received their orders. Muller was quickly on hand to explain the plans to the English speaking Preston's.

"My friends," he began, "Herr Hoffman has been kind enough to organise transportation for our party. Mrs. Preston, Master Edward and Miss Julie will come with me in the first car and we will travel to your hotel. The gentlemen will travel with Herr Hoffman. I understand you are both to attend a meeting with important Party delegates…"

"Bollocks to that!" John interjected. "I'm not going anywhere with that swine."

Andrew shot his brother an angry look.

"What the hell is the matter with you, John?" he demanded.

"I'm not going to be their bleeding poster boy again!" John replied indignantly. "They'll be no repeat of that bloody disgraceful debacle in Dunkirk. The bastards will have to shoot me first!"

His older brother's furious defiance was obviously very unsettling for Andrew. Yvonne watched her husband closely, expecting an angry reaction. However, Andrew appeared to be paralysed in shock, and for once in his life the man was left speechless.

Yvonne was worried about how the Germans would respond to her brother-in-law's outburst. You couldn't just say what you really felt, not in this country. Luckily, only Muller himself had heard John's defiant little speech. Yvonne was surprised because the German captain wasn't angered by the words of his English adversary. Instead, Henrich appeared to be amused by the whole affair. She even detected a faint smile on the German man's lips. This moment could have been a dangerous one, but Muller soon took control of the situation, as he ushered the family through the turnstiles and out onto the street beyond, where two dark coloured Volkswagen sedan cars awaited them. Yvonne and her teenage children were shepherded into the back seat of the first vehicle, and soon they were on the move.

The drive through central Berlin was short but eventful. One of the young soldiers they met at the train station was driving; a skinny blond haired boy with hazelnut eyes. He sped through the streets with a purpose, as other traffic yielded and made way.

Yvonne guessed the other drivers recognised their Volkswagen as being a government vehicle on official business. Presumably this is why they allowed their car right of way. Maybe the Nazis expected her to be impressed by this 'VIP' treatment, but Yvonne couldn't have cared less. She was in no hurry to get to her final destination.

Their escort, Captain Muller, sat in the front passenger seat. He frequently turned his head to speak with Yvonne and her children, to indicate points of interest or tourist attractions. Muller's smile was presumably meant to put the family at ease, but Yvonne couldn't tell whether the German was genuine or not.

Was he nothing more than a charming sociopath? Yvonne had fallen for such a man once before, and she'd vowed never to do so again. She smiled back at Muller and exchanged meaningless pleasantries, but deep down she just wished the German would shut up and leave her alone.

Yvonne sat in the middle seat with her teenage children on either side of her. This wasn't her preference, but it was better than having Edward and Julie fighting the whole time. Julie was in one of her moods. Fourteen was a difficult age for a girl, and she was a bolshie young lady at the best of times. Edward was staring out of the right hand side window, his eyes wide open and filled with excitement and wonder. Her son seemed thrilled to be in the German capital. This was all one big adventure for the boy, and Edward was so eager to please his father. He still looked up to his dad and viewed him as some sort of hero.

Yvonne couldn't bring herself to tell Edward the truth about his father, as tempted as she often was to do so. Her son would find out the truth himself soon enough, and God help him when that day came.

At first, Yvonne had little interest in seeing the streets of Berlin, as they whizzed through the city in their fast Volkswagen sedan. However, eventually her curiosity did get the better of her. She stared out of the left and right back seat windows, looking over the heads of her children. She was surprised and impressed by what she saw. She had expected Berlin to be much the same as London was these days; grimy and decrepit, with the signs of decay and decline evident on every street corner. The reality was quite different. Berlin appeared to be filled with expensive boutique shops, selling the latest fashions and consumer goods. She saw bakeries, their windows displaying full loaves, cakes and buns. Next, the car passed a butchers selling fresh cuts of high quality beef, venison and pork. There was no offal or black bread for sale here, nor were their long queues of housewives waiting outside, anxiously clutching a hold of their ration cards and praying that stocks would last. At first sight, Berlin seemed very different to her hometown. This city was affluent and well fed. In contrast, the London she'd left was impoverished and half starved.

The shops and businesses were busy and seemingly successful, and the streets were tidy and well ordered. But this wasn't all. The Berliners themselves looked like a better class of people. The men strode confidently along the pavements with their heads held high. Their demeanour and body language suggested a self-assured attitude and an industrious demeanour. Yvonne compared these German men to their English contemporaries, the thousands of shabby and down trodden individuals who queued for hours outside of the Labour Exchange, collecting their meagre dole money and searching for jobs which were never there. The male Berliners wore lavish, tailored three piece suits or immaculate military style uniforms of various types. And then she saw the women.

Yvonne had heard much about German women. Andrew frequently spoke of blonde haired maidens wearing pigtails and lederhosen; pure Aryan virgins with ample bosoms and child bearing hips. Yvonne had always been disgusted by her husband's sick sexual fantasies, and she paid little notice to his pro-Nazi ramblings. She had held her own preconceptions about how German women would look. She imagined hard faced, humourless sourpusses with broad shoulders and almost masculine features. Aryan maidens and miserable old bats; Yvonne didn't see either type of women on these Berlin streets. The girls and ladies she did see were attractive, elegant and sophisticated. They wore the latest fashions, the type of which was only available to the very wealthy back in England.

She watched on enviously as their long floral dresses flowed in the gentle summer breeze. She glared with jealousy at their designer high heeled shoes and flamboyant headwear, and suddenly she felt extremely self-conscious. She looked down at her own dull and conservative dark dress and worn old jacket. She hadn't been able to afford any new clothes in years. She was just glad to be inside the car, as opposed to out on the pavement. She couldn't have dealt with having those women staring at her, judging her with an arrogant contempt.

So this is Germany. She hadn't expected this, but now it made perfect sense. Germany had won the war. They had conquered all of Europe and must have accumulated vast wealth and fortune. The German people were arrogant because they were winners. They had defeated every country on the continent and now they were enjoying the fruits of their many victories. In that moment, Yvonne felt as if her husband had been right all along. Perhaps the Germans really were superior. Certainly their Empire appeared to be in its ascendency, while the British Empire was clearly in crisis. It brought her no joy to admit that Andrew could be right. Nevertheless, Yvonne did feel just a glimmer of hope in that moment. Perhaps their new life in Germany wouldn't be so bad after all. Maybe she could make this work for her family, for her children.

The car sped onwards. The traffic was busy in this part of town. Their driver soon grew tired of waiting so he turned off the main road and onto a side street. If the German driver thought this detour would hasten their journey, he was sadly mistaken. The route was blocked by a parked truck and the street was too narrow to pass it. Two young workmen wearing overalls were unloading building materials from the back of the stationary vehicle. They didn't appear to notice the Volkswagen sedan at first. A moment later the impatient driver beeped his horn and furiously shouted at the men, demanding that they move their truck and clear the road. Both workmen looked back nervously at the sedan. Yvonne reckoned the boys were intimidated by what was clearly a government car on official business.

One of the men raised a hand apologetically. Both of the workers quickened their pace, as they rushed to unload their bags of concrete and assorted building equipment. In the meantime, they could not move forward, so there was nothing to do but wait. The driver sighed aloud and swore in frustration, but a stern couple of words from Captain Muller were enough to silence the man.

Yvonne and the kids took the opportunity to look out of the car windows and take in the scenery, such as it was. There was a large building site on their right hand side. Yvonne looked upwards and saw scaffolding as far up as the eye could see. In front of the site stood a tall fence with barbed wire on the top. It was hard for her to tell what exactly they were constructing; maybe an office building or a block of flats. She had noticed a lot of building work going on all across Berlin. She was curious and decided to ask Muller why this was.

"Our capital is being rapidly rebuilt by the government," Muller explained. "The Fuhrer plans to make Berlin the greatest city in the entire world, and he has commissioned the Reich's chief architect, Herr Albert Speer, to design the New Berlin and to oversee the works. These constructions you have seen are minute in comparison to the Welthauptstadt Germania project, which we shall see later today."

Yvonne's curiosity was satisfied. It made perfect sense, of course. Germany was a wealthy, victorious and dominant country, full of energy and new ideas. They needed a magnificent and world class capital city in order to reflect the great ambition of the German people.

Yvonne suddenly realised how her thoughts were becoming so similar to the ideas communicated by her Nazi-loving husband. This realisation frightened her considerably.

Their wait went on for the next couple of minutes. Yvonne's attention was again drawn to her right hand side, whenever she saw the gate leading into the construction site swinging open. It was only then that she noticed how strong and high the gate and fence actually were. And the barbed wire on top of the barrier was razor sharp. Clearly whoever was in charge of this construction project was keen on security, and Yvonne would soon discover why.

A moment later a number of individuals began to exit the building site and slowly walk out across the road. Around ten or so people tumbled out through the gate, and more soon followed.

Yvonne immediately noted the physical appearances of this new group. They looked very different from the well dressed and self-assured Berliners she had seen thus far.

In sharp contrast to the affluent city dwellers, these people looked dirty, hungry and tired. Their clothes were ragged and filthy. Their demeanour and body language was also very different, as they shuffled along with their backs slumped and heads down. But the most shocking aspect was their physical condition. These people were thin, many showed signs of malnutrition, and several wore bandages or walked with crutches.

The group were mostly men of various ages, but Yvonne saw some women too...and children! God help those poor children. Yvonne had known and lived amongst the working poor of East London, but this lot was in an even sorrier state than the East Enders. If they reminded Yvonne of anyone, it was the ragged and desperate refugees they had seen on the dockside back at Dover. The memory chilled her to the bone.

She sat forward in her chair and asked, "Who on Earth are these people? They look bloody terrible."

Henrich glanced over at the ragged group, whose number had now swelled to approximately one hundred. They passed in front of the Volkswagen, not daring to look upon the passengers inside of the sedan car.

Henrich appeared nervous and uncomfortable in this situation. He obviously hadn't expected to run into these poor wretches on this afternoon's drive.

"These people are guest workers," he finally answered, after a moment's delay. "They come from many countries, but mostly from Eastern Europe..." He paused briefly and looked as if he was about to elaborate, but then simply added, "They work on the construction sites, helping us to build the New Berlin. They work on sites all across the city..."

Muller would say no more, but Yvonne was in no way satisfied by his explanation. These poor sods certainly didn't look like 'guests' to her, more like slave labourers. How did they come to be here? Not by choice surely.

These people came from counties which had been conquered and colonised by the Nazis, so why in God's name would they come to Berlin voluntarily, to help build a new capital for their hated German enemy?

It made no sense. It was more likely the case that the Eastern Europeans were prisoners, taken from their homes under duress and forced to work for their Nazi masters. This was surely the dark side of Berlin, the part that their 'escorts' hadn't wanted them to see.

Yvonne silently scolded herself for her naivety. The Germans may be wealthy and over indulged, and their capital was ever growing. But it was all based on a lie.

The masters were living happy because they had foreign slave labour to do all the work for them. Henrich had spoken of construction sites all across Berlin. How many such people were working in this city? Thousands? Tens of thousands? And what about the rest of the German Empire? Yvonne shuddered to think.

As if to confirm her worst suspicions, she saw another smaller group of men exiting the site through the front gate. There were half a dozen in total and they confidently marched out of the construction site, following the mob of trudging workers. The six men were all dressed in dark uniforms. They were large, muscular, neat and clean shaven. Their appearance was in stark contrast to that of the Slavic males. Yvonne guessed that the half dozen were native Germans. They all carried elongated objects in their hands which, at second glance, she recognised as being batons. Clearly these men were guards, or perhaps 'overseers' would be a better description of their role.

The overseers descended on the much larger group of slave workers. They split up, each taking control of a section of people. They shouted furiously at the Slavs, screaming out orders in harsh German. Many of the workers looked visibly agitated and most quickened their pace as they crossed the road. Those who didn't or couldn't speed up were 'motivated' by a hard baton strike to their back. Yvonne winced every time she saw a hit. This clearly was a well-practised technique. There were only six overseers controlling over one hundred slaves. If the Slavs had wanted to, they could surely have overpowered the heavily outnumbered Germans. But the slaves looked so cowed and submissive that Yvonne couldn't imagine them rebelling against their Aryan masters.

Only then did she notice that both her children were also transfixed by the terrible scene unfolding on the street in front of them.

Edward looked on with a mixture of curiosity and bewilderment evident in his young eyes. Julie sat forward in her seat. Her mouth was wide open in shock, and the look on her face was one of disgust and fury. Yvonne knew how strongly her daughter felt about injustice and people being treated unfairly. She was also very clever, so had surely realised what was going on here.

Yvonne was worried that her daughter would open her mouth and say something unwise. She knew that the Germans wouldn't take kindly to any criticism of their society or practices.

"Schnell! Schnell!" the guards screamed, as they continued to lash out with their batons without receiving even the slightest provocation. Several of the put upon Slavic workers yelped or cried out in pain, but the majority simply took the abuse and made their way to the assembly point on the far side of the road.

Yvonne spotted one elderly man who could have been in his 60's or 70's. It was hard to tell. He walked with a bad limp and with the assistance of an old crutch. Clearly the poor old fellow was struggling to keep up with the rest of the group, and he soon fell behind the others.

A few of the workers looked back sympathetically at their struggling comrade, but not one attempted to help him. Presumably they were all too afraid of their overseers to take the risk.

The limping old man soon fell further behind the rest of the group, and he came to the attention of one of the German guards. The baton-wielding thug screamed at the poor old fellow. He demanded that the stricken individual quicken his pace, even though he was clearly physically incapable of doing so. Yvonne wondered what kind of hard, back breaking labour the Nazis had forced this pitiful, elderly man to participate in. She shuddered to think.

Predictably, the aged slave was unable to catch up with the rest of the group. The German guard gave up on his shouting and instead approached his victim with a malicious intent, his baton raised high and ready to strike. Yvonne and her children could only watch on in shocked horror as the violent scene played out in front of their very eyes.

The old Slav saw his assailant approaching but, to Yvonne's astonishment, he made no attempt to defend himself, or even to flee from the inevitable attack. Instead, he stood up tall on his crutch and looked his attacker straight in the eye. The German took no heed. He raised his baton and savagely struck his victim across the face. The old man dropped his crutch and fell to the pavement. He raised his hands up to his face, as crimson blood spilled from the fresh gash on his forehead. The guard was not satisfied. He raised his baton up and struck the man, again and again and again....Yvonne felt every hit. She saw the blood and heard the sickening cracks of bones breaking. It was a ghastly spectacle to watch, and yet she could not avert her eyes from this violent scene.

It suddenly occurred to her that her children were also being exposed to this brutal savagery. As a mother, she wanted to shield her offspring from such horrors, but she was powerless to do so.

The scene was too much even for the masculine Edward. His eyes were wide open in shock and his face was pale. Yvonne was worried that her son was about to vomit all over the back seat of the car, but thankfully the boy managed to control himself. Predictably, Julie reacted with indignant outrage after witnessing the savage attack.

She could not hold her tongue any longer.

"They can't do that!" she cried out, with a raw emotion evident in her voice. "They can't treat that poor man like this! He hasn't done anything to anyone! Someone has to stop them!"

Captain Muller had remained ominously silent throughout this whole ugly incident, but he reacted promptly to Julie's angry outburst. The German officer turned around sharply in his seat and he glared sternly straight at Julie.

Yvonne knew her daughter. The girl was rebellious and not easily intimidated. She met Henrich's glare and remained defiant in the face of his rebuke. Muller saw he was getting nowhere with the girl and turned to Yvonne.

"Your daughter needs to be careful about what she says," he warned. "This is not England. We use different methods here in the German Reich."

But Julie started off on another angry rant.

"You Nazis are a bunch of thugs and bullies! And..."

"That's enough, Julie!" Yvonne interjected.

Her daughter shot her a look of surprise and annoyance. "But mother…," said Julie.

"But nothing!" Yvonne replied firmly. "We will talk about this later."

Julie wasn't happy, but she obeyed her mother and did not utter another word. Yvonne felt guilty, because she knew Julie was right. What had happened to this elderly man was a bloody disgrace, and she was sure this wasn't just an isolated incident. At the same time, however, Germany was a dangerous place. As Muller had pointed out, you couldn't just criticise the government in this country. There was no freedom of speech. Yvonne didn't know what the Nazis would do to her daughter, but she was determined not to let any harm come to either of her children. Protecting her offspring was always a mother's first priority.

When the beating finally stopped, the victim lay motionless on the pavement. He was at least unconscious, and probably more seriously injured. His wounds looked severe. The German guard couldn't care less. He seemed pleased with himself, in fact, and sauntered away from his battered victim, waving his bloodied baton in the air, a sick and sadistic smile on his lips.

The other five guards were keeping a close eye on the hundred or so Slavs assembled on the other side of the street, and Yvonne wondered how they would react to the savage beating of the most vulnerable of their number. Some looked angry or upset, but the majority appeared numb and emotionless. It was as if this violent scene was something they saw every day of their lives, and perhaps it was.

By now, the delivery truck had finally moved on, and the street in front of them was clear. Their driver put his foot down on the accelerator pedal and the Volkswagen sedan sped onwards. Yvonne looked into the rear view window and saw the broken body of the elderly Slav. God knows what would become of him now, she wondered, and she felt sick.

She would not forget what had happened here today, on an obscure backstreet of central Berlin. She had seen the true face of the Nazis, the violent brutality which lay just underneath the false façade of the seemingly affluent and successful German capital.

And what would await her family, when they finally reached their new home? Yvonne dreaded to think.

Her worst nightmares couldn't prepare her for the horrors still to come.

# 6/ 'Beer Hall'

JOHN PRESTON HAD SUCCEEDED in his modest ambition of temporarily escaping from his Gestapo escorts. The Krauts had wanted him to go along to some sort of Nazi meeting or rally, but John was having none of it. They had tricked and coerced him into participating in that humiliating spectacle back in Dunkirk.

The terrible memory of his shameful submission would likely haunt him for the rest of his days. John couldn't go through that again, he just couldn't.

Hoffman and his young henchman had attempted to shepherd the two Preston brothers into a waiting car, after they left the train station. Andrew had gone along willingly, of course. The bloody fool actually thought he was going to meet Adolf Hitler. John had other ideas.

He took advantage of the heaving mass of commuters pushing out through the turnstiles. He was able to blend into the crowd and quickly disappear before the Gestapo men even realised he was missing. He felt ever so slightly pleased with himself as he strolled down the city street and avoided the suspicious glares of so many native Berliners. It was a small victory on his part. He knew he wouldn't be free for long. The Gestapo probably had spies everywhere in this city and John stood out like a sore thumb. The authorities would catch up with him soon enough, but if he managed to win just a couple of hours of freedom, he would be happy. In fact, there was only one thing he wanted to do right now. He wanted to find a quiet backstreet pub somewhere and get himself a pint.

It took him longer than expected to achieve his objective. Eventually, he escaped from the large crowds and found himself in a quieter, shabbier part of the town. It was there that he found the type of establishment he'd been looking for. He saw the run down old building with its smoky windows and decrepit signage. This business stood in sharp contrast to the other establishments he'd seen during his short walk through Berlin city centre. He had been to a lot of towns and cities during his time in the Army and he knew there were always pubs like this, hidden away in dark corners and well away from prying eyes.

He recognised just one word on the sign above the door - 'Bier Haus'.

He reckoned this old place would suit him just fine and sauntered in through the front door, feeling some degree of trepidation.

He adjusted his eyes to the dim light and breathed in the thick smoke as he stifled a cough, before realising the establishment was nearly empty. This wasn't much of a surprise given that it was a weekday afternoon.

The few patrons in the bar appeared to be regulars, all men and mostly of an advanced age. He saw old lads with white hair and wrinkled skin, dressed in worn-out old suits. Some wore military medals on their civilian jackets, so he assumed they must be veterans of the 1914-18 war.

Everyone was staring right at him. They obviously weren't used to seeing strangers in their pub. Their glares were suspicious, if not outright hostile. He reckoned it was not a good idea to advertise the fact he was an Englishman. Some of them had probably fought against his father, back in the Great War.

There was one patron who appeared friendly, a balding fellow with a gut belly who sat at the far end of the bar. He looked pretty worse for wear. The chap greeted John by raising a tankard of beer and succeeded in spilling half of the contents on the floor. He followed up by uttering a sentence which would have been incomprehensible to John even if he spoke fluent German.

John ignored the drunk and made his way to the bar. The landlord was younger than most of his patrons, possibly in his late 40s. His hair was turning grey, he had bags under his eyes and his skin had a yellow tint to it, probably as a result of years of heavy smoking. The barman looked a lot like the establishment in fact; worn out and past his best.

The proprietor was not welcoming. He glared at John, looking him up and down with suspicion and contempt. There was no greeting, just a single word of cold acknowledgement.

"Ja?" said the landlord.

John was in no mood for conversation himself, and, in any event, his command of spoken German was limited. He replied simply by giving the man his order.

"Ein großer Bier," said John, trying to disguise his English accent but probably failing miserably.

The German barman looked at him with a heightened suspicion. An uncomfortable moment passed but, in the end, he grunted in acknowledgement and shifted across to the pumps, where he poured a beer.

The glass was banged down unceremoniously on the counter and John was surprised by the sheer size of the tankard, which was almost twice the size of an English pint. He promptly paid for it with a few of the Reichspfening coins the Germans had given him as spending money before finding a quiet booth in a dark and abandoned corner.

He sat down in his booth and took a deep breath as he enjoyed his temporary respite. He remembered another pub at another time…the public bar in King David's Hotel, Jerusalem. The day of the bombing…the day when his Elaine had died.

John had so many bad memories he wished he could erase. But this was impossible. The ghosts of his past would stay with him always.

*You should be bloody ashamed, Sergeant Preston!*

That's what the Colonel had said to him on the day they left Dover, and his former CO had been spot on. John did feel

115

thoroughly ashamed. Right now, he wished the ground would open and swallow him up.

He tried to drown his sorrows by drinking his beer, and was pleasantly surprised by its fine taste; it was definitely stronger and more flavoursome than the English variety, but this wasn't a huge surprise because he had heard that German ale was better, and had long suspected that the English pints were heavily watered down. Perhaps being able to get a decent pint was just another spoil of victory; this he could at least appreciate.

Nursing his beer, he could hardly believe his life had turned out this way. If only he could go back in time just a couple of days, he would have made a better decision and he briefly considered leaving the pub to seek out the British Embassy to apply for sanctuary and repatriation back to England.

He quickly rejected the foolhardy idea. It was unlikely he would make it to the Embassy without being picked up by the Gestapo or local police. Even if he did reach the consulate, he doubted the UK authorities would accept him, given his status as a traitor to Britain. But, ultimately, he could not abandon his sister-in-law, his nephew and his niece to an uncertain fate in this hellish country and he arrived at the grim realisation that he was trapped. There was no way out for him. His ugly situation left him feeling utterly depressed. All he could do was drink.

Suddenly, a ruckus from the far side of the bar drew his attention. He looked up and saw his friend at the bar, the portly and balding drunk who had greeted him when he entered the pub. The heavily intoxicated man had managed to stand up, though he was swaying back and forth, waving his tankard in the air, and singing aloud.

"Links, links, links, links," he sang. "Die Trommeln werden gerührt! Links, links, links, links – Der Rote Wedding marschiert!"

John knew enough German to get the gist of the ditty. Links meant 'left' or 'to the left', Rote was 'Red' and marschiert translated as 'to march' or 'the march'.

He was surprised, because the lyrics sounded like they were from a Communist song. Why on Earth would this fool be singing a Red ditty in a Nazi pub? Was he mad or just plain stupid?

John wasn't the only customer who took notice of the drunkard's impromptu singsong. The landlord shouted at him to stop at once and several of the army veterans stood up from their seats, angrily shaking their fists or walking sticks.

The drunk either didn't notice or didn't care. He sang louder, eventually reaching the final chorus. "…Proletarier, ihr müsst rüsten – Rot Front! Rot Front!" *Red Front*, the battle cry of the Bolsheviks, the mortal enemies of National Socialism.

John couldn't help but flash the drunkard a smile and a wink, as the old fellow proudly finished his defiant political anthem. His fellow pub patrons were not as appreciative. They jeered and booed, but he didn't care.

The drunkard simply waved his hands dismissively and fell back down on his stool, before he lifted his tankard up to his mouth and started to drink. John was slightly disappointed by the sudden end to the bar room drama, but he didn't have to wait long for his next surprise.

The front door of the pub swung open and the barman nodded curtly and greeted Captain Henrich Muller.

The bastard had found him. John had hoped to have more time before his German chaperones tracked him down. He hadn't even had the bloody time to finish his pint!

Muller strode across the bar room floor towards John and said, "Good afternoon, my English friend. You are a difficult man to find, Ja?"

"Not difficult enough, apparently," John replied, in a sarcastic tone.

Muller's smile grew broader. He stood over the table, saying, "I suppose you wouldn't believe me if I told you I was a regular patron of this establishment?"

This time it was John's turn to smile. "Somehow," he answered, "I don't think this is your kind of pub."

"You'd be surprised," Muller answered coyly, and without elaborating.

"I suppose I'm in trouble then?" John asked, although he did not bother to wait for an answer. "I hope you'll at least let me finish my beer?"

"Actually," said Henrich. "I was hoping to join you for a drink. It is my round, as you say in England."

John was baffled and dumbstruck, but he gladly accepted Muller's offer of a beer. After all, this would be the first time a German had ever bought him a pint. Henrich proceeded to the bar and returned shortly after with two large tankards in each hand. He laid the beers down on the table and took a seat facing John. Next, he raised his tankard and said, "Prost, Sergeant Preston."

John paused for a moment before accepting Muller's apparent show of friendship. He raised his own tankard and clinked it against that of his compatriot.

"Cheers, Captain Muller," he replied.

John felt more at ease in that moment. Muller was his enemy on paper but, right now, he felt like a friend. And maybe the German captain was the only friend he had left.

"I thought you were travelling with Yvonne and the young ones?" John asked.

"Yes," Muller replied coolly. "We brought them to the hotel where they are currently resting. Your brother is attending the planned meeting. The idea was for your entire family to meet this afternoon to attend the Party rally. I'm afraid your actions have disturbed our timetable, Sergeant Preston. Herr Hoffman is not overly pleased with you…"

"What's he going to do?" John asked, in a dismissive tone. He tried not to show his fear.

"Don't concern yourself, Mr. Preston," Henrich replied. "I can deal with Hoffman. I'm just thankful that you didn't attempt to flee to the British Embassy. If so, I wouldn't have been able to help you…such a rash action would have earned you a one way trip to Prinz-Albrecht-Straße."

John shuddered at the very mention of the notorious Gestapo headquarters, where brutal tortures and summary executions were said to take place on an almost daily basis. He thanked his lucky stars that he hadn't acted on his earlier impulse to seek out the UK consulate.

"Your brother was quite annoyed by your disappearance," stated Henrich. John simply nodded his head in acknowledgement.

"You and your brother are quite different, I believe…" Muller was trying to start a conversation, but John wasn't keen. He didn't like the German officer probing even further into his family's affairs. He decided to change tact.

"Do you have any brothers?" John asked.

He was surprised at Henrich's reaction to his question. A terrible sadness seemed to come over the German. He averted his eyes, looking down at the floor. There was an awkward pause before Muller finally answered.

"…I did have a younger brother," he muttered, "but he died…"

John felt sorry. He may be a German, but Henrich was still a human being. He wondered how Muller's brother had died. Was he killed during the war? He didn't feel comfortable asking, so he remained quiet. Muller was the one who eventually broke the silence.

"How long were you in the British Army?" he enquired, curious.

"The best part of fifteen years," John answered, as he was grateful for the change in subject. "I went back into service in 1941, after my stint as a POW. They said I wasn't fit for overseas service again, because of the injury I got at Dunkirk. Instead of fighting the Japs in Burma, I got stuck back in Britain with the old lads in the Home Guard. They finally gave me my honorary discharge in 1945."

Henrich nodded his head and John realised he had probably been lucky, given that Muller had surely fought on the Eastern Front during those years he was posted in peaceful Britain.

"What about you?" John asked. "How did you end up in the Army? Did you always want to be an officer?"

"No," Muller responded, with a sly smile on his face. "Serving in the Wehrmacht was never my ambition. I was born into a middle class family in Munich. My father was a merchant, but he served as a colonel in the 14-18 war…"

"My old man was a corporal in that war," John added. "He got gassed during the Somme offensive. Never was quite the same after that."

"My father was always bitter over Germany's defeat," Muller added. "He was also furious over the Treaty of Versialles."

"So," John concluded, "your father wanted you to join the Army?"

"Yes, ultimately he did," Muller confirmed. "I enjoyed a good standard of education - private school followed by a degree in Law and English at Munich University, not to mention a year spent in Cambridge…"

John could hardly relate to Henrich's early life. He was an East End working class boy and had received only a basic education. His options had been limited. He'd worked long hours in the docks for several years, but his craving for adventure had driven him into joining the Army…that, and the desire to prove himself to his father.

"I wanted to train to become a lawyer and to work in London, or perhaps New York. But it was not to be. Hitler came to power in 1933, and he soon began a programme of vast rearmament. My father supported the Nazis. He believed Hitler would reverse the humiliation of Versailles and lead Germany to great victories over the Bolsheviks and the Western democracies. My father said it was my duty to join the officer corps and serve my country. So this is what I did, albeit with some reluctance. For us Germans, duty always comes first."

In spite of himself, John was engaged. He wanted to hear more of the German captain's story.

"Which campaigns did you fight in?" he asked.

"I served as an untested lieutenant during the invasion of Poland," Muller answered. "This was my first experience of battle. In spite of my nerves I performed adequately. In Poland I earned my first and last medal, and I was promoted to full captain soon after the campaign. As you know, I fought in the French campaign. Next came Operation Barbarossa. Nothing prepared me for the intensity of the hard fight against the Bolsheviks. The Russians are not an elegant race, but they are fierce and ruthless warriors. At first the Russian soldiers were more afraid of their Red masters than they were of us, but this didn't last. My division was in the push for Moscow. We fought for the city street by street, losing many, many men in the process. Our spirits were raised after we heard the news of Stalin's death. Thank God we held the city before the onset of winter. If not, tens of thousands of our men would surely have frozen to death."

John sat back and listened intently. He tried to imagine how bad it must have been for Muller and his comrades, to fight the ferocious Reds and brave the notoriously brutal Russian winter. He didn't envy them one bit.

"Fall Blau commenced in the spring of 1942. We had Moscow but we needed the southern oilfields in order to continue the war. Our division fought at Stalingrad. This was our toughest fight yet, worse even than Moscow. We fought the Reds for every street, every building, and every room. And then the Russians counterattacked; two pincer assaults across the Volga. For a time it looked like we would be encircled and destroyed. But the Soviets didn't have sufficient reserves to push home their attack. Our forces were able to stabilise the front. The last resistance ended in the city, and our southern forces seized the Baku oil fields soon after....still, we were lucky. Many of Hitler's plans were foolhardy and reckless, no matter what the Party historians write in their books."

John was shocked by Muller's forthrightness. He didn't believe it was the done thing to criticise Hitler's battlefield strategies, especially given the German Fuhrer's apparently well-deserved reputation as a military mastermind. He cautiously glanced at the bar behind him, checking that no-one had overheard the captain's last statement. The only man in earshot was the bald headed drunk. The fellow was totally out of it, swaying back and forth on his stool, trying his best not to fall to the floor.

There was just one thing that John didn't understand. He wanted to ask Henrich Muller a pertinent question but he restrained himself, as he imagined his inquiry could cause offence. However, Henrich appeared able to read John's mind.

"You're probably wondering why I am still a captain at my age, given my considerable combat experience during the war. I do not usually tell this story. To speak of such things is unwise in today's Germany. Nevertheless, the beer has loosened my inhibitions...and, in spite of my instincts, I feel I can trust you,

Sergeant Preston. It is a strange thing, to make friends with a former mortal enemy."

John could relate to that. He felt a connection to the German soldier, something he had not expected.

Muller paused and took a deep breath, as he mustered the courage to continue.

"Joachim…that was my brother's name. He was ten years younger than me. A good natured and kind spirited child…but he was, how do you say, slow. My parents realised early on that there was something wrong with Joachim. My father had money, so he was able to send him to a special hospital outside Munich. Joachim spent many years there, living amongst children with similar issues. We went to visit him as often as we could. The facility was a hellish place from our perspective, but Joachim seemed happy there.

"The situation changed when the Nazis consolidated their power. It started in the years before the war. The Party began distributing propaganda posters, stating how a patient with a hereditary defect would cost the Reich sixty thousand marks throughout their lifetime. The Nazis claimed people such as Joachim were a drain on society. I was worried, but my father was still an ardent supporter of the Party, so he was unconcerned. In August 1939 we received news that Joachim was to be moved to a new facility. He was fourteen years old, but the doctors said his developmental age was only four. They were unhappy with his progress and claimed a hospital in Bernburg was pioneering a new treatment which would help Joachim. My parents had no reason to disbelieve the specialists. At that time, I was deployed on the Eastern Front, preparing for the Polish offensive. To my eternal shame, I barely gave poor Joachim a thought at that time…"

Henrich paused. He sighed and shook his head. John could see the man's grief. This was still very raw for Henrich. He didn't know why the German was spilling his guts out to him. Maybe Muller just needed to tell his story to someone.

John heard the drunk kicking off again at the bar. He began yet another rendition of Rot Front, although his lyrics were less coherent than before. John ignored the drunkard's singing. He listened up and heard the sound of boots thumping against pavement. He guessed that there was a march going down the street – Hitler Youth or SA.

The Nazis loved their marches and rallies. It was just like the newsreel footage he had seen back in England.

Muller needed a long gulp of beer before he could continue his tale of woe.

"…I was still in combat when I received the news. Joachim had passed away….they told us that he died from pneumonia."

"I'm sorry mate," John said, with a genuine sympathy in his voice. "That must have been hell, to lose your brother so young…"

The din of the march grew ever louder. The drunk had to raise his volume just to be heard over the racket. The Communist chanter and the Nazi marching band…it was like two opposing sides in a war, exchanging artillery fire across the void.

"Unfortunately, this wasn't the end of the affair," Henrich added, in a tone which was more angry than sorrowful. "My mother and father were devastated, of course, as was I. I was grieving, but also suspicious. Joachim had been perfectly healthy the last time I visited him. The cause of death made no sense. I wanted the truth. I was a war hero by this time, a decorated veteran of the Polish campaign. I had connections within the Party and was able to make discreet enquiries. I pushed my father to do the same, even though he was reluctant to pry. Eventually, we found out that dozens of children had died on the same day at this so called 'hospital' in Bernburg. In all cases, the cause of death recorded was 'pneumonia'."

John was shocked. He didn't know where this story was going. He wasn't even sure that he wanted to hear the conclusion.

"Finally, we discovered the truth," said Henrich, as he tried in vain to control the raw emotion in his voice. "…Joachim…and many others… were murdered by the government. They called the program Aktion T4. The Nazi's plan involved the mass murder of the cripples, the retarded, and the mad….all ages were targeted, from children to pensioners. It didn't matter to them. They considered these people a drain on society, so they wiped them out…"

"My God!" John cried. "That's monstrous!"

"Indeed," Muller replied solemnly. He seemed relieved to get it off his chest, to unburden himself and tell his terrible story.

"And they got away with this?" asked John.

"Of course," Henrich replied. "Some relatives objected, of course, and so did we. I received several visits from the Gestapo. Threats were made against me and my family. In the end, though, I listened to my father. He said we shouldn't pursue the matter. Joachim was dead and there was no way to bring him back. Our duty is to the Reich, he said. The Party has to make the tough decisions for the good of Germany. Sacrifices have to be made. It is difficult to bear, but we must move on... I listened to my father and obeyed his wishes. For this, I will never forgive myself..."

"What happened after that?" John prompted, as he was eager to hear more.

Henrich shrugged his shoulders. "I was still a soldier of the Reich, and there was a war going on. We invaded the Low Countries and France in late spring 1940. As you know, Sergeant Preston, combat is all encompassing. Your entire focus is to fight and survive. I threw myself into the midst of battle. My loyalty was not to Hitler and his Nazis, not even to Germany, but to the men who I fought alongside..."

John nodded his head in a display of understanding. He shared this common experience with Henrich. Both men knew the hell that was war. They had both seen firsthand the dark instincts and impulses which men experienced during the intensity of battle, but also the loyalty and heroism.

"Barbarossa commenced in May 1941. My conduct on the battlefield and my father's Party connections might have secured me a staff officer position far away from the frontline. However, the Nazis remembered the problems I had caused them over Joachim's death. They knew I wasn't a loyal Party man any longer. This is why I was sent to serve in the shock battalions, fighting in the most intense battles on the Eastern Front. They expected me to die, to be killed in action...but I survived, against the odds. The war ended, but I was denied permission to leave the Wehrmacht. They refused to promote me, or to give me a position of authority. Since I speak English, I was assigned as a liaison officer for British defectors…and so, here I am…" Henrich finished his life story and took another drink from his tankard.

He looked John in the eye and flashed him a forced smile. "At least…," Muller added, "at least I am no longer on the Eastern Front…"

John was confused. "But the war in Russia is over, is it not? Moscow, Leningrad and Stalingrad were all German victories…Surely it must have ended there?"

He was asking these questions more out of hope, rather than any expectation of a positive answer.

"On the contrary, Sergeant Preston," Henrich responded. His expression was deadly serious. "These battles were won, but the war continues even to this day. This is the truth which Herr Goebbels wishes to hide from the German people."

John was extremely concerned by what he was hearing from the German captain. He opened his mouth to ask what Henrich meant, but he was distracted by a sudden clamour directly behind him.

It had been all quiet right up to this point. The previous march had ended some minutes earlier, as presumably the Hitler Youth or whoever had moved on to join up with the main rally. But now there were boots on the pavement right outside the door of the pub. He could hear the shouts of several men, serious men who meant business. It was clear to John that these newcomers held a malicious intent. He turned his head around and looked anxiously towards the pub's entrance. A moment later the door was kicked open.

Men in Nazi uniforms piled into the bar. They moved in tight formation, a well-organised and practiced assault, executed with typical German efficiency. Four men in dark black garb now stood in the middle of the pub's floor. All had weapons drawn, small black pistols of German design. Each man looked determined, deadly serious. These boys meant business. Their predatory eyes scanned the interior of the establishment. The Nazis were looking for someone, hunting down their prey.

John felt a sickening fear rising up from the pit of his stomach. His mind was racing, as he imagined the worst. They were here for him, he thought, as the panic overcame him. Hoffman had sent these bastards to arrest him. Or maybe it was Muller they were after. He'd been talking too openly about his brother's murder, about Hitler's mistakes on the Eastern Front. You couldn't just say things like this in Nazi Berlin.

John was frozen in fear as he looked to the squad of Luger wielding thugs in uniform. There was bugger all John could do. If he tried to run or fight, the Krauts would surely shoot him dead, so he awaited the inevitable.

The Germans scanned the room, searching out their target. Suddenly they all focused on an individual. There was a sudden shout and then the snatch squad moved in.

They darted towards the bar as one, and roughly grabbed hold of the bald headed drunk. He was so far gone he probably didn't know what was going on.

When he did finally try to protest, one of the Nazis struck him hard on the back of the head with the butt of his pistol. He shrieked in agony as blood poured from the deep gash in his skull and he fell off his stool and landed heavily on the tiled floor. A moment later the squad of secret police dragged their man up onto his feet. They roughly slipped a pair of handcuffs on him and frog marched him out of the pub.

The ugly incident had only lasted a few seconds in its entirety. John felt ashamed, because he had simply sat in his chair and watched. He'd made no attempt to aid the victim.

The other patrons in the pub barely reacted to the violent intrusion into their afternoon's drinking. They looked up for a moment before returning to their beers, cigarettes and newspapers. They didn't care....had probably seen it all before, so many times.

The landlord lifted up the discarded tankard from the bar top and used a cloth to wipe away the spilt beer. After that, it was back to 'business as usual', as if nothing had ever happened.

Why had the Nazis arrested this man? What the hell had he ever done to anyone? The bloke was nothing more than a harmless old drunk. John knew the type. Was it because of the song? John reckoned so. This was enough to get a geezer lifted here in Hitler's Berlin. An old drunkard singing communist songs he remembered from his youth. Even such a small act of defiance was too much for the Nazis to bear. But how had they found out? Someone must have grassed the fellow up. Perhaps one of the regulars had slipped out to inform the police, or, more likely, the landlord himself had put in a call to the Gestapo. He was bound to have a phone behind the bar. The bastard. Germany was full of state informers. Everyone was watching everyone else, stitching each other up over any old rubbish. This was his brother's utopia…the ultimate police state.

John looked back towards his companion for the first time in several minutes. Henrich had not reacted to the assault and arrest. The expression on his face was dead pan and emotionless. This was all routine for him. Living on the edge…never knowing when or where the Gestapo would come for him.

"We should go," Muller said. "If not, Hoffman and his men will come looking for us."

John nodded in agreement. He had seen enough. The men left their table and promptly exited the pub, strolling out onto the quiet and well-ordered Berlin streets beyond.

# 7 / 'The Knights of Albion'

ANDREW PRESTON WAS FURIOUS with his brother. He was fuming all the way through their car journey, as the chauffeur driven Volkswagen sedan sped through the streets of Berlin.

Andrew was getting treated like royalty, what with his own car, driver and police escort. Hoffman was in the passenger seat, and Andrew was seated in the rear, just like a visiting dignitary or a leading industrialist...someone important, worthy of respect and special treatment. He was touring the greatest city on Earth, the capital of the mighty German Empire, and he was on his way to meet with top Party officials, perhaps even the Fuhrer himself.

This should be one of the greatest days of Andrew's life, but his ungrateful sod of a brother seemed determined to ruin everything. John had slipped away at the train station. He'd blended in with the mob of daytime commuters and had simply disappeared, wandering off into the congested streets of Berlin. Hoffman hadn't been happy, that much was obvious. But there was nothing to be done. John would turn up at some point. In the meantime, they had to get going, otherwise Andrew would miss his appointment.

He should have known John would pull a stunt like this. His older brother had kicked off in the train station, just before they'd exited through the turnstiles. John was still unhappy because of the rally in Dunkirk. He'd been sulking the entire trip, all the way from Northern France. Andrew didn't understand why his brother was so upset. All they had made him do was stand up on a stage and give a salute. What was so bloody bad about that? Yes, Andrew knew his brother had fought against the Germans during the war. John was always at pains to remind him of this fact. His older brother had his pride, but pride always comes before the fall. John had fought for the wrong side, and he had lost.

Why couldn't he just accept this reality? The Germans were superior…this much was self-evident. If John didn't believe it, why didn't he just take a look around Berlin? He could see for himself the wonders being built by the pioneers of National Socialism…the new wonders of the world…they were all here, right in the heart of the Reich.

Why did no-one in this bloody family appreciate what Andrew was doing for them? John had been nothing back in England…just another ex-soldier discarded by an unappreciative socialist government. His brother had been left a broken man after the Zionists murdered his woman, and it was Andrew who dragged John out of his hole of self-pity. His wife was an ungrateful bitch. Andrew had always been faithful to his missus, he had supported her and their children all these years…and still she sought to undermine and embarrass him at every opportunity.

It would be different now they were in Germany. Wives respected their husbands here in the Reich. She would learn her place. And Julie…she was a wild one alright. His daughter was far too outspoken and rebellious. This would never do. If they had stayed in London, the silly little girl could have ended up courting a Wog or, worse yet, a Yid. Out here she would marry a pure Aryan boy and give birth to strong blond haired, blue eyed babies. This was his daughter's destiny, and Andrew would make sure she followed the path which nature intended for a young woman. He was grateful for Edward at least. His son was becoming a fine young man, loyal and respectful, as an adolescent boy should be. Here in Germany, Edward would fulfil his full potential. He had great hopes for his boy.

Andrew tried to put thoughts of family to the back of his mind. He wouldn't let these ingrates ruin his big day. The man wanted to take in every detail of this great city, so he was disappointed, because their car sped through the streets so quickly that it was near impossible to see any sights. No matter. Andrew had been promised a visit to Welthauptstadt Germania during his stay in Berlin. Here he would see firsthand the magnificent construction projects commissioned by the Fuhrer and built by the genius architect, Albert Speer… the Avenue of Splendors; the Great Hall and the Arch of Victory, the greatest monuments on Earth, dwarfing the inferior constructions in Paris, London and New York. Andrew couldn't wait to see this. But first, he needed to get through this afternoon's conference.

They hadn't told him who he was meeting. Andrew didn't like this uncertainty. He preferred to know what was happening, to have control over his own affairs. Would the Fuhrer himself be present? Andrew hoped so. He had to admit to feeling a bad case of the nerves. This was probably the single most important event of his entire life. He couldn't afford to muck it up…

The car turned a corner and drove down a wide throughway. Andrew saw old buildings, attractive architecture dating back from another era. He was uncertain of the geography of Berlin. He didn't know where they were, or where they were going to. He looked out through the side window of the car, and up towards the street sign attached to an adjacent building. He read the German name; Prinz Albrecht-Strabe. He only had to think for a second before he made the connection in his brain. He knew this street. Everyone did.

This was the location of the infamous Gestapo Headquarters. The impressive looking 18th century palace on this street had been taken over by Himmler's SS in the mid 1930's, but the house had proven too small to accommodate the rapidly expanding secret police apparatus. Therefore, several adjacent buildings had been taken over, and now the sprawling Gestapo complex dominated the entire street.

Andrew remembered hearing about this place while he was back in London, during his days with the BUF. He and his comrades heard the stories of Jews and Communists arrested and tortured in the infamous underground chambers maintained and manned by the most sadistic elements of the Nazi machine. He wasn't keen on this sort of thing. He had fought the Communists in the streets of East London and had mercilessly beaten Zionist prisoners in Palestine. Nevertheless, it took a special breed to become a torturer. The Gestapo were rumoured to use horrific measures, a vicious mix of medieval brutality and modern day 'enhanced interrogation techniques'. Andrew realised that such measures were necessary. The enemies of the Reich had to be dealt with severely, and without mercy. Nevertheless, he didn't want to be involved himself. He'd never thought he would ever actually visit this place.

Andrew hoped their car would drive on past the Gestapo HQ. Instead, the driver parked their vehicle outside the front of the building. Hoffman presented his ID papers to an armed guard on duty and promptly exited the car. The side door was opened by the guard, and Andrew was ordered to exit the vehicle. He hesitated for a moment. He couldn't fathom why they had brought him here. This was the place where the enemies of National Socialism where sent. Here, they were interrogated or tortured by the Gestapo before being shipped to a concentration camp or put in front of a firing squad.

Andrew Preston was not an enemy of the Fuhrer. He was a loyal fascist and avid supporter of the Reich. He'd defected to Germany, for God's sake! He didn't like this. His nervousness had now turned into panic. He continued to sit in the car, refusing to get out. Hoffman barked an order in harsh German. Andrew realised he was being ridiculous. Surely his German friends meant him no harm. There must be a logical explanation for all this. He finally climbed out of his seat and stepped out onto the pavement.

Preston forgot that Hoffman didn't speak his language. He asked the policeman a question in English, saying; "What are we doing here?"

In spite of his supposed lack of English, Hoffman apparently did understand the question. He answered with just one word, saying, "Meeting."

In the absence of any other options, Andrew followed his German escort. He ascended the front steps and passed the armed guards on duty. Next, both men passed through the solid oak doors of the Prinz-Albrecht Palais, which were opened up for them by the guards on duty.

They entered the unassuming building which served such a secret and sinister purpose.

The interior lobby was large and spacious, with marble tiled floors and classical pillars. Andrew got the impression that the interior of the Palais had been grander in the past, that the décor had been more appealing in years gone by. In all likelihood the Gestapo had gone for a more minimalist style of decoration, stripping the walls and the floors bare.

This building had been altered in order to better fit its current purpose. Prinz-Albrecht was not a place of warmth or beauty, but of pain, violence and fear. Other than this first impression, Andrew was surprised by how unremarkable the interior of the building was. He knew what they did here, however, if he hadn't been pre-warned, he might have thought this place was just a normal government office. There was even a reception at the front, manned by a hard faced, middle-aged woman wearing wide rimmed spectacles.

The security was the giveaway. It was subtle, but an observant man such as Andrew could see the suited guards stationed throughout the lobby, with the telltale bulges under their jackets, which could only be made by concealed side-arms. Two fully uniformed troops armed with sub machine guns stood guard just behind the reception. They checked Hoffman's credentials before saluting their superior officer and waving both men through the cordon.

Hoffman led his visitor up a wide staircase, as they ascended to the upper floors. Andrew felt a great relief because, as far as he knew, the torture chambers were located in the basement of the building. He hadn't really thought Hoffman was going to stitch him up or arrest him. It would make no sense. Nevertheless, he needed to keep his wits about him, especially when his own family were causing him so many problems. The two men walked down a narrow and dimly lit corridor without windows. They eventually came to a non-descript doorway, no different from the many others they had passed on their short walk down the corridor. Hoffman knocked on the door before turning the handle and opening it up. He motioned Andrew to enter, almost shoving him into the room. Hoffman did not follow him inside, and the door was shut tight behind him.

Andrew looked ahead into the small office room. There was a table with an empty chair set in front of it. A pot of coffee and several china cups were set upon the table top. Behind the desk sat three men. All of them stood up as he entered the room. Andrew raised his right arm and cried 'Heil Hitler!' The three repeated the phrase, but with little enthusiasm. He was greatly surprised, because he recognised two of the trio; one man he knew from his past, and another he recognised from newsreel footage, and photographs published in papers back in England. These were the last couple of men he expected to meet here in Berlin.

The man who spoke first was dressed in a fine tailored grey suit, waistcoat, white shirt and dark coloured tie. The fellow was well groomed and could be described as handsome. He talked in a well clipped, upper class English accent. His tone was patronising and condescending. Clearly he thought of himself as the most important person in this room.

"Ah, Mr. Preston, I assume. Welcome to Berlin, my good man." He held out a hand across the table, which Andrew accepted without thinking. The fellow's palm was soft and smooth. Andrew reckoned the man had never done a hard days graft in his whole life.

"Allow me to make the formal introductions," the man continued. "My name is John Amery…"

Andrew had been spot on with his identification. The man looked just like his photograph. John Amery, eldest son of Leo Amery. His father had been the Secretary of State for India and Burma…an upper class member of the British political establishment. John's story was well known back in England. He'd been born in Chelsea and educated at Harrow, up until the point when the headmaster had chucked him out. John had been considered a difficult child, constantly living in his father's shadow. He'd been involved in a number of unsuccessful businesses in his early 20's and had married a former prostitute, bringing further shame to his long-suffering family. Amery was an avid anti-Communist. He claimed to have fought with Franco's forces during the Spanish Civil War. This account was later exposed as a lie.

Amery had been living in France during the German invasion of that country. Later, he was granted a visa to enter Germany, where he presented himself as a British Fascist and Anti-Communist. He came to Berlin and somehow managed to get close to Hitler himself, and was thus permitted to remain in the German capital as a 'guest of the Reich'. Back in Britain, John Amery was considered an arch traitor. He'd been sentenced to death in absentia for treason, although this sentence was later revoked under pressure from the German government.

Nevertheless, Amery didn't seem to have any intention of returning to England. Why would he, when he had such a good life out here? Andrew had never thought much of the man. He reckoned Amery was dishonest and manipulative, a selfish upper-class cad who would do anything to save his own skin. True enough, Andrew had never met the fellow before, but his first impressions did little to change his opinion of him.

Amery continued by introducing the two men standing on either side of him, both of whom were dressed in the uniform of Wehrmacht officers.

"And these gentlemen are Lieutenant John Codd and Lieutenant Thomas Haller Cooper. Although I believe you and Cooper are already acquainted?"

"Yes...," Andrew replied hesitantly. "We were both members of the BUF in London, back in the late 30s. Good to see you again, Mr. Cooper."

Cooper merely nodded his head in acknowledgement, as his dark eyes glared straight through Andrew. Here was a serious man. Andrew had always admired Cooper, ever since he met him at a Blackshirt rally in '38. Cooper was a determined and committed individual, bred from good stock. They had spoken on several occasions and Cooper had told Andrew his story. Thomas was a fellow Londoner, born and raised in Chiswick. He had an English father and German mother. After he left school, Thomas had applied to join several institutions, including the Metropolitan Police, Royal Navy and RAF. He was rejected by all of these forces, with his German mother being the reason given on each and every occasion. Blatant discrimination against the Aryan people, that's what it was.

Naturally, Cooper had been left bitter and resentful as a result of this unfair treatment. He had therefore channelled his energies towards the British Union of Fascists. Cooper had been a good man for the Blackshirts, up until the summer of 1939, when he suddenly disappeared from London. Andrew had always been curious as to what had happened to his friend.

"Long time, no see, mate," said Andrew. "What have you been up to all these years?"

Cooper shrugged his shoulders before answering in a cool, 'matter of fact' tone of voice.

"I left England to take a job with the German Labour Service in Stuttgart. I was caught there whenever war was declared. They interned me as an enemy alien for a short while, but then my mother produced documents proving I was a pure-blooded Volksdeutsher, so I was released. Later, I joined the SS and fought on the Eastern Front...was honoured for bravery in battle..."

He pointed to the medals neatly displayed on his jacket.
Andrew nodded his head. He felt a great respect for his former colleague. Cooper had fought on the Eastern Front alongside his Aryan brothers. He had helped to crush the Jewish and Bolshevik swine, securing the conquests which had provided much needed Lebensraum for the Aryan people. Thomas Haller Cooper was a hero in Andrew's eyes.

The next man to speak was John Codd. His accent was a thick Southern Irish brogue.

"Tell me, Mr. Preston," Codd began, "is your brother John not here with you?"

"No," Andrew replied, as he attempted to hide his embarrassment. "John is here in Berlin, but regretfully he was unable to attend our meeting..."

"Pity," Codd replied. "I've met your brother before and hoped to see him again. Like John, I served with the British Army in France and was taken prisoner. We were both held in Stalag 3-B at Lannesdorf, and our paths crossed on a few occasions..."

"You didn't return to Britain after the peace settlement?" Andrew enquired.

"God no," Codd responded. "I'm an Irishman first and foremost. I volunteered my services to the Germans, as I wanted to fight for the cause of Irish Freedom, and reckoned the Fuhrer was the best man to get this done. They assigned me to the Abwehr, trained me up in espionage and the like...the Germans wanted to send me on an undercover mission in the North of Ireland, but this operation got cancelled after the peace treaty was signed. After that, I joined the SS...and now I'm an officer, serving in the independent Irish company attached to the Free Corps. Not a bad job for a farmer's son from County Laois!"

Codd smiled and winked at Andrew. He did not reciprocate. Andrew didn't think much of John Codd; the Irishman struck him as being a shameful opportunist, the type who would serve any country or army, if he thought such service would be of benefit to himself.

Codd, the turncoat, and Amery, the cad. Cooper was the only honest and decent man in this room, the only one of the trio Andrew respected.

"So, Mr. Preston," said Amery. "Now the introductions are over, perhaps you would like to take a seat? Please help yourself to a coffee, and then we can get started. I don't expect this meeting to take very long..."

"Excuse me, Mr. Amery," Andrew interjected, as he ignored the offer of a hot beverage. "I was led to believe that I was meeting top Party officials this afternoon..."

Amery screwed up his face in annoyance. He clearly didn't appreciate the implication.

"No offence to you good gentlemen," Andrew added in the way of apology, even though he didn't really mean it. "But I was hoping to meet with Himmler, Goebbels or Groening...or perhaps with the Fuhrer himself..."

Amery responded with mocking laughter. "Good God man!" he exclaimed, "Surely you don't think Herr Hitler has the time to meet with the likes of you? The Fuhrer is a busy man, Mr. Preston. He has an entire Empire to run, in case you didn't realise!"

Andrew was taken aback, humiliated even. He was almost lost for words.

"I just thought…" he finally spluttered.

"You think too much, Preston," Amery spat back. "You're a foot soldier, not a leader. Just remember your place, old boy…"

Andrew's embarrassment turned to raw anger. He clenched his fist under the table and had to fight the strong urge to reach across the desk and give the bastard a bloody good slap. How dare he!

Andrew remembered the stories about the Amery family. The rumour was that John Amery's grandmother was a Jew. Yes, that would make perfect sense. Amery's deceitfulness and cowardice could easily be explained by his origins, by his inferior bloodline.

Why on earth would the Fuhrer trust such a man? Andrew just couldn't understand it.

He knew he had to control his temper. Andrew had to remember where he was. Hoffman was probably standing outside the door, just waiting for him to slip up. Andrew wouldn't be riled by Amery.

He nodded his head and reached out for the mug and pot, suddenly deciding he needed a coffee after all. He poured the hot beverage into the china cup, not bothering to add milk or sugar. A strong black coffee would do him just fine. He needed to keep his wits about him.

"Don't worry, Preston," Amery added, as an aside. "You will see the Fuhrer later on, when he speaks at the rally. We'll try to get your family close to the stage."

Andrew mumbled a half-hearted thanks before Amery continued. "Well, my good man, you are at the beginning of your journey east, and our benefactors felt it would be prudent for you to meet with a few of your fellow countrymen, before you leave Berlin. As you may already know, I am a personal friend of the Fuhrer and the founder of the British Free Corps. All my idea, old chap…not that I'm one to blow my own trumpet!

137

*Yeah, bloody right*, Andrew thought, but didn't say, A bastard like Amery would gladly take all the credit for an idea, regardless of whether he deserved it or not.

"We started off small," Amery explained. "Only about fifty odd men, all ex-Prisoners of War. It was difficult for the boys back then. But we've grown in strength over the years. Now the BFC is brigade sized…four thousand troops organised into a mechanised infantry formation. The boys have seen some action out East, our friend Cooper will tell you…"

*Yes,* Andrew thought, *but I bet you've never been anywhere near the front, have you, Amery?*

"…add to that the twenty thousand British and Commonwealth citizens who are already living in the Eastern territories, mainly in Southern Ostland province, where your own family are headed. More and more English families are coming over every month. Of course, our people are just a part of a much bigger picture. There are approximately five million Germans and 'Germanized' Europeans living in the colonies now; General Government, Ostland, Ukraine and Muscovy. We are building a mighty new Empire, Mr. Preston. Our settlements and plantations will rise up from the ashes, a great network linked by Autobahns. One day, a man will be able to drive his Volkswagen from here in Berlin right up to the Ural Mountains. Of course, there is still much to do, and many challenges still face us. There are dangers, Mr. Preston…I will not lie to you. This is why all male settlers of fighting age must be armed, and are required to serve in the local defence militia. Men such as you and your brother will be required to serve and to fight…"

"We understand this, Amery," Andrew replied sternly. "We will both do our duty to the Reich, as will my son, when he comes of age."

"I'm sure you will, Preston," Amery replied, in a patronising tone. "Of course, we would have liked to speak with your brother face to face. What a shame he has been detained on other business. John Preston is the soldier in the family, as I understand it."

Andrew once again struggled to contain his anger. He was

sick and tired of people going on about John as if he was some kind of bloody war hero, and as if Andrew was nothing in comparison.

"It is true that John is an ex-soldier, and he fought at Dunkirk…"

Amery cut him off abruptly.

"Forgive me for asking, my good man. But my colleagues and I are somewhat concerned. We fear that your brother may be experiencing divided loyalties…perhaps he regrets his decision to defect?"

"Absolutely not!" Andrew replied firmly, without a second's hesitation. "John is loyal to the Reich, and he will do his duty!"

The strength of Andrew's defence of his brother surprised even him. In spite of everything, he was still fiercely loyal to John.

"Good," Amery replied, as apparently his concerns were addressed. "Very good. And you have some military experience yourself, I'm led to believe?"

"Yes," Andrew answered. "I served in the Colonial Police in Palestine, during the Emergency of '45 to '47. The Yids rose up against the government, using terror tactics against our people…bombings, kidnappings, murders…any kind of underhand and immoral tactic. What more would you expect from the Jews? We fought the bastards, kept a lid on their rebellion. But, our weak government made us fight with one hand tied behind our backs. The politicians should have let us slaughter the scum. Instead, they choose to accept a shameful surrender to terrorism…"

"You call that a bloody war?" interjected Cooper, as he spoke for the first time in several minutes. "I've heard all about Palestine. Nothing but a petty squabble over a few scraps of land. Palestine wasn't a real fight…nothing like the Eastern Front!"

Andrew was left gob smacked by Cooper's unwarranted attack on him. Why would his old comrade humiliate him like this? What the hell was his problem?

Andrew shot Cooper a dirty look, but he was met by a dark, steadfast glare which chilled him to the bone. Thomas was a different man now. Whatever he had seen out in Russia had clearly changed him for the worse.

Amery picked up on the heightened tensions in the room and sought to change the topic of conversation. "Speaking of Palestine," he began, "I myself have held several productive meetings with Amin al-Husseni, the Grand Mutfi of Jerusalem. He lives here in Berlin, did you know? In exile from his homeland. The Grand Mutfi is a close confidant of the Fuhrer...a very clever man, is al-Husseni."

Amery's anecdote was meant to calm Andrew, but instead the comment left him fuming. He considered it a personal insult that the Fuhrer would meet with an Arab, but not with a pure Aryan such as him. He could no longer contain his anger. "He may be clever for a Wog," he spat, "but he is still a member of an inferior race."

"Well quite," replied Amery, after an uncomfortable pause.

Andrew wasn't done yet. He hated Amery and sought to push him into an argument. "If it had been up to me," Andrew said firmly, "every single Jew in Palestine would have been taken out and shot. Every single bloody one of them..." Andrew was thinking of Amery's rumoured Jewish ancestry, and he hoped his controversial opinion would drive his adversary to reveal his true self. To Andrew's great disappointment, Amery did not react with anger. Instead he actually smiled and stifled a laugh.

"Funnily enough," said Amery, "the Grand Mutfi had a similar idea. Perhaps you have more in common with the Arab than you care to admit? You know, our conversation reminds me of the advice Hitler once gave to Lord Halifax, on how to deal with the Indian Independence Movement. As I recall, the Fuhrer advised Halifax to shoot Gandhi, and, if this did not suffice to reduce them to submission, shoot a dozen leading members of the Congress, and, if that did not suffice, shoot two hundred...and so on, until order is established. Sound counsel, I think we can all agree. If only Halifax and my father had listened...maybe Britain would still have India."

Andrew could agree with Amery on this point at least. He nodded his head and confirmed his fellow Englishman's suspicions. "The British Empire is crumbling," he stated, as a matter of point.

"Regretfully so," Amery agreed. "But luckily the German Empire is at the height of her power. These are exciting times, Mr.

Preston. The future is coming, and your family will be at the very centre of this new dawn."

Andrew liked what he was hearing. John Amery was an idiot in most respects, but he knew the score. Germany was in the ascendency, and Andrew had surely made the right decision in bringing his family out here.

"Well," Amery concluded, "I think we have detained you here for long enough, Mr. Preston. I'm sure you are eager to meet up with your family." He glanced at this watch. "And the Party rally will be commencing soon. You don't want to miss seeing the Fuhrer, I am sure…" Andrew stood up and shook hands with each man in turn, noting that Thomas Cooper's farewell was the coolest of the three. This unsettled him somewhat. He made to leave the room but, before he did so, his curiosity got the better of him. He turned around and looked past John Amery, addressing his final question directly to his old BUF comrade, Thomas Haller Cooper.

"Tell me, Cooper," he said, in an apprehensive tone. "You've fought on the Eastern Front, and I respect you for that. What I want to know is what it's like out there now. What are me and my family walking into?" The other men in the room reacted to the unexpected question. The Irishman, John Codd, laughed aloud. John Amery looked visibly annoyed, probably because Andrew had deliberately bypassed him to speak directly with his subordinate. Cooper himself glared back at Andrew with those dark, dead eyes. He spoke in a hard and stern voice, like a strict headmaster remonstrating with an unruly pupil.

"You've no idea, old friend," Cooper answered, "no bloody idea of what awaits you; may God have mercy on your family."

Andrew felt a cold chill run through him. He looked Cooper in the eye for just a moment, but he was unable to hold the man's gaze and averted his eyes to glance down at the floor. He turned around and went for the door, without uttering another word. He just wanted to get away. Hoffman was standing in the corridor, waiting for him, but there would be no sympathy from the cold and emotionless Gestapo man and, for the first time in his journey, he began to have serious doubts about what he would find out in the East.

# 8/ 'Fuhrer'

YVONNE AND EDWARD LEFT the hotel just after three o'clock. Their accommodation was luxurious; it was undeniable. The hotel was 5 Star. Yvonne's room came complete with a grand four poster bed with satin sheets. The suite included an open balcony, with majestic views of the city streets…not that she had bothered to look out the window.

Yvonne hadn't seen luxury like this for many years and, had the circumstances been different, she may have appreciated the accommodation, but she could not enjoy her beautiful surroundings, not after what she had seen on that back street. This was all a false façade, she knew this now. The real Berlin was Eastern European slaves and brutal SS guards beating them senseless.

They were served a delicious dinner of veal steaks, Lyonnais potatoes and a selection of glazed vegetables, all washed down by the finest French wines, and freshly squeezed fruit juices for the youngsters.

Yvonne and her children hadn't been served such a grand meal in years, but none of them could enjoy their lunch. She pushed the food around her plate and was barely able to eat a bite.

She kept thinking of that poor old man on the street, beaten to a bloody pulp by those Nazi thugs. Would he survive his severe injuries? Yvonne didn't think so. She didn't eat the food, but did drink the wine. She needed the alcohol as an anaesthetic, to help her to forget. She just wanted this terrible day to end.

Muller had disappeared after lunch, and she hoped she and her children would be left alone for the rest of the afternoon. No such luck. Their young German driver insisted that the family had to attend the Party rally occurring in the city centre, which would be addressed by the Fuhrer himself. Yvonne argued with the boy, but to no avail. At least he didn't insist on Julie accompanying them.

Yvonne's daughter had not reacted well to the events of earlier today. Julie had been very upset by the whole ugly affair and so she had taken to her hotel bedroom, refusing to leave. Yvonne had managed to persuade their German escort that her daughter was ill, so she was unable to attend the rally. She had hoped her son would also stay in the hotel. He was shaken after the incident in that back alleyway, but he was still filled with a boyish curiosity and sense of wonder.

Edward didn't want to miss the opportunity to see Hitler speak. He'd spent years listening to his father talking about Hitler, describing the German leader like he was some sort of God amongst men. Edward didn't want to disappoint his father. He was afraid of Andrew, afraid of letting him down.

Mother and son sat side by side in the back seat of the Volkswagen as the driver sped through the streets of Berlin. Yvonne didn't wish to observe the city scenes on this occasion. She had seen enough of the German capital.

They drove only a relatively short distance before the car came to a halt. The driver parked on a corner. He exited the vehicle and opened the back door for Yvonne, explaining in rough, broken English that he could go no further because of the large crowds on the street. He would wait here until the rally was over, and would then drive them back to the hotel.

Yvonne and Edward stepped on to the pavement, the driver pointing them in the direction to go. She was confused and concerned about what lay ahead, but she saw the excitement in her son's eyes, the boyish grin on his lips. This was all still a big adventure to him. Off they went, rounding a corner to see three familiar faces.

143

Her husband Andrew, brother-in-law John, and their escort Henrich Muller were standing on the pavement awaiting their arrival. Muller smiled faintly and nodded his head, greeting both Yvonne and Edward with his usual display of good manners, but it seemed artificial.

Her husband appeared uncharacteristically subdued. She had expected Andrew to be carrying on like a child at Christmas. He was finally going to see his hero in the flesh, his beloved Fuhrer. But Andrew looked distracted, as if he had something serious on his mind. Perhaps something unpleasant had occurred at his afternoon meeting. She didn't bother asking.

John didn't look much better. He greeted Yvonne without much enthusiasm. She could see sadness in his eyes and could smell alcohol on his breath.

"Well, my English friends," greeted Muller, "now that everyone is here, we can proceed to the meeting place. The rally will take place in front of the Brandenburg Gate. I'm afraid we have a bit of a walk ahead of us. The crowd makes it impossible for us to proceed by car. Please, follow me."

As they started walking, Yvonne's attention was captured by a large structure on the far horizon. She turned her head and looked up, astonished by what she saw: the Brandenburg Gate, an impressive arch like structure consisting of a row of ornate columns and a beautifully sculptured crest at its head.

However, the Gate itself did not hold Yvonne's attention. What left her awestruck were the gigantic structures behind it. A long avenue of grand buildings spread across the horizon, towering above the surrounding city. This entire area was apparently one vast construction site, a work in progress, with towering stone columns rising up far into the blue summer skies.

The structures were covered by vast exoskeletons of scaffolding. A second arch stood about a mile or so to the left of the Brandenburg Gate. This structure was much taller and wider than the Brandenburg, perhaps four or five times as tall. The arch was draped in an enormous Swastika flag. But even it was dwarfed by the vast building being constructed to the far right hand side of the avenue.

The hall was gigantic, and the dome must have been hundreds of feet high. The roof was unfinished, leaving the structure exposed to the elements. Scaffolding reached up to the highest point, and flocks of tiny birds flew in and out of the open dome.

"Impressive, isn't it," said Muller. "This is the centre piece of Speer's Welthauptstadt Germania project. The Grand Avenue is three miles long and four hundred foot wide. At the far end, we are constructing a huge railway terminal, which will serve as a transport hub for train services heading out to the Eastern colonies. The monument you see is named the Arch of Triumph. The arch was constructed to celebrate Germany's victories during the war, and to commemorate the sacrifices made by our men on the battlefields of Europe. On the right hand side of the avenue is the Fuhrer's presidential palace. This building is still under construction, so our leader is yet to move in. And finally, on the far right side of the avenue, you will see the master piece of our capital...the Ruhmeshalle, or Hall of Glory. When completed, our Great Hall will be the largest single building in the world, 1,000 feet high and capable of accommodating 150,000 spectators..."

"It's amazing," uttered Andrew. "More beautiful than I could ever have imagined."

Her husband and son were awe struck by the enormity of the occasion and Yvonne had to admit she was impressed herself. She was curious to find out more.

"Tell me, Captain Muller," she enquired, "when will this construction project be completed?"

"Herr Speer has assured the Fuhrer and the German people that the project will be completed by the end of 1950," Muller answered. "He has drafted in thousands of additional workers in order to ensure the deadline is met."

*Thousands of workers.* Yvonne realised what this meant. She had seen firsthand how the Nazis treated these workers; she wondered how many men, women and children were being used as forced labour and how many had died in the process.

They walked on towards the historical Bradenburg Gate and Reichstag building, both now dwarfed by the vast constructions rising up behind them. Soon the road began to fill up with other pedestrians, hundreds and then thousands of them, all walking in the same direction as the Preston party.

Yvonne assumed these people were also attending the Party rally. She looked around to observe the mass of people. She saw men, women and children, all well dressed and turned out, confident and self-assured, just as Yvonne had come to expect from the affluent and arrogant citizens of Berlin.

Some in the crowd, elegant and stylish women, gave them strange looks, probably thinking they didn't fit in here, but Yvonne didn't care anymore. She knew that the affluence of Berlin's women was built on the blood, sweat and tears of so many abused and enslaved peoples. She would much prefer her and the children to be poor and destitute, rather than live a life of wealth and luxury based on such an horrific system; she could hold her head up high.

"So many people..," Edward muttered, under his breath.

"Actually," Muller responded, "today's rally will be a small one, compared to those of the past. The authorities expect twenty five to thirty thousand attendees this afternoon. There was a time when such events would attract crowds of one hundred thousand, or more. Alas, it seems today's Germans are not as dedicated to their Fuhrer's vision as they once were."

Yvonne detected a hint of sarcasm in Henrich's voice. She was beginning to wonder just how committed the captain was to Hitler's regime.

They moved forward, and the crowd thickened. There were people on every side of them now; a crush of humanity. Yvonne felt claustrophobic. She made sure Edward was close, as she didn't want him to get lost in the mob. Before long the stage came into view, standing just in front of the Brandenburg Gate. It was a vast platform, much higher and longer than the stage they had seen back in Dunkirk. She estimated that the platform stood about thirty foot high and was around one hundred or more foot long. A podium had been placed in the centre of the stage. It was dwarfed by the sheer size of the platform on which it sat. There were huge speakers set up on both sides of the platform. But what really caught her eye was the immense banner which hung above the podium. It was the largest flag she had ever seen, with the Swastika emblem set against the blood red background. It chilled Yvonne to the bone. She had come to think of the Nazi flag as representing the very epitome of evil, the banner of a savage Empire, built upon a bloody foundation of conquest, slavery and mass murder.

The Germans present at this rally apparently did not feel the same way. Excitement was in the air. It was like electricity, flowing through every man, woman and child present in the crowd. It was as if the fascist supporters were under some kind of spell, a mass form of hypnosis which kept every one under control, and blinded them all to the evils perpetrated by this regime.

Every face in the crowd looked to the podium, and then the man of the hour came into view.

A phalanx of uniformed soldiers marched out onto the stage in a diamond formation, all acting as one, totally committed to guarding their leader. On reaching the podium, they broke formation and formed a defensive line on the stage, facing out towards the assembled crowd.

One man strode confidently forward and there was a roar of applause and cheers from the audience. Yvonne had to cover her ears. She looked up and saw him for the first time: Adolf Hitler, the man who had conquered all of Europe in just a few short years. He was arguably the most powerful leader on the planet at this time, a man who inspired both fear and devoted admiration, depending on one's point of view.

For years Yvonne's husband had spoken of Hitler as if he was a demigod, a man who had risen up to a new level of greatness, leading his nation to world domination. She glanced across to Andrew and saw the expression on his face. His eyes were wide with wonder, his mouth open. He was in complete awe of his hero. Her husband clearly shared the feeling of the German crowd. Hitler was his Messiah. Andrew had been waiting half his life for this moment, and now he was here. Yvonne didn't know how to feel. Should she be happy for her husband? Maybe this momentous event would change him for the better. Perhaps all of his frustration and anger would now fade away. Deep down, though, she knew that such hopes were foolhardy.

Yvonne's first impression of Hitler was one of disappointment. She was under-awed by the man's physical presence, or lack thereof. True enough, she was standing far back from the podium, and so all of the men on stage looked small from her perspective. Nevertheless, it was obvious that Hitler was not a physically imposing character. He wasn't particularly tall or well built, and he appeared stooped, like it was a struggle for him to even stand up. He wore a khaki uniform and peaked cap, complete with a Swastika armband. And, of course, Yvonne had been used to seeing Hitler's image for many years; in the papers and news reels and the like. She had never been impressed by Hitler's appearance. He wasn't an attractive man, not in Yvonne's eyes. She could never understand why the German women seemed to go so crazy over him. She guessed that, in his case, power was an aphrodisiac. And then there was the Nazi ideal of manhood, the pure Aryan; tall, blond haired, blue eyed, muscular and well built. This was everything that Hitler was not. How had such a man ever come to rule over this country?

Hitler marched up to the podium. He didn't acknowledge the men standing to either side of him, the fanatical bodyguards whose loyalty to their leader was beyond question. He looked up to the crowd in front of him, the thousands of devoted followers here to see their Fuhrer. His eyes were piercing. It was an odd and unnerving thing, but it seemed as if Hitler was looking straight at Yvonne herself, like he was picking her out from the thousands of others present. This was impossible, of course, but it was how she felt in this moment. There was a second's pause, and then Hitler began to speak. His voice was powerful and penetrating, his volume greatly enhanced by the huge speakers on either side of the stage.

Yvonne was not a native German speaker. She knew some words and phrases, but didn't understand much of what Hitler was saying. Nevertheless, she was surprised to find herself hanging on the Fuhrer's every word. His speech was mesmerising. She didn't know what it was, but Hitler was clearly a passionate and very skilled orator. She guessed this was a big part of his appeal. As before, it seemed to Yvonne that Hitler was speaking directly to her. It was an eerie and unsettling feeling. She wondered whether every person present in the crowd felt the same way. She concluded that they must do. This was how Hitler got to them. He was like a fisherman, reeling in a thousand different catches simultaneously.

She glanced across to the rest of her family, curious to see how they were all reacting to Hitler's speech. Did they feel the same way as she did? Her husband was still lost in his little fantasy. Andrew was entirely focussed on his beloved Fuhrer. He stared directly at Hitler, listening intently to the German leader's every word. His complete devotion and admiration to this tyrant was frightening.

Edward was similarly in awe of Hitler. He replicated his father's stance and facial expression to a tee. Yvonne shook her head in disappointment. When was her son ever going to learn? Her brother-in-law John seemed less than impressed. He alone stood in defiance of Hitler, refusing to join in the sycophantic applause and hero-worshipping.

The speech went on. Yvonne continued to listen. She didn't understand much of what Hitler was saying, but she did get the general gist of his speech. The German leader made several references to Juden or the 'Jewish enemy', and the inevitable triumph of the Volks, the German and Aryan people. It was all pretty standard stuff. Just 'run of the mill' Nazi propaganda. No wonder fewer and fewer people where turning out for these silly rallies, she thought.

Hitler then started speaking on other matters, but Yvonne's limited knowledge of the German language was soon exhausted, and she struggled to follow the meaning. Captain Muller noticed that and he moved closer to her and began to whisper in her ear, providing a translated summary.

"The Fuhrer speaks of the Fatherland's victory over the Jewish-Bolshevik criminals, the fall of Moscow and death of Stalin," Muller explained. "He states that the next great battle for the German people will be against the Americans, a nation he describes as being corrupted by Negroid and Jewish blood. He claims that the money men and bankers in Wall Street are all Jews or puppets of the Jews, and that they orchestrated the 1929 Crash in an unsuccessful attempt to destroy the German economy. And now

149

the American President Truman is increasing his country's military spending, building US bases across the world in an attempt to challenge German power..."

This made sense to Yvonne. With Russia defeated and Britain in decline, it seemed as if America was the only country left in the world which was capable of standing up to the Nazis. Hitler would never say so directly, but it seemed he felt threatened by American power, even if he did think of their people as inferior.

The speech continued. Once again, Muller was there to provide the translation. "...And now the Fuhrer speaks of great scientific advances, which will allow the Fatherland to match and exceed the Americans in the fields of weaponry and technology."

Yvonne wondered what Hitler meant by this last comment. She knew little about military weapons, so she didn't dwell on the statement.

Soon after, the Fuhrer's speech reached a frightening crescendo. Hitler started to play act on the stage, whipping the crowd up with his erratic behaviour. He began to scream and gyrate like some kind of madman, waving his arms in the air and shouting out with such anger. The crowd responded to his bizarre and unsettling behaviour, and they replicated his passionate show of hatred.

Yvonne observed such people on every side of her; men, women, old and young...even children dressed up in their Hitler Youth uniforms. They acted in unison, as if they were all a part of one gigantic machine. Every attendee raised their hands to give the Nazi salute, and each one cried out 'Seig Heil! Seig Heil!' over and over again. The noise was unbearable. Yvonne couldn't take it, she couldn't stand this visceral display of animalistic savagery. She wanted to run away, but there was nowhere to go...no escape from this. To her horror, she observed that both her husband and son were participating in this grotesque display. Both Andrew and Edward had apparently been swept up with the rest of the Nazi supporting mob. They'd been entranced by the sheer, terrifying magnetism of Hitler, and the fierce fanaticism of the hateful crowd.

She turned away in disgust, her attention suddenly captured by an incident happening directly behind her.

There was a small gap in the crowd, now filled by a half dozen middle aged women, all of whom carried placards. They were clearly Germans, but their physical appearance and whole demeanour was very different from the others, as was their clothing; they were all dressed in black, from head to toe.

Yvonne looked into their faces and saw their emotional exhaustion and the sorrow in their eyes. However, what really drew her attention were the large cardboard placards carried by each of the women. The signs looked like sandwich boards; they hung over the shoulders and covered the entire torso and each bore a photograph of a young man. Six different boys, all not much older than Edward, all dressed in military uniforms. They all had boyish grins and a childlike innocence in their bright eyes.

There were German names printed on each sign, just above the photographs...Berndt Strauss, Eric Dieter, Gustav Boll, Jurgen Schweinsteiger, Max Koch and Otto Reinhart. Unremarkable names, Yvonne supposed, but clearly they meant something to the women and she quickly realised the connection: they were mothers, the boys were their sons. Under each photograph was written a date and a place name - Warsaw, Minsk, Moscow, Archangel, Tambov, and Kazan.

Muller turned to Yvonne to confirm her suspicions, "They are mothers of young men who have been killed on the Eastern Front. Their grief has removed all of their fears. "

The unexpected presence of these women clearly concerned him. Yvonne could empathise with them. Their loss was heart-breaking and she tried to imagine how she would feel, if Edward was killed in a war. It was too awful for her to even contemplate.

Then a terrible realisation struck her: according to the dates on the placards these boys had all fallen in either 1947 or 1948 when, if the Nazis were to be believed, the war in the East was over, and the colonies were peaceful and pacified. This was clearly an untruth. Young men were still dying out there in the East, and probably many more than the half dozen portrayed on these placards. Yvonne felt both angry and fearful. The Nazis had lied to them all, and there was no telling what dangers awaited her family as they headed into what was obviously still a war-zone.

By now, others in the crowd had noticed the six grieving women. Several were temporarily distracted from their slavish worship of the Fuhrer, as they turned around to confront the female protestors.

Yvonne wondered how the Nazi faithful would react to this small protest made by middle class German women; mothers struggling with their grief and asking for nothing more than a recognition of their suffering. She hoped the rally attendees would respect their dignity, but once again she was disappointed.

A section of the crowd broke away from the main rally and surrounded the group of protesting mothers, spitting and screaming obscenities, but it drew no reaction from the targets of their abuse, which only served to aggravate the attackers all the more.

A couple of men stepped forward and attempted to physically rip the placards off their backs. Several frenzied scuffles ensued and Yvonne saw a young boy of about ten dressed in the uniform of the Hitler Youth join the melee. He was soon accompanied by a group of female Nazis who immediately pounced on the hapless and grieving mothers, striking them with closed fists and handbags. The situation was becoming very ugly and Yvonne was scared.

She looked across to the German captain who was clearly upset by what was happening, but he made no effort to intervene. She saw that John was as horrified as she was by the unprovoked attack. He moved forward, preparing for a fight, but suddenly a number of men emerged from the crowd, all easily recognisable as plain clothes Gestapo officers.

The civilian attackers instinctively backed off, but then the unexpected happened. The officers pounced on the group of mothers, snapped each of them in handcuffs and marched them away.

Yvonne looked up and saw a familiar face, standing just a few yards behind her: Hoffman, the sinister Gestapo commander and unwanted escort. She had thought the secret policeman had left her family alone for the afternoon, but no such luck. He had always been there, watching them from the shadows. The men who had made the arrests were surely under his command. This was

Hoffman's job, assaulting and dragging off innocent housewives and mothers...so-called Enemies of the State.

The Gestapo man was staring straight at Yvonne, his dark and intense eyes cutting right through her. She looked away, spotting her husband and son who were oblivious to what had just played out in front of her.

Both Edward and Andrew were still engrossed in Hitler's ranting, their arms raised in salute as they chanted, 'Heil Hitler! Heil Hitler!'

Yvonne felt as if she was about to be physically sick. She didn't care about Andrew anymore, but the sight of her only son behaving in such a manner was too much to bear. She didn't want to end up like those other mothers, holding a placard displaying the picture of her dead son. But it seemed as if her worst nightmare was fast becoming a reality.

She knew she had to do something, and quickly, otherwise her son would be lost to her forever.

# 9/ 'The City of Death'

JULIE PRESTON HATED HER family. Yes, she knew that this statement was a cliché. Julie also knew she was a fourteen year old girl, and everyone was always telling her she was too young, and didn't yet know how the world really worked. But Julie considered herself much more mature than most girls of her age – silly little things who only thought about dresses, boys and dances. Unlike her contemporaries, Julie wasn't blind to what was going on around her. She knew exactly what the Nazi brutes were capable of, but none of her family would recognise their true nature.

Julie wasn't usually given to outbreaks of teenage angst, although she did have her moments. Nevertheless, the girl felt she had many legitimate reasons for feeling angry with her parents. She thought very little of her father and considered him as nothing more than a bully and a violent patriarch. Andrew Preston was a man obsessed with control and power. Since he'd never held any real power in his whole life, he took his frustrations out on his family. Julie was disgusted by her dad's slavish devotion to Adolf Hitler and his brutish Nazi foot soldiers. She despised everything that the Fascists represented and stood for. Julie considered herself as an anti-Fascist, having befriended several young socialists and Jews back in London; illicit relationships formed in secret defiance to her father's hateful beliefs.

Louis had taught her everything she knew about socialism, Marxism and the solidarity of the people. Her Louis, oh how she missed him...

She had few good memories of her father. Those she did retain were all from early childhood...back in the days when she was a clueless little girl bouncing on Daddy's knee, and not mature enough to form her own opinions of the world. Her more recent experiences with him had not been good. Julie argued with her father frequently. She just didn't respect him anymore.

He could not cope with any level of defiance and often reacted violently to her insolence; she had been on the receiving end of several beatings - slaps, fists and belts. She didn't care anymore. Bruises would heal, and that brute was never going to beat her into submission. Julie knew the truth. Her father was nothing but a cowardly bully, and Julie wasn't frightened of bullies...not anymore.

In contrast to her own behaviour, Julie's older brother always went along with whatever their father said and did. It was pathetic. Edward seemed to be obsessed with pleasing his father, and with emulating the man's revolting fascist ideals. Her brother's unquestioning devotion to their old man angered Julie no end. She was constantly fighting with her brother, but there was no talking to Edward. He wouldn't change his views, so Julie had decided to ignore him.

When growing up, Julie had formed a close kinship with her long suffering mother. This was partly because she knew that her mother had borne the brunt of their father's violent temper over the years, and she had done her best to shield Edward and Julie from the worst of the fights. Edward had always buried his head in the sand, but Julie knew the truth. Also, Julie had always considered her mother to be an intelligent and enlightened woman, at least compared to the other members of the Preston family.

In more recent years, Julie had felt able to have frank and personal conversations with her mother, to share many of her deepest feelings and to seek maternal advice. However, Julie no longer felt this way. She no longer trusted her mum and she felt betrayed by her.

Julie blamed her mother for not standing up to their father. She shouldn't have allowed their entire family to be dragged away from their home, and forced against their will to move to Nazi Germany. She just couldn't understand why her mother would have allowed this. Julie was extremely disappointed in her.

She also felt very let down by her uncle John. She had always looked up to her uncle. She'd considered him to be a good and decent man, a brave soldier who had fought the good fight against the Nazis...unlike her own father, who had spent most of the war in prison. But then Uncle John had agreed to go along with his younger brother's insane plan. How could he be so weak? How could he betray his country and everything he stood for? Julie didn't understand at all. Why was she the only one who could see the truth? Were the rest of her family stupid?

She was still haunted by the terrible memory of that poor man getting beaten up by those Nazi thugs on a back street in Berlin. She'd been unable to sleep for two night's straight because she was still so upset and angry. And what had her mother said, whenever Julie had spoken out in protest at the poor man's treatment? She had told her to shut up.

This had been the final straw for Julie. She had refused to attend the ridiculous Hitler rally later that same afternoon and had locked herself away in the hotel room, crying for hours; not just due to what she had witnessed, but also because of what she'd lost – her life and friends back in London...and her one true love.

Julie could tell something was wrong when the rest of her family arrived back at the hotel that evening. Her father and brother were both ecstatic. They kept on going on and on about their beloved 'Fuhrer'. The men's sycophantic admiration of this mass murdering psychopath made her feel physically sick. However, both her mother and uncle were behaving very differently. They both seemed shaken and upset. Julie guessed the two had witnessed something unpleasant at the rally. She asked her mother what had happened, but she'd refused to tell her. Julie didn't care anymore. She no longer felt any love or loyalty towards her treacherous family. Young Julie had already come to a personal decision. She was going to escape and run away at the first opportunity. She didn't just want to flee from her oppressive family and this Nazi nightmare. Julie also yearned to make her way home to England. She knew her journey would be difficult...maybe near impossible. But she was determined to try, because the boy she loved was back home in London.

Louis was older, sixteen. Most boys of this age were immature and stupid. Julie knew this much. Teenage boys were usually after only one thing when it came to girls. Her mother had warned her about such boys; she'd warned her daughter to stay clear of them and to always be careful. Her mum had met her dad when she was a teenager herself, and she'd apparently been swept off her feet by his charm and good looks, mainly because she didn't know any better at such a young age. Her mother didn't want Julie to make the same mistakes as she had. Louis was different, though.

They had met one night at a youth club on the Old Kent Road and had got to talking. Louis was intelligent and compassionate. He cared about people and about important social causes, and he'd taught Julie all about progressive political ideologies; Marxism, Trotskyism...the revolutionary principles of liberty, equality and fraternity. Julie had been blown away by his great knowledge of such things. He was a member of the Young Socialists, and felt very passionately about their cause. Julie greatly admired his romantic commitment to social justice.

He was also very handsome, what with his soft, olive coloured skin, his beaming smile, hazelnut eyes and shining black hair. Louis was also half-Jewish, his mother having immigrated to England during the 1920s. As far as Julie's father was concerned, Louis was probably the most unsuitable partner for his only daughter. Then again, this was all a part of the attraction as far as Julie was concerned.

Louis was not like the other boys his age. He was the perfect gentleman; kind, respectful and considerate. He didn't pressurise Julie into doing anything she didn't want to do. They had kissed and fondled a couple of times, but that was as far as it had gone. Julie was still a virgin. She didn't feel ready for sex, and Louis had respected this. They had spent their all too brief time together going to the pictures, walking in the park or just talking about so many meaningful topics; literature, poetry, music, politics, life and love. Julie had fallen for him in a big way, but their time had been cut painfully short.

Julie knew how her father would react if he ever found out about her and Louis. Therefore, she'd kept their relationship a total secret, even from her own mother. But, only a few short weeks later, her father had announced that their family was leaving England to move to Germany. Julie had been totally devastated. She'd argued fiercely with both of her parents, provoking her father's violent temper. But she realised that such arguments were ultimately futile. Her dad would never change his mind.

Instead, she'd met with Louis and had told him the bad news. He'd been as upset as her, and the young couple had soon decided to run away together. Julie had been ready and eager to leave with her love, but, at the very last moment, Louis had changed his mind. He'd told Julie they couldn't run away, that it wasn't practical to do so. He said that she should go with her family. Julie was left confused, upset and angry by her boyfriend's sudden reversal. She screamed and argued with him, but Louis had calmed her down and explained his decision. He said they were destined to be together, and seas, mountains and borders couldn't keep them apart. Their separation would only be temporary. Louis had promised he would find a way for the two of them to be together – that she just needed to trust him. Julie had reluctantly agreed to his terms. She did trust Louis, but it was still torture to be parted from him.

She missed him so much and, given everything which had happened over the past few days, she was even more determined to escape from this nightmare and find her way back to England.

After a night's stay in Berlin, the family had re-boarded the train to continue their journey eastwards. Julie had been biding her time and was careful not to kick up a fuss, lest she give away her secret plan. The train travelled through eastern Germany and Prussia, before it crossed the border and entered the territory known as the 'General Government'. Her uncle had told her that these lands were once part of Poland, the country which England had gone to war to defend. And now the nation no longer existed.

Julie looked out the carriage window to take in the views of the Polish countryside as the train sped through these lands at a great pace. It didn't stop and she could see why. This country was dead. Gone were the tidy, well organised and affluent towns and villages of the Fatherland. All she could see were ruined and abandoned settlements, burnt or overgrown fields and so many heavily fortified German military bases. The towns they passed through which were still standing seemed largely abandoned. They looked like ghost towns, with their eerily empty streets and crumbling buildings. This was the General Government, otherwise known as 'Gestapo Land'.

Julie saw many German soldiers, but very few Polish civilians. She wondered what could have happened to this country. Julie knew there had been a war here, and she could only conclude that the Germans must have destroyed the entire Polish nation. She spared a thought for all of the poor people who once lived here, before the Nazi invasion. She reckoned they had all been shipped off to work as slave labourers inside of Hitler's Reich, just like those she had seen back in Berlin.

After several hours, the train arrived in the suburbs of what appeared to be a large city....or at least, what had once been a substantial conurbation. And again, the signs of devastation were everywhere. There was hardly a single building undamaged, and many had been completely demolished or destroyed. The small number of people they spotted appeared to be thin, ragged and filthy – as if they were barely surviving. They peeked out from behind ruined buildings to sneak a look at the train speeding by. They showed their heads only briefly, before ducking back into cover, like frightened rabbits retreating down to their subterranean warrens.

The military presence was also heavy, with German Army billets positioned every couple of miles along the track; heavily armed soldiers manning machine guns behind concrete pillboxes.

"Which city is this?" asked Julie, as she spoke for the first time in about an hour.

"This is Warsaw," Captain Henrich Muller answered, in a solemn voice. "Once the capital of the Polish Republic and now ruled as part of the Reich's Generalgouvernement or 'General Government' province."

"What happened here?" asked her uncle John. He spoke with an accusatory and suspicious tone.

Muller hesitated for several seconds before he finally answered. His facial expression was grim.

"There was an uprising," he explained. "Back in the spring of 1943, communist terrorists attacked our troops and attempted to take control of the city. The battle was fierce, and much of the city was destroyed in the fighting."

"How awful," said Julie's mother. Hers was a reflex display of feigned sympathy. This angered Julie no end.

"Regrettably," said Muller. "Regrettably, the Reich has been unable to rebuild Warsaw to date. We currently lack the finances and resources to do so."

Julie noticed the subtle and silent gestures exchanged between Hoffman and Muller. The German captain seemed about to say more, but one sharp glare from the Gestapo officer was enough to quieten him. There followed a tense silence for the next moment, until Julie's father deemed it appropriate to add his own comment.

"Bloody Poles!" snarled Andrew. "Sub-human Slavs, the lot of them...they're all treacherous swine, don't you know? Always eager to bite the hand that feeds them."

Julie scoffed aloud in a mocking gesture. She did so without thinking, but luckily her father hadn't heard her. She waited for someone else to challenge her father, but no-one did. Julie was left fuming, but she knew she had to control her emotions. If she lost her temper now it would scupper her whole plan.

How could any of her family believe the rubbish Muller was telling them? There had probably never been a battle here but, even if there had been, this was no excuse for the Germans to destroy an entire city. And it was clearly a lie that Germany could not afford to rebuild Warsaw. The Nazis must be spending a colossal amount of money in order to construct those grotesque, giant structures in Berlin. And how many Polish workers were being forced against their will to work in the German capital, while their own capital city was left in ruins? Julie was so sick of all these lies, and all of the hypocrisy, but she wouldn't have to put up with this for much longer.

Their train was due to stop in Warsaw overnight while they waited for new supplies and additional passengers. Unlike their stopover in Berlin, none of the passengers were permitted to leave the train, and so they all had to sleep on board.

Julie could not sleep, however. Fully dressed, and with a rucksack packed with all her belongings, she lay on her bunk, staring up at the carriage ceiling, working out the beginnings of what would be a daring plan for escape come dawn.

She made her move when she eventually saw the first glimmers of daylight creeping in through the small carriage window, carefully climbing out of her bunk, doing so as quickly and as quietly as possible, not wanting to wake her brother nearby. But she need not have worried. Edward was a heavy sleeper. She took one glance at him, put on her shoes, grabbed her bag and slipped out into the corridor.

With no one in sight, she moved off, trying to think of her next step to freedom.

Earlier, she had observed their German guards, one in particular, an older man with grey hair and stripes on his sleeve. He appeared to be more senior than the others and she had noticed he carried a set of keys around his belt, master keys, she reckoned.

She needed them.

She got her chance when she came across the guard farther down the carriage. He was fast asleep in an otherwise empty passenger compartment and her eyes immediately focused on the set of keys dangling from his belt. Talking a deep breath to compose herself, she tip-toed her way toward him, praying he wouldn't awake from his slumber. She reached out to slip the keys from his possession, her hands trembling with fear and trepidation.

*Please, God, don't let him wake up. I'm dead if he does! Please...please...please.*

Holding her breath now she gently worked the keys from the man's belt and quickly melted from his presence, elated and terrified at the same time.

She then made her way to the catering area, stocking up on food supplies before staff turned up to cook breakfast. She grabbed bread rolls, cheese, ham, German sausages, apples and pears, piling them all into her rucksack. She also nabbed two flasks, filling up one with orange juice and the second with apple juice.

With enough to sustain her for a few days on the run, and with the sun slowly rising in the early morning sky, she made her way to the exit door, quickly found the key to unlock it and stepped out on to the still empty station platform.

From here…well, from here she hadn't really given it much thought, the cold realisation only now dawning on her. Once clear of the station, then what? She could stow away on a train heading back in the opposite direction, or she could try to make her way north to the Baltic coastline to get a boat to anywhere other than Germany, preferably back home to the safety of England.

She cautiously glanced up and down the platform. There were two armed soldiers in the distance, but they clearly hadn't spotted her and for that she was thankful.

She was about to move off in the opposite direction when she felt a firm hand on her shoulder. Horrified, she turned round, unable to breath.

"What the hell are you doing here?"

It was Edward. He looked tired and dishevelled.

"What does it look like? I'm leaving, Edward," she replied sternly and defiantly. "I'm running away, and there's nothing you can do to stop me, so get back on to the train before anybody notices you are missing."

"But you can't!" Edward cried frantically. "This is madness! You're going to get us all into so much trouble!"

Suddenly, Julie heard loud voices. She glanced down the platform to see the two armed soldiers rushing towards her. In an instant, she broke away from her brother and took off, running as fast as her legs would carry her, ignoring the frantic cries of protest from her brother. Before long, she reached the far end of the platform where a short flight of stairs opened up an escape route for her. But her relief was short-lived, for when she got the station exit, she found herself confronted by a locked iron gate.

The soldiers were closing on her. She could hear the thump of heavy boots behind her, but she didn't dare to look back. Just when she was about to surrender she remembered the keys.

The gate swung open on the third attempt and she made a dash for freedom, unaware that Edward had somehow evaded capture and was now by her side.

"The key...give me the key!" he yelled, grabbing it from Julie's hand and then rushing back to re-lock the gate just before the arrival of the soldiers. The Germans could only look on as brother and sister quickly disappeared from view.

They didn't know how far they had come, or for how long they had been running. All they knew was that their lungs were burning and their legs aching.

Julie was the first to stop. Leaning against a wall, she was fighting for air. Edward came to her side, his face bright red and his breathing laboured, but they had succeeded in losing their pursuers, for now at least.

Looking around her, Julie could only see abandoned buildings, shell and bullet riddled concrete ruins and rubble strewn streets. The whole of the city was derelict and empty.

"Where the hell are we?" asked Edward and Julie shot him a hard look before moving off again. "Where are you going?" Edward cried. "This is madness, Julie! We have to go back!"

"You should go back!" Julie retorted. "I'm going on." Edward followed her.

Suddenly, Julie's attention was drawn to movement away to the right. It was a boy. He'd darted across the empty street and disappeared behind a brick wall, and she set off to investigate.

Edward called after her, telling her to stop, but she paid no heed and quickened her pace when the boy came back into view. She urged him to stop, but he kept on running, and soon she found herself in the remains of a gutted building where she was confronted by a group of other ragged and frightened children, refugees by all accounts. She couldn't begin to imagine the horrors they had been through.

Edward came up behind her.

"We shouldn't be here," he kept repeating, "We shouldn't get involved."

Julie ignored him and turned back to the children, asking if any of them spoke English.

One boy stepped forward, cautiously strolling towards her. He was probably the eldest of the group and Julie reckoned he had assumed a leadership role over the younger children. He was perhaps the same age as Julie, but it was difficult for her to tell for sure, because the poor boy was so malnourished and his growth had probably been stunted. He was pale and thin, and his clothes were a state, but, in spite of his desperate condition, there was still a bright twinkle in his eye, still a dash of hope in his tired and hungry face. Julie instinctively liked the boy. She looked down to his torn and soiled clothing and noted the faded yellow star sewed onto the front of his filthy jacket. Julie wondered what this symbol meant, and why he continued to wear it. She looked him in the eye and spoke, even though she felt slightly foolish in doing so.

"Good morning," she said, in the way of a formal greeting. "My name is Julie....what is yours?"

The boy seemed to understand her. He smiled, flashing his broken yellow teeth through his dried up lips. "Abraham," he replied.

"We are from England," explained Julie. "Is this your home?"

His reply was incomprehensible and Julie guessed he was speaking in Polish. There was sadness in his eyes and he kept on pointing to his jacket, drawing her attention to the yellow star. Julie guessed that the symbol meant something to him, that it represented an important part of his identity. When he spoke again, he repeatedly lifted his hand up to his mouth and made a gesture which intimated the act of chewing. Julie understood instantly, and she mentally scolded herself for being so thoughtless. They wanted food. These poor kids were starving! Julie didn't hesitate. She had taken food from the train for herself, but their need was much, much greater.

She dropped her rucksack down to the dusty ground and began to open up the bag, but to her great annoyance, Edward made an attempt to stop her, reaching out to grab the bag from her, but she was having none of it. She shoved him away, leaving him visibly shocked and subdued.

Julie opened the rucksack and invited the children to take what they wanted.

The children rushed to the rucksack and tore into the supplies. Abraham allowed them a few seconds grace before he too relented and joined in.

Julie and Edward both watched on, awestruck as the seven half starved refugees ripped through the small quantity of food. It was as if they had never eaten before. Bread rolls and slices of cheese and ham were shoved into mouths, pears and apples were rapidly demolished. It was a feeding frenzy.

The moment was suddenly disrupted by the heavy stomp of boots and seconds later Julie, Edward and the children found themselves facing a squad of bulky and heavily armed German soldiers, all dressed in the standard grey uniforms and the distinctive steel helmets of the Wehrmacht.

Abraham ran towards the younger children in his care, many of whom were screaming and crying. He took charge, herding them towards the open back door of the shattered building, but more soldiers arrived to block their escape route.

One of the Germans stepped forward and lashed out at Abraham with his rifle. The butt struck him in the belly and he doubled over in pain. The soldier then grabbed him by the jacket and dragged him across the floor, tossing him roughly into the corner of the room.

Some of the other soldiers turned on the children, poking and prodding them with their rifles, as Abraham got to his feet again. It was too much for Julie to take. Her rage overcame the fear she had previously felt and she threw herself at the gun-wielding soldiers, but it was to no avail. Moments later she – and Edward - were being dragged away by two of the Germans, one of whom whispered in her ear, "Calm down!"

It was Captain Muller.

Suddenly they were back out on the street, and Julie could no longer see what was happening behind the walls of the ruins.

A few seconds later there was a chorus of chilling screams, the desperate cries of children, followed by the sound of gunfire.

Then silence.

Finding her voice again, Julie turned on Muller, yelling, "You killed them...you murdered Abraham and those children...shot them all..."

"NO!" Muller responded sternly. "We did no such thing! We simply fired warning shots to scare them off. These children are not meant to be in this district. They are unharmed and will return to their families."

"You are lying!" retorted Julie, kicking Muller in the shin, trying to break free from his grasp.

She almost succeeded, but then a second soldier grabbed her right arm, and she was overpowered. Minutes later, she was being dragged back to the train.

# 10/ 'Destroyer of Worlds'

JULIE HAD BORNE THE brunt of her father's fury. True enough, Andrew Preston had been angry at both of his children, but Julie got the worst of it. He had screamed in her face, told her she was a disgrace of a daughter and that he was ashamed of her.

Julie could have laughed at this comment, and so she did. She talked back to her father, which was never a smart idea. He had reacted violently to her continued defiance, slapping her hard across the face. Julie knew he would have done a lot worse, had they not been in a train carriage filled with strangers. She had repeated her belief that the German soldiers had committed a cold blooded massacre of innocent children.

Muller continued to deny the allegation, but Julie knew he was lying. Predictably, her father did not believe her. He demanded to know whether she had actually seen anybody being shot. Julie had to admit that she had not. As far as her father was concerned, the matter was now closed.

Edward and Julie had both been locked in their sleeping compartment as a punishment for their unauthorised foray into Warsaw. Julie knew this wouldn't be the end of the matter. Her father would not let her off so easily, and he had a long memory. Edward blamed his sister for the whole affair, so now he was refusing to speak with her. She was totally distraught. Her escape attempt had failed, and she was unlikely to get another opportunity. She may never see her Louis again. Worse still, she realised that her own actions had indirectly led to the deaths of seven innocent children. Julie felt devastated, and she did not know how she was going to live with herself.

She lay on top of her bunk, unable to sleep. Their train had left Warsaw many hours ago, and now it was night time once again. The darkness filled up their small cabin. Edward was snoring. For some reason, Julie found the noise comforting. Her mind was racing. She knew she would not be able to get even a wink of sleep on this night. She needed some sort of distraction from the horrific memories trapped inside her head.

She climbed out of her bunk, making sure to be as quiet as possible, and crept across the cabin floor to the small window, which was covered up by a black-out curtain. She lifted the blind ever so slightly. Edward grunted, but did not stir. She looked out to the rolling countryside. To her disappointment, she was unable to see much in the way of scenery. It was nearly pitch black and the night's moon was nothing more than a slender crescent. There were only a few artificial lights visible on the far horizon. However, when she looked up, she saw hundreds of stars in the sky, many more than she could ever remember seeing back in London, and she was temporarily enthralled by the vast beauty of the galaxy.

Suddenly, there was an immense flash of light on the extreme far horizon. The illumination was as bright as the sun and she was forced to cover her face to protect her eyes. For a brief moment, it looked like daylight. When she opened her eyes, she saw that the light was fading. It dimmed and finally disappeared, as darkness returned to the land. Julie had never seen anything like it and wondered what could have caused such an intense light. A thunder storm perhaps? Surely not, as the flash was many times brighter than any lightning strike she had ever seen. She stayed by the window for some time, as if expecting a repeat of this extraordinary event. But there was nothing more to see, and eventually she returned to her bunk to suffer a restless night.

John Preston sat down to breakfast in the dining car at 8am sharp, alongside his brother and sister-in-law, Captain Muller and the ever present Gestapo man called Hoffman.

There was a wide selection of foods spread out in front of them; fruit, bread, cheese and meats, all to be washed down by fruit juice, tea or coffee.

John wasn't hungry. All he could manage was a mug of strong, black coffee. He sipped at his hot beverage without much enthusiasm. The others picked at their food. There was no conversation. The group were still dealing with the ugly aftermath of Julie's and Edward's escape attempt in Warsaw.

His brother was still furious. John could tell as much from the livid look on Andrew's face. His whole demeanour was that of a man in a state of constant rage. John didn't like this side of his brother. He could tell Yvonne was feeling uncomfortable in this situation, although presumably she had had to deal with her husband's anger on many previous occasions.

John knew that neither child had had anything to eat since at least yesterday morning. He decided that he should speak up and persuade his brother to see reason.

"You know," he said calmly, "you know, Andrew, it would be best if the children were to get washed and dressed. A bit of breakfast would also do them some good..."

Andrew shot his brother a hard look, and said, "They're being punished...this was my ruling...are you telling me how to raise my own children?"

"No, of course not..." John replied defensively. He was desperately trying to figure out what to say next, but luckily Yvonne intervened.

"But Andrew," she protested, "today is a big day. We'll be disembarking from the train and beginning the final leg of our journey. That's what you told me, isn't it? The children will need to be washed and prepared, and they'll need a good breakfast to keep them going..."

Andrew grunted. "All right," he finally answered. "But they can bloody well wait until I'm finished eating before they come to the table. I'm too disgusted to see either one of them."

All parties seemed satisfied by this compromise. John got

back to his coffee, and to his own inner thoughts. He vividly remembered the grim scenes they had all witnessed back in Warsaw. He was having serious doubts about the state of affairs on the ground here in Eastern Europe. He had seen war. He knew the devastation that could be caused by artillery bombardment and aerial bombing. Nevertheless, the sheer scale of the destruction he'd witnessed in Warsaw was truly shocking. He couldn't recall seeing even a single undamaged building in the city. What kind of battle could have caused this?

John recalled hearing of a popular uprising breaking out in Warsaw, back in the spring of 1943. The accounts of the fighting which reached London were inevitably heavily censored. Poland was firmly under Nazi control, and there were no outsiders on the ground that would have been able to provide an independent account of events. Furthermore, by 1943, few Britons were interested in news coming from the continent. Britain's war had been over for three long years by that point. The conflict was a humiliating memory for almost all Englishmen, and few wanted to be reminded of 'Britain's darkest hour'. The British Empire had gone to war in order to defend Polish independence, but this honourable goal was soon forgotten after Halifax had made peace with Hitler.

The devastation John had observed in Warsaw appeared to have been caused by systematic bombardment and probably by controlled explosions using dynamite. The Wehrmacht would not have needed to use such overwhelming force in order to put down a simple rebellion by poorly armed Polish civilians, so he could only conclude that the Nazis had purposefully demolished the city, either in retaliation for the uprising, or because it had always been their intention to level the Polish capital.

As for the city's former citizens, John could only assume they had been forcibly relocated, enslaved or murdered. Whatever the case, he was convinced that he had witnessed evidence of an unprecedented war crime committed by the Nazis. What's more, his niece Julie returned to the train with a very disturbing account of an alleged massacre carried out by German soldiers. He had taken the time to carefully consider Julie's allegations. He knew that teenage girls were prone to having overactive imaginations. At the same time, he knew that his niece was a sensible and intelligent young lady. John was unconvinced by Henrich Muller's explanation of events. He already knew that the Nazis had murdered Henrich's younger brother, along with thousands of other disabled German children. If this was what they were capable of doing to their own underage citizens, John was sure they would not hesitate to shoot down Polish and Jewish children. He shuddered to think how many innocents had met a similar fate.

His grim musings were interrupted by Muller, resuming the role as the family's appointed guide and advisor.

"We have passed the old border," Muller explained, "about a mile ago. Before the war, these lands formed the frontier between Poland and the Soviet Republic of Belorussia. Today, this is the internal boundary between Generalgouvernement and Reichskommissariat Ostland – the latter province is, of course, our final destination, and your family's new home."

Andrew grinned like a Cheshire cat. John nodded his head without much enthusiasm. He couldn't see much difference between the two provinces of the Greater German Reich. As with Poland, most of Belorussia's borderlands appeared to be barren and deserted. This didn't bode well.

John tried to imagine how these lands must have looked seven years ago, when the Nazi onslaught had begun. In May of 1941 Germany and her allies had launched the largest land based invasion in military history, Operation Barbarossa – over three million Axis troops attacking over a front of thousands of kilometres. John attempted to put himself in the place of the Soviet soldiers and peasants, the hapless individuals who found themselves trapped in the eye of the storm, as the most vicious and deadly war machine of all time fell upon them, during that terrible spring and summer.

"Can we see a map of the territory?" Andrew enquired, with his face full of a nauseating enthusiasm. "I'd like to see exactly where our new home is located."

Muller shook his head, saying, "I'm afraid not, Mr. Preston. The old maps are of little use these days. Most of the former Soviet villages cease to exist, as do many of the smaller towns from the pre-war period. Instead, they have been replaced by a network of Wehrmacht forts and settler plantations. This is the new order, out here in the East."

"So, what happened to the former population?" John asked. "There must have been millions of Soviet citizens living in these lands."

The question clearly made Muller feel very uncomfortable. He broke off eye contact with John, and stared out through the carriage window, taking in the ravaged countryside as their train sped onwards. There followed a pause of several seconds, before the German captain finally answered.

"Some still live here, working for the Wehrmacht or the Volks settlers. The majority have emigrated further East, out to the Ural Mountains and beyond. Siberia and Central Asia are the new homelands of the Slavic and Jewish peoples."

Henrich didn't elaborate. His answer had been far from convincing. John thought it was ludicrous for the Nazis to claim that millions of Russians had voluntarily immigrated to lands thousands of miles distant. Reports from Eastern Europe had been sparse to non-existent for many years, but John and the others had seen much during their long train journey, and a very unsettling picture was beginning to emerge.

John knew that Muller was holding something back, but he did not push the matter. He noted that the Gestapo man Hoffman was still sitting at the back of the car. The secret policeman was listening intently to every word spoken. By now, it was clear to John that Hoffman did indeed understand English, regardless of what they had previously been told.

Just then, John's attention was drawn towards the rear of the train car, as the door was flung open and two strangers sauntered in.

Both men were young, perhaps in their early to mid-twenties. They were both wearing the uniforms of the Waffen SS. The men looked to be the very epitome of the Aryan soldier, the blond haired, blue eyed and perfectly physically formed young men of the Reich. The newcomers fitted this stereotype, so John assumed they were both Germans. He only realised his mistake after he heard the boys speak.

"Good morning," said both men in turn, as they greeted the Preston family and their German escorts. They spoke English with a heavy and distinctive accent. John recognised their drawl. They were South Africans. Introductions followed. The soldiers seemed to know of the Preston family, even though none of them had previously met. The men politely shook hands with Andrew, Yvonne and Henrich, but they snubbed John, refusing to acknowledge him or even look in his direction. He wondered why this was.

The South Africans introduced themselves as Jan van der Merwe and Pieter Steyn. Afrikaners. Perhaps this was the reason for their hostility. John didn't like it, but he held his tongue. Van der Merwe and Steyn both took their seats at the table and began to tuck into their breakfast.

A few moments passed before Yvonne struck up a conversation. "So, Mister van der Merwe and Mister Steyn…" she began.

"Please, Mrs. Preston," interrupted Steyn, "call us Jan and Pieter. We're all friends here, after all."

The South African then shot John a hostile look, but he wasn't going to let this Boer upstart intimidate him.

"Well, my new friends," Yvonne continued. John could detect the cutting sarcasm in her speech, although apparently the South Africans could not. "How did you come to be in our company?" she asked.

Steyn smirked. "That's a long story," he replied, before he took another mouthful of food from his plate.

"We're cousins," said van der Merwe, as he took up the mantle. "Grew up on farms right next to each other back in the Transvaal province. Our families have farmed those lands since the days of the Great Trek…"

"Our families are committed Boer nationalists," added Steyn, after he had chewed and swallowed. "Our ancestors fought against the British Empire during the First and Second Freedom Wars. We were brought up to honour their memories. Our people

173

never forgot the atrocities committed against us by the British, and we yearned for the chance to fight back against our oppressors. For myself and Jan, the opportunity came during the spring of 1942, when the Afrikaner people rose up in rebellion."

So, this is their story, John realised. The cousins were rebels, guilty of treason against the Empire. The two Boers must have known that John was a former British soldier. This was why they were treating him with such hostility. He listened with interest as Steyn told the next part of their story.

"When the English occupied our towns, many of us retreated into the bush, where we continued the fight." He shrugged his shoulders. "It went on for many months. We hit the English whenever we could, mounting ambushes and attacking isolated forts. Our people helped us, fed us and gave us shelter. We both ended up in serious bother after we shot the Magistrate."

Van der Merwe laughed aloud at the mention of the violent act.

"That bastard had it coming! He came into our district, taking the hard line and sentencing our brave soldiers to hang. The word came down the line - the bastard had to go, and the two of us got the job. It was a pleasure to put down that filthy vermin!"

John felt the anger rising up inside him. These animals had committed cold blooded murder, and now they were sitting here, laughing about it. It took all of his inner strength to retain his composure.

"Unfortunately," Steyn added, "unfortunately there were witnesses to the shooting, and the two of us were soon identified. The Brits put a bounty on our heads. We had to go on the run, because we'd have faced the noose if caught. The resistance network aided our escape. We were smuggled on board a freight ship out of Cape Town, worked our fare up past the Horn of Africa and through the Suez Canal. We made it to Naples, and eventually to Germany. The Fuhrer has welcomed many hundreds of exiled Boers into his Reich. He greatly admires our prowess in battle. Jan and I joined up with the Waffen SS. We've just attended an intense training course at a Wehrmacht base in East Prussia. We were bussed down from there and met the train last night during a stop off in a border station. And now, we're heading out East…just like your own family."

"Well," answered Andrew, his voice full of hearty enthusiasm. "It's an honour to meet you both."

"It's good to meet you too, Mr. Preston," answered van der Merwe, "and your charming wife. It's a pity I can't say the same about your brother."

Once again, the South African gave John an aggressive look. This time, he rose to the bait.

"What's your bloody problem, mate?" he demanded. "Is there something you want to say to me?"

Van der Merwe was definitely the most obnoxious and unpleasant of the duo. He eyeballed John, and was clearly trying to provoke a fight.

"You're a bloody English soldier, aren't you?" he demanded.

"I was," John answered defensively. "So, what of it?"

"Me and my cousin don't care much for the likes of you…hate your bloody guts, in fact. The British Army have slaughtered our people, burnt down our farms…we killed many of your lot during the Transvaal rebellion. I wish we had killed more. As far as I'm concerned, the only good English soldier is a dead English soldier!"

John was enraged. He could hold back no longer. There was no way he would let this Boer bastard disparage the good name of the British Army. He stood up from his chair and pointed accusingly towards both of the South African cousins.

"You two are nothing more than bandits and murderers! You're both lowlife vermin and should be hung for treason!"

Van der Merwe and Steyn both rose up from their chairs, pushing their breakfast plates aside. They screamed abuse and threats, but John didn't care. He was more than willing to take them on. The confrontation seemed destined to escalate. Yvonne was visibly upset. She retreated into the far corner of the carriage.

Henrich seemed taken aback by the sudden escalation. He clearly hadn't foreseen this potential dispute. To everyone's great surprise, it was Andrew who intervened in the role of peacemaker.

175

"Now come on lads!" he shouted. "There is no excuse for this! Let bygones be bygones…these battles are in the past. We are all servants of the Reich now…on the same side. We're all Aryans. The Jews, Communists and Yankees want us to fight amongst each other. That is their goal. We must stay united!"

His brother's speech was a load of bollocks. John knew as much. However, the brief intermission had given him time to think. It wasn't exactly a smart idea for him to start a fight with two younger and fitter men. He was relieved to see that the two South Africans appeared to be pacified after hearing Andrew's words. They both grunted a reluctant agreement and sat back down. John soon followed suit. Van der Merwe glared threateningly towards John, as if to say 'this isn't over'.

All present went back to their breakfasts, but the atmosphere was still extremely tense. Yvonne soon made her excuses and left the table, as she mumbled something about seeing to the children. Only the men were left now. Not a word was spoken. John silently prayed for a distraction. He soon got one.

A young German soldier rushed in through the back door of the kitchen car. His entry was so quick and dramatic that all present looked back in his direction. John recognised the German as being a new addition to their security detail. He had replaced the rather incompetent older geezer who had allowed Julie and Edward to escape, after falling asleep at his post.

The young private rushed to Hoffman's side. He had an excited, almost euphoric look in his eyes. John and the others watched on with great interest as the soldier whispered frantically into Hoffman's ear. The Gestapo Chief listened intently to his subordinate's hushed report. John was astonished to see the sudden change in expression on Hoffman's face. For the first time since they had met, the Gestapo man actually smiled. The secret policeman looked positively ecstatic. When the young private finished his report, Hoffman leaned across the breakfast table and communicated the news to his fellow officer, Captain Muller.

The Gestapo man spoke so quickly that John struggled to understand the German. He did recognise a couple of words, including 'bomb', 'test' and 'success'. Muller feigned a smile as he heard the news, but John could tell that Henrich did not share his colleague's enthusiasm. Hoffman was still in a state of intense exhilaration several minutes later, when he left the kitchen car, muttering something about making a radio call to Berlin. John, Andrew and the two South Africans were all anxious to hear the news which had caused so much excitement.

"Well," Andrew asked impatiently. "What the hell is it?"

Muller sighed before answering with a heavy heart. "We just received a confirmation from the OKH Command. The Wehrmacht's weapons development section has successfully tested the Fatherland's first atomic bomb. The detonation took place late last night in the Pripet Marshes, not far from our current location."

"Bloody hell!" exclaimed Andrew. "That's bleeding fantastic news!"

The two South Africans joined Andrew in an impromptu celebration. All three men stood up and shook hands, before cheering with joy.

"No one can stop us now!" Andrew proclaimed, "Soon, the Reich will rule the entire world!"

John felt a cold shudder. The grim news brought back unhappy memories. He vividly recalled hearing of America's first a-bomb test, which had occurred two years previously. John had been in Jerusalem at the time. He'd heard about the Manhattan test just before the King David's Hotel bombing, the day when his Elaine had died. The nuclear detonation had been a terrible omen back then, and John feared the successful German test would herald yet more suffering and pain. The destructive capability of these new weapons truly terrified him. For two years America had been the only country in the world to possess these dreadful bombs. As much as he hated nuclear weapons, John did believe that the American atomic arsenal had kept the Nazis in check for the past 24 months. But now it appears that Germany would be able to match the military power of the United States.

John remembered Hitler's speech in Berlin, his talk of conflict with the Americans and the development of new weapons and technologies. He now recognised the German leader's discreet reference to the upcoming atomic test. Hitler's belligerent words seemed to make war more likely, and John dreaded the prospect of a conflict fought with such terrible and devastating weapons.

He shook his head in despair and looked across the breakfast table and saw his friend Henrich Muller. The German captain held his head in his hands. He clearly shared John's feeling of impending doom.

His brother and the South Africans continued their sickening celebration. John had seen and heard enough. He quietly slipped away from the group, ignoring both the trio of rejoicing fools and the despairing Wehrmacht officer. He rushed out of the dining car and retreated back into the empty passenger carriage. He wanted some time alone to contemplate the momentous events of this morning.

He took a seat and looked through the carriage window, out to the rolling landscape beyond. Soon the train began to slow and, after a few moments, the locomotive pulled into a heavily fortified station. The platform was occupied by a number of well-armed combat troops, wielding machine guns behind concrete barricades. They pulled up to the platform and came to an abrupt halt. A moment later another train arrived on the adjacent platform, coming from the opposite direction and halting right next to their own locomotive.

John glanced through the windows of the adjacent train. He was shocked to see the carriage packed full of wounded German soldiers, their injuries ranging from missing limbs and bandaged head wounds to severe burns and facial disfigurements. It was clear they had been evacuated from the battlefields of the Eastern territories.

What lay ahead was a bloody war-zone. Depressed, he retreated to his sleeping compartment.

# BOOK THREE

## BLOOD AND SOIL

# 11/ 'Plantation'

THE PRESTON FAMILY'S LONG train journey was finally at an end. They had travelled hundreds of miles, and had seen some amazing sights, but Andrew Preston knew the best was still to come. Their locomotive had ended its drive in the city of Minsk. From there, the family was rushed through the station and directed towards a convoy of waiting vehicles. Their luggage and possessions were loaded up, and then the Preston's were on their way.

They would travel the final part of their trip on board a convoy of armoured cars and APCs, along with a platoon of well-armed Wehrmacht troops.

Andrew noted the disposition of the convoy, which included a machine gun wielding armoured car, two trucks loaded with soldiers, an infantry carrying APC and four motorcycle outriders. His wife had made a sarcastic comment regarding the number of armed troops and tanks required for a simple drive through the Russian countryside. Andrew had told her to 'shut up', as she clearly didn't know what she was talking about. He felt a great excitement on this day and was determined not to let his family's continued negativity ruin his big moment.

True, it did seem a bit odd to him that the Wehrmacht had allocated such a large force simply to escort his family on their drive south. This did not worry him, however. He knew that the Germans liked to be well prepared for any potential scenario. Also, he considered the size of their escort as evidence of his family's importance to the National Socialist regime.

The territory they were currently travelling through was called Reichskommissariat Ostland. It was one of the four military-run provinces which made up the German territories of the East (the other three being Ukraine, Moskowien and Kaukasien). Andrew knew the land they were currently travelling through had been conquered by the Wehrmacht during their rapid advance in second half of 1941. Apparently guerrilla resistance had been a problem for several years, but this was now a thing of the past. The Reich's Colonization Office had assured Andrew that this district was completely pacified, and was now a safe area for civilian settlement. He had no reason to disbelief them.

Andrew had hoped to see some of the countryside during their drive south, to get a feel for these lands. He was told that this province was now home to over one million German settlers, along with tens of thousands of Aryans of other nationalities - including Dutch, Danes, Norwegians, South Africans and, of course, Englishmen. This was the Lebensraum or 'Living Space' which Adolf Hitler had long spoken of. Once, this vision had been little more than a fantasy, but the military genius of the Fuhrer and the sheer brilliance of the German soldiers had made this dream into a reality. Andrew had hoped to see the land and so he was disappointed to discover that his family would be travelling in an armoured APC without any outward-facing windows in the rear.

But nothing would dampen his good mood, not even his lingering anger with both of his teenage children. He hadn't forgotten about their illegal foray onto the dangerous streets of Warsaw. He had no doubt that his daughter was the ringleader in that incident, but he was also disappointed with his son. Edward was the elder; he should have been able to stop his young sister from taking such a rash and foolhardy course of action. He should have done better.

Andrew had no doubt that his son had learnt his lesson. He'd make a man out of the boy yet. His daughter was another matter. Julie continued to defy and rebel against him. This would never do. Andrew had been unable to properly punish his daughter for her intolerable insolence and defiance. He couldn't do so on the train because they were always surrounded by people. But he would not forget. The girl had to learn her place. She must fulfil her role as a woman and cease chasing after childish fantasies.

Right now, Julie was sitting opposite him in the back of the APC. He shot his daughter an angry look, just to remind her he was still in charge. She returned his glare, her eyes ever defiant.

His children's failings were of little concern to him at the moment; they would be dealt with soon enough, but not today. Because on this day, he was ready to fulfil his destiny. After years of hard slog for low wages, constant police harassment, spells of imprisonment and so much humiliation suffered at the hands of socialists and members of inferior races....after years of misery in the slums of the East End....today he will get what he really deserves from life. He will be granted his own plantation and a substantial plot of agricultural land. He will also have his own workforce of subdued Slavs to do his bidding – a small army of servants, both domestics and farm hands. And he will rule the roost. He will hold a position of authority, something he has always yearned for. The days of working under some idiotic manager are over. From now on, he'd be his own boss.

Nonetheless, Andrew had little to no experience of farming or rural life. He was an East Ender born and bred, and the only time he had tried his hand at agriculture was on his old man's allotment, but he wasn't overly worried. The Reich Office had assured him that previous farming experience was not necessary, as he would receive all of the required training at a local agricultural college run by the Colonial Ministry.

Besides, it's not like he's going to be doing any of the 'donkey' work himself. The Slavs would do all the back breaking labour. That's what they were there for – peasants and serfs; bred for brainless menial work, to slave away for 12 hours a day, seven days a week, out in the fields. Aryans were born to conquer and rule, this was the destiny of their race. And Andrew was an excellent administrator.

He had always worked as a clerk, rising from his humble upbringing to obtain a coveted white collar job. He would have excelled in this role back in England, had not the socialists and Jews conspired to prevent him gaining promotion. Out here it would be different. He would take care of the accounts and the paperwork for his plantation, running the enterprise with a super efficiency which even the Germans would admire. Yes, he was determined to make this business a great success. He knew it would all come together once they arrived at their new home. Yvonne will settle down and stop complaining…and, if she doesn't, he'd bloody well divorce her and send her back to England. After all, he could always remarry. He could take a young bride…one who was more docile and respectful. She would have to be young and beautiful, and capable of bearing many children. Yes, that would be good – to father a whole new family of Aryan youngsters. Andrew smiled at the thought.

His wife noticed him smirking. She was sitting at the far end of the vehicle's rear, remaining silent during their road trip. She glared at him, with a look of confusion on her face.

*If only you knew*, Andrew thought. *If only you bloody well knew!*

He returned to his fantasy as the military vehicle sped onwards, dreaming of his future.

In his mind, years had now passed. His brother John had finally settled down, having married an attractive and sensible German Frau. John had a son of his own now, and another baby was on the way. His brother had given up all of his demons. He'd forgotten all about England and the war, and now he was eternally grateful to him.

Julie was there too. She was a young woman now, no longer a child. She'd gotten married to a handsome young German officer from a good family. All of her immature ideals had been forgotten. She was content now – a happily married woman who would soon have children of her own. She would make a good mother.

And there was Edward…good old Edward, Andrew's first born…his loyal and brave son. Edward looked smart in his Waffen SS uniform. He was home on leave, fresh from fighting the Russian guerrillas in the Ural Mountains. His son was almost at the end of his term of military service. He had fought with distinction and had won many medals, all of which were proudly displayed on the breast of his jacket. Perhaps he would even win the Iron Cross…why not? Edward had recently gotten engaged, and he would be married as soon as he received his honourable discharge from the Wehrmacht. Next he would be granted his own plantation and acreage. Edward would settle down with his wife and start his own family. Andrew was very proud of his son.

His fantasy continued. More years had passed. Andrew was an old man now, but he was content with his lot. All of his family were around him – children and grandchildren. He was the old patriarch of the family and the youngsters all looked up to him, seeking his wisdom and guidance. He happily sat back while his grandchildren played around him, and his docile and obedient Slavic servants tended to his every need. And, although he may not have long left in this world, Andrew would die happy. He had lived a good life and had built a secure and prosperous future for his family. All this had come to be because of his own efforts, and his vision. Andrew could rightly feel proud of himself.

Reluctantly, he returned to the present. This was Andrew's dream, but there was still much work to be done before it could be achieved. His journey continued.

The convoy finally arrived at its final destination. Most of the family had dozed or read during the long journey, but Andrew had been too excited to do either.

The vehicle came to an abrupt halt before one of the accompanying German soldiers opened up the back of the half truck, allowing sunshine and fresh air to flood in.

Andrew was first to make his way out. He soaked up the atmosphere and, after his eyes were adjusted to the bright sunshine, he admired the stunning scenery and majestic country views. It was a fine summer's day, with blue skies, a powerful sun and hardly a cloud to be seen; it was a moment to savour. He turned his head and saw a vast forest on the horizon; an immense wood of tall and mighty oaks, stretching out as far as the eye could see. He was greatly impressed by the sheer grandeur of this picturesque scene… a view of almost unadulterated natural beauty.

He had never seen the like. He'd lived his whole life in London and had only enjoyed the occasional trip out to the Essex countryside or Epping Forest. And to think that all this land was his to rule over. Andrew felt like one of the mighty Kings of old, experiencing elation like nothing he had ever felt before.

Until reality struck.

He turned his head to the left and spotted a dilapidated building just yards away. At one time it had been a two storey farmhouse, but now abandoned. The walls were still standing, but the paint had long since peeled away, leaving nothing but a grey and depressing semi-ruin. The brickwork was beginning to crumble, and many slates were missing from the roof. Most of the windows had been removed or smashed, and the front door was hanging off its hinges.

"Welcome to your new home," said Muller.

Andrew's heart sank. He refused to believe it.

"You must be bloody joking, mate!" he exclaimed.

"I'm afraid not," Muller answered. "The farmhouse has seen better days, it is true….the farm was owned by an affluent Belorussian peasant family before the war, but the original owners were arrested and deported in the late 1930's, during Stalin's Purges. They were accused by the NVKD of being 'kulaks'. I believe the farm has been unoccupied for roughly a decade now, and, as you can see, the buildings have fallen into a state of disrepair."

"Disrepair!" Andrew exclaimed, in an incredulous tone. "Bloody disrepair! Is that what you call it?"

"You can't expect my family to live here!" cried Yvonne. "It's falling apart!"

Muller shrugged his shoulders.

"It's not so bad. The farmhouse still has four walls and a roof. This is more than many of the farms out here on the frontier. I acknowledge there will be some work involved in repairing the house and the sheds…"

"And who will do this work?" Andrew demanded angrily. He was quickly beginning to lose patience with the German officer.

"You will, of course," answered Muller, as if this was the most obvious thing in the world. "It is your responsibility to maintain your own farm and land."

Andrew couldn't believe what he was hearing.

"But this isn't what I was told!" he exclaimed. "We were promised a good home and a high yield plantation…"

"You were promised a house and a plot of land, nothing more," Muller replied sharply. "The Fuhrer is determined to build up a strong race of peasant warriors to hold the Eastern frontier. He expects the settler families to be self-sufficient and self-reliant."

Andrew was becoming more and more exasperated. He didn't want to hear what Henrich Muller was saying. Was he really serious?

"But," Andrew pleaded, "but, how are we supposed to farm the land and tend to the livestock? We'll be spending all of our time fixing this bloody house!"

Muller shook his head and stifled a laugh.

"Mr. Preston," he answered, "there will be no crops or livestock here, not this season anyway. As you can see, the land is overgrown. There haven't been any crops on this farm for years. As for livestock…you are in no position to tend to cattle or sheep at this time. Besides, there are so many predators out in the woods…" He pointed to the tree line behind them. "…packs of wolves and brown bears. If you kept animals, they would surely make easy prey. No, Mr. Preston, your focus must be to repair the farmhouse and cut back the forest, to clear the fields. This land will not produce a crop this year. The weather is good right now, but winter comes in quickly here in Russia. You'll need to have the house rebuilt long before the first snowfall. You should also stock up on firewood. The winters are very harsh in this country."

Andrew kept hoping this was all some kind of terrible nightmare. He kept expecting to wake up…but this was no dream and he suddenly felt extremely agitated.

"But how will we live?" he pleaded. "Will we not starve?"

"No...no," Muller replied. "It won't come to that. You and your brother will serve in the local defence militia. In return for this mandatory military service, you will both receive a modest salary and sufficient rations to feed both your family and your workforce....Mein Gott! I almost forgot to tell you about your workers! Here they come now..."

Muller pointed across the grass to a group of figures approaching; four darkly clad civilians escorted by one uniformed German soldier armed with a Mauser rifle. The civilians were all dirty, thin and pale. Andrew could tell from the look of them that they were all Slavs.

One was just a boy – little more than ten years old. He was small and thin. Andrew didn't reckon he would be much use as a worker. Beside the boy stood a middle aged man. He sported an untidy and dirty beard, and his eyes were sullen and hungry. The man was stooped and appeared to be in physical pain. He looked weak, like a strong gust of wind would blow him over. It was difficult to tell his exact age, but he was surely in his 40's at least.

There was one woman amongst the group. She was dressed in a long dark shawl which covered the top of her head. Her face was wrinkled, her eyes dimmed and almost lifeless. She was elderly, probably in her 60's or 70's. Andrew wondered what she had lived through during her long existence – the days of the Tsar, the Bolshevik coup, Lenin, Stalin's Purges, the War, and now into the era of the New World Order...the age of Lebensraum. He felt a grudging respect for the woman.

There was a young man, too, probably in his early 20's. As with the others, his clothes were ragged and torn, and he certainly could do with a wash. But his physical condition was better than the rest. Unlike the others, he smiled at Andrew, with a rebellious defiance in his eyes. Trouble. One to watch.

"His name is Sergei, said Muller. "You're lucky to have him, because he speaks both English and German. He will translate your instructions for the other workers."

"It is a pleasure to meet you, sir," said the young man. "It will be my honour to serve you and your family."

Andrew clenched his teeth, but said nothing. Trouble.

"Allow me to introduce my comrades," Sergei continued. "This is Maria," he said, nodding towards the older woman. "This is Yuri. And the boy is called Ivan. Myself, Yuri and Ivan will do the repairs to the house, and Maria will work for your wife, doing the domestic chores."

Andrew turned to Muller, saying, "Is this it? Four good-for-nothings! I was promised a full workforce!"

"These workers will suffice to rebuild the house and see your family through the winter," Muller replied. "You will be allocated more people next year, when hopefully you'll in a position to begin farming the land."

Andrew threw his head up and looked to the sky above. He was beginning to realise that the Germans had misled him. He had not been told the whole truth about this enterprise and he felt greatly angered by the deception. However, he knew there was little he could do right now, and he didn't want to lose face in front of his family.

"Can I see the inside of the house?" he asked meekly.

"Of course," Muller answered. "This is your home now, after all."

Andrew turned back towards his family. John was nowhere to be seen. Edward looked worried and Julie was typically disinterested.

"Stay out here while I inspect the premises," he said.

His children obeyed the order, but his wife did not. Yvonne stepped forward and followed him.

For once, Andrew felt unable to stop his wife. However, he made sure to get to the front entrance before she did. He marched up to the front door and attempted to open it. As soon as he touched the knob, the rotten wooden door came off its hinges and fell down heavily to the ground.

"Christ!" Andrew swore aloud.

He climbed over the door and walked into the front room. It stank of damp and mould. The walls were covered with filth but were otherwise bare, absent of any trace of paint or wallpaper. There were several pieces of dilapidated furniture strewn around the room – a few chairs, a writing desk and a dining table. All of these aging pieces looked on the verge of falling apart. There was an old fireplace in the far corner which clearly hadn't been lit for many years. The hearth was filled up with rubbish and debris, and the mantelpiece was cracked and covered in many layers of grime and dirt.

Andrew was left speechless. Muller stood in the doorway as he offered an explanation regarding the sleeping arrangements for the family.

"The bedrooms are upstairs. Unfortunately there are no beds at the moment, other than one old frame in the master bedroom. But, I've been assured that fresh mattresses will be delivered by the end of the day."

"This place is a bloody tip!" protested Andrew. "It's worse than the slums of bleeding Whitechapel!"

Just then, a large rat scuttled across the living room floor and Andrew shook his head in dismay.

Yvonne didn't say a word. She simply stared at him, with her eyes full of resentment and anger. It was as if she was saying, 'I told you so!'

Andrew was furious, but there was nothing he could do, because deep down he knew she was right. This place was a hellhole, but, for the Preston family, it was now home.

John Preston had deliberately held back from engaging in the heated conversation between Henrich Muller and his brother Andrew. He realised that his brother was deeply disappointed by the state of the so-called plantation. John was equally unimpressed by the condition of the farmhouse and land, but he was not overly surprised, as he knew the Nazis had lied to them all from day one. He lingered outside of the house, awaiting Henrich.

Now that their long journey was finally over, he was determined to obtain answers from the German captain before he disappeared from their lives forever. He was sure that Muller knew the truth about what was happening out here on the Eastern frontier.

When Muller emerged, he seized his opportunity, grabbing the captain's right arm, yelling, "You bloody well lied to us!"

"Not exactly," mumbled Muller.

"But there is much you haven't told us!" John snapped back. He wasn't going to let the German off so easily.

"Yes," Henrich reluctantly admitted.

"Well?" retorted John.

"Not here," Muller said. "Come for a walk with me."

They strode towards the far tree line. John had little choice except to follow the German officer. He guessed that Henrich wanted to be far from prying eyes and ears before he said any more. This seemed like a reasonable precaution. The two men had walked for about one hundred yards before Muller finally deemed it safe to speak freely.

"Generalplan Ost is failing," he whispered. "Everyone knows as much, but no-one will admit it. Questioning the Fuhrer's judgement is considered heresy in the Reich. This country is a wreck. Years of savage warfare has removed much of the population and destroyed most of the infrastructure. Safety and security are also significant concerns. Fewer and fewer Germans are prepared to move to and settle in the Reich's Eastern territories. This is why the Party is making great efforts to encourage emigration from other countries, including England."

"So, what's to be done?" John asked; he was deeply troubled.

"As I told your brother," Muller replied resolutely, "you must make the best of it. Rebuild the farmhouse and see out the winter. Your situation should improve by next spring." He briefly paused, before adding a hushed aside, "We will leave you an ample supply of weaponry – shotguns and hunting rifles to see off bears and wolves, and Mausers and Lugers for defence against partisans. They're still out there, you know. No matter how many sweeps are conducted by our troops and militiamen, many guerrilla fighters continue to slip through our fingers. We will leave you guns and ample ammunition. Under no circumstances should you allow any of your workers access to the weapons. You should be armed every time you leave the farm. I would also recommend keeping your weapons close by whilst you sleep. This is a dangerous country, John. You must remain vigilant."

John was chilled by the German's stark warning, but he made sure to thank Muller for his sound and pragmatic advice, knowing it would ultimately fall to him to protect the family.

He looked to the tree line and the massive primordial forest beyond. Who or what was out there? He wondered.

Time would surely tell.

# 12/ 'The Hunt'

IT HAD BEEN TWO weeks since the Preston family first arrived at their new home, namely the worse for wear plantation located to the north of the massive Pripet marshes. Only a fortnight had passed, but to young Edward Preston it had seemed like an eternity. They had all been flat out for the entire two weeks, working hard throughout the long summer days, before they crashed down exhausted on their uncomfortable and lumpy mattresses, come nightfall.

The delegation of the heavy workload had been their first challenge. Edward's father had initially insisted that all of the manual labour should be carried out by their four Russian workers. This had been the way of it for the first two days, but it soon became obvious that the Russians weren't able to do all the hard graft by themselves.

Sergei was a good worker, but Yuri was fairly useless and Ivan was just a young lad. The old woman was called Maria. Edward felt odd calling her 'Maria', because he would usually address older people by their surname and proper title. But he didn't know her surname, or whether she was married or widowed. Maria was at least as old as Edward's grandmother, but she still had a lot of energy for her advanced age. She had washed all the family's clothes using water extracted from a well and heated in a pot over an open fire, and had used an old mangle to dry them. She had prepared decent meals for the family by cooking over a wood burning stove. As if this wasn't enough, Maria would also work all day helping to clean out the dirty interior of the house. She was a tough old lady, no doubt about it.

Sergei had worked on the repairs to the house, with help from Yuri and Ivan. They had done the best they could – chopping down trees for firewood, boarding up the open window frames, scraping the mould off the walls, setting traps to catch the rodent vermin, reaffixing the front door and replacing missing slates on the roof. This had gone on for two days, but Edward's father had not been happy with the slow progress. There had been a big row about this on day three. His Dad said the 'Slavs' were lazy and feckless and needed to 'pull the finger out'.

Sergei and the other Russians hadn't said a single word in their own defence, although, in fairness, Sergei was the only one of them who understood and spoke English. Instead, it had been his uncle John who had stood up for the Russians. John had argued that there was too much work for the Slavs and so the family would all have to chip in and do their bit. Andrew hadn't been happy about this suggestion, but in the end he had agreed with his older brother.

Edward had been relieved, because he didn't like seeing his uncle and dad fighting. The confrontation had been very unsettling for him to witness. Besides, Edward didn't mind the manual work. In fact, he was happy to have something to do – to keep himself busy. He didn't fully understand why his father disliked the Russians so much. Edward didn't have any real problem with any of the Slavs. Sergei was the only one who could speak English, and Edward chatted to him whenever his father wasn't around. He thought Sergei was a nice enough fellow, but his dad really seemed to hate him. Edward knew the Slavs worked for their family, but his dad had always told him that a boss should treat his employees with respect. But, now that he was the boss, he seemed to be going back on his previous beliefs. Edward felt his father was being hypocritical, but he didn't dare say so.

There was a tension between Edward and his father. The son knew why. His dad was still disappointed with him because of that whole ugly debacle back in Warsaw. Edward got angry every time he thought back to that day. It had been Julie's fault. Edward was still furious with his little sister as, once again, she'd gotten him into deep trouble. Why couldn't she just be a good girl and do as she was told? He really hated his sister sometimes. It was a terrible thing to think, but true nonetheless. He felt it unfair that his father had punished him for Julie's bad behaviour. Still, he did respect his dad's position.

True enough, Edward should have done better – he should have been able to stop his younger sibling, to control her and make her obey. This was the man's role – his father had taught him as much. Unfortunately, it just didn't come naturally to him. Edward was ashamed of himself, and he fully understood why his father was disappointed in him. He was an inadequate son – a weak boy who couldn't stand up for himself. This was how he felt right now, but Edward was determined to change his fortunes. He was going to better himself…he would become a man and would make his father proud.

Today's hunting trip would mark the beginning of Edward's transformation. Today he would begin to win back his father's trust and confidence.

Andrew had made the decision just the night before. They had all been working too hard, he said, and they deserved a break. He'd insisted that the men should trek out into the woods for a hunting trip where there would be hares, polecats, deer and moose for the boys to pursue. The family were still waiting to receive their allocated Volkswagen from the German Colonial Office, but there was no reason why they couldn't hike out into the forest for a day's hunting.

Andrew told Edward they were leaving at dawn and returning home at dusk. They would bring guns, rucksacks, food and water with them, and would bring back whatever they could carry. They could hardly drag back a dead moose, he had joked, but a few rabbits or a cut of venison would do just fine for their tea. Edward was very happy to be invited on this trip. It was also good to see his dad so enthusiastic about spending time with him – father and son together.

Uncle John was coming too. There had been a bit of an argument between the two brothers on this point. John wasn't too keen about the whole expedition. He said it wasn't wise to be traipsing out into the forest without taking reasonable precautions. Uncle John believed that there were Soviet partisans hiding out in the woods, and so their party risked unwittingly walking into an ambush. Edward didn't like the sound of this. He was nervous enough already about the trip, since he didn't want to disappoint his father.

The risk of embarrassment or failure was a worry for Edward, but his uncle's talk of savage Russian guerrillas was truly terrifying. However, his father had simply laughed off his older brother's concerns. He was certain that there were no guerrilla fighters left in this district, nor had there been for many years.

Uncle John didn't seem convinced. He said he was also worried about leaving the women alone in the house with only their Slavic workers for company. Edward's father had conceded this point but had also promised they would all be home before nightfall. He insisted that Yvonne and Julie would be fine. Besides, they weren't entirely without support.

One of the few pieces of modern technology which the Germans had left the family was a two-way radio set. All of the Preston's had received rudimentary training from Muller's men in the use of the radio. They'd been instructed to contact the closest German military outpost in case of any serious emergency. The outpost had a mechanised rapid response unit on standby and a field hospital ready to receive any wounded or sick settlers. Edward hoped that his family would never need to avail of the outpost's hospital or military forces, but he was glad to have the Germans looking after them, just in case.

Edward had been the first one up and dressed on that particular morning. He was up out of bed before 5am, which was shortly before the break of dawn. He took a walk outside the farmhouse and enjoyed watching the majestic sunrise on the eastern horizon – the mighty orange sphere gradually emerging over the top of the hills and above the tree line.

This country was beautiful. One could see as much if you took the time to appreciate it. Why didn't his mother and sister understand this? Edward did not know.

He returned to the farmhouse to find Maria preparing breakfast in the kitchen. In the absence of any supply of gas or oil, Maria had to cook the food over a wood burning stove. The Germans had left behind many cans of dried and preserved foods – spam, sardines, corned beef and assorted tinned vegetables and fruits. The German Army delivered pounds of butter, loaves of bread and pints of milk and packets of loose tobacco once a week, but this was their lot. It wasn't the best of diets, but Edward was used to going without back in ration-plagued Britain.

Besides, this situation was only temporary. Their farm would be up and running soon enough, and then the family would be growing their own food and slaughtering their own livestock. It would be smooth sailing from that point onwards. Edward and his family would be living like Kings.

Soon, the rest of the family emerged from their respective bedrooms. His father and uncle both wore the same dark green camouflage gear supplied by the Germans. They looked like soldiers, as did Edward, in his near identical outfit. His father had told him that their clothes would help them blend into the background as they stalked their prey. Edward knew next to nothing about hunting, so he would take his lead from his father and uncle.

The men sat down at the kitchen table while they waited for Maria to serve their morning meal. Edward's mother came in a couple of minutes later. She was dressed and made up, but she didn't quite look herself. Edward could see the lines of worry which cut across her face. He didn't like seeing his mother like this. What was the matter with her?

Soon Maria brought them their breakfast, which consisted of half stale but toasted bread with butter, cooked corn beef and mugs of weak tea. Edward tucked in. They would bring a packed lunch with them, but he needed the energy for this morning's hike. Maria left the room after serving their meals. His father didn't allow the servants to eat with the family. The meal was eaten quickly. His father was the only one who spoke during the breakfast. He was clearly very excited about the day ahead. Uncle John and his mother said nothing.

They left straight after breakfast. Edward cleaned his plate and grabbed his packed rucksack, before making to leave the kitchen and join the men outside. But, before he left the table, he had to say goodbye to his mother. To Edward's surprise and embarrassment his mum became overly emotional in that moment. She hugged him and held him tight before she whispered in his ear, saying, "Be careful, Edward, I love you."

Edward pulled away. He refused to meet her eye and did not utter a response before he left the room. He was annoyed with his mother and could not understand why she still treated him like a child. Why was she becoming so emotional anyway? He was only going away for a few hours!

The three men walked out of the farmhouse and assembled on the rough gravel track which led back to the main road. Their plan was to proceed on foot towards the tree line, where they would enter the immense primordial forest which covered such a vast area of land. However, there were some additional items to collect before they left the farm.

Edward's father led them to a locked steel shutter located outside of the main farmhouse. The shutter door was the only entrance to a small subterranean bunker which could not be accessed from the house itself. In contrast to the rest of the complex, the steel shutter looked brand new, as did the large and sturdy looking padlock which secured the entrance.

Andrew and John held the only two keys for the padlock. John opened the lock and pulled away the heavy door, exposing the inside of the bunker to the morning sunlight.

Edward peeked inside and he felt a surge of excitement when he saw the contents of the underground dugout. On the left hand side of the bunker stood a rack loaded up with weapons – elongated firearms such as rifles, carbines and shotguns. Below the long guns lay a collection of pistols and revolvers. Edward didn't know the makes and models, but he assumed they were manufactured in Germany. On the right hand side of the dugout stood boxes of ammunition, all stacked up on top of each other. It looked like there were enough bullets and shells here to fight a small war.

Edward watched on in awe as Andrew and John entered the small armoury and carefully examined the weaponry.

"We should take Mausers and spare magazines," said John.

"Why?" asked Andrew. "We're only going hunting; there's no need to bring military rifles."

"And what if we run into the partisans?" John answered back.

Andrew rolled his eyes in frustration.

"Oh, for God's sake!" he exclaimed. "Not this again! I've told you John, there are no guerrillas left in this district! Besides, the Mausers are too heavy for us to carry. It's a country hike, not a bloody forced march!"

John thought about this for a while, and eventually he nodded his head in agreement. "All right," he said. "But you and I will take a Luger pistol each, with two spare magazines each."

"Fine," answered Andrew. "Now, can we please get going?"

Edward watched on as the two men gathered up the weapons and ammunitions. He didn't like this talk of dangerous partisans running around these woods. His father said there were no partisans out here, but his uncle disagreed. Who was right and who was wrong? Edward couldn't tell.

In the end, the men took the weapons most appropriate for their hunt. Andrew took a long hunting rifle with a sniper's scope attached. John selected a double barrelled shotgun, and he put on a bandolier to carry spare shells, making him look a bit like a bandit from the Old Wild West.

Andrew picked out a gun for his son. He handed him the weapon along with a handful of spare bullets.

"It's a .22 single shot rifle," he explained. "You'll have to reload after every round fired. It's not the most powerful of guns, but a straight shot will be enough to take down your prey."

His father's eyes were full of expectation. Edward knew this was his opportunity to impress him, to make him proud. He felt very nervous, but he was also determined to see this through. He grasped hold of the rifle and pocketed the spare bullets. His father grinned at him, and Edward returned the smile. He noted his uncle securing the shutter door behind him, and checking the padlock several times to make sure it was locked.

Now the men were fully armed and ready for the day ahead. They set off across the fields and towards the tree line. Edward looked back over his shoulder only once. He saw his mother standing on the porch, seeing them off. He didn't wave to her. Now his focus was entirely on the forest ahead.

The mighty trees towered above them, standing dozens of foot tall, with their branches and heavy foliage partly blocking out the sun. The forest had a foreboding presence, having stood for maybe hundreds of years. Edward wondered what dark and sinister secrets lay within the boundaries of this ancient forest. He felt a cold chill running down his spine as the party of three entered the forest, but he had to admit that there was an awe-inspiring beauty to this woodland.

The scene reminded Edward of the books he had read as a child, such as the Grimms Fairy Tales and Tolkien's The Hobbit. There was an enchanting side to this forest which evoked Edward's childlike fantasies of elves, fairies and halflings. But there was also a more sinister side - goblins, trolls and hideous ogres hiding in the shadows and waiting to ambush unwary travellers.

He needed to get these childish fears out of his head. There were no such things as trolls or orcs...but there were wild animals out here, packs of wolves which they heard howling during the night...and then there were armed partisans who may or may not exist. But, he knew he'd be fine as long as he stayed close to his father and his uncle.

If Edward's dad shared his fears he didn't let it show. Andrew talked continually throughout their hike.

"This is great, isn't it? It's bloody fantastic, to be out here in the wilderness...taming the frontier. This is how men should live...no more smog filled cities and terraced streets for our family! It will just be a short hike this first time. We won't go too deep into the woods on this trip. We're just dipping our toes, getting to know the lie of the land. We'll be able to go further afield once we get our car. We'll get you driving, too, Edward. It's about time you learned. Just imagine the girl's faces when we come back with fresh venison and rabbit…we'll be eating well tonight, let me bloody tell you!"

Edward found his father's constant chatter tiresome and distracting, but he didn't dare to tell him so. In the end, it was Uncle John who succeeded in silencing his younger brother.

"You know, Andrew," he said, in a surprisingly patient tone of voice, "all this loud talking is going to scare off the game. Perhaps we should stay quiet for a bit."

"Yes," Andrew answered apologetically, "Yes, you're quite right John. Sorry."

Edward was impressed. He couldn't remember the last time his father had apologised, for any reason. The next part of their hike was concluded in relative silence; the only sound they heard were the songs of the birds high above them.


The party had been hiking for several hours before they broke for lunch. Edward had enjoyed the hike and the natural beauty of the Belorussian forest. However, the hunt itself had been a dismal failure. They had seen next to no wildlife and had not come close to killing even a single creature.

Andrew had taken a few pot shots at fast moving hares and rabbits, but to no avail. He had cursed with every shot missed. Edward was yet to fire his rifle. In a way he was relieved. His only previous experience of firearms had been a couple of sessions of target shooting back on the farm. Edward wasn't a particularly good shot. He found the gun heavy, and his hands shook as he aimed. He hadn't liked the loud crack of the gunshot or the powerful kickback of the rifle. He wasn't a natural, but his father had insisted that he'd get better with practice. Edward just hoped that he didn't fail at the critical moment.

John was the navigator; he'd charted the journey using the detailed topological map given to them by the Wehrmacht. He had planned the route meticulously, utilising navigation skills learned during his many years in the British Army.

By lunchtime they reached a small flowing river which meandered through the forest. The scene was picturesque, serene and peaceful…which was more than Edward could say about his father. Andrew's cheery demeanour was long gone, and now he was in a foul mood.

The three men sat by the river bank and unloaded their packed lunches. Edward opened the top of his flask and eagerly drank his lukewarm and thin vegetable soup. Next, he tore into the sardine sandwich which Maria had made for him. The lunch wasn't the greatest he had ever eaten, but he was starving after a long morning of hard hiking.

"I just don't understand it!" exclaimed Andrew. "This forest should be full of wild game, but we've hardly seen a bloody thing!"

"We've been unlucky today," John answered calmly, "but there will be other opportunities."

"We're not giving up yet!" Andrew shot back angrily.

"We'll have to, if we want to get home before sunset," John responded. "Besides, we might run into some game on our way back."

The trio finished their lunch in silence. They rested for a time before they picked up their gear and started off on the long trek home.

They had been walking for about half an hour when they saw it. Some 50 feet in front of them stood a solitary deer, grazing out in the open, seemingly without a care in the world.

The deer hadn't noticed them. John raised a finger up to his lips, indicating that they should remain as quiet as possible. The trio crouched down low and crept forward slowly and carefully. Edward had heard that deer had very acute hearing, and even the crack of a twig under your boot could be enough to give you away. He was particularly careful, as he definitely did not want to be the one to give the game away.

He saw his father moving forward, his face screwed up as he focussed on his quarry. He began to raise and aim his rifle before apparently having second thoughts. He turned towards Edward and whispered softly in his ear, "This one's for you, son. Shoot it down. Kill it."

Edward experienced a sudden outbreak of panic. This was the opportunity he had prayed for, the chance to prove himself, but now that the moment was finally here, he was terrified of the potential for failure.

He slowly pulled his rifle down from his shoulder and took aim. The firearm felt so heavy. His hands were shaking and his vision blurred. He could not focus.

John leaned over and whispered some helpful guidance, saying "Control your breathing, deep and slow breaths. Focus on your target...nothing else."

Edward tightened his grip on the rifle. He looked down the sights of the gun and focussed on the animal. This was the first time he had looked at the deer in great detail. The animal was sleek and slender, with brown and white speckled fur and big dark eyes, a peaceful and innocent creature. He didn't feel right shooting at it. After all, what had the deer ever done to him? It seemed very unfair to kill a defenceless animal in such a manner. But he knew he had to dispel such thoughts from his mind.

Compassion was weakness, that's what his dad had always told him. Men were natural hunters...this was their instinct. If he didn't kill the deer right now, his father would never forgive him. He felt sorry for the poor animal, but it was going to get shot one way or another, so he might as well be the one who did it.

Edward controlled his breathing, just as his uncle had taught him, and he aimed. He paused for just a second, his finger poised on the trigger. This proved to be a critical error. Suddenly, the deer's head shot up. It glared directly at Edward. For a brief moment, their eyes met across the abyss. Edward panicked. He pulled the trigger and fired...too soon. The gunshot was deafening, and the kick back of the rifle slammed into his shoulder, causing him to yelp. The bullet went high above its target. A split second later, the deer took off. It ran at great speed, heading out of the clearing and back into the forest. Edward's heart sank. He didn't want to see the disappointment in his father's eyes. Instead, he made an instantaneous decision. He would not admit defeat so easily. The hunt was still on. He dropped his rucksack, lifted his rifle, got up off his knees and started to run.

He sprinted after the deer and didn't look back. He heard his uncle calling out his name, telling him to stop. Edward ignored him. He would come back to his father and uncle with the body of the dead animal slung over his shoulders.

He darted through the clearing and followed the deer past the tree line. The deer was fast and he was forever left in its wake. But Edward was smarter than this beast, and he knew he'd find a way to catch it.

The chase reminded him of the incident a couple of weeks earlier, when he'd pursued his sister through the urban jungle of Warsaw. That day had ended in humiliation and shame, but today Edward would return triumphant. He kept running, as the hunt continued.

Edward's legs were tired and the backs of his calves ached. He was perspiring heavily and was out of breath. In the end, he had no choice but to stop. The deer was long gone.

He silently rebuked himself. What on earth had he been thinking? How had he ever expected to catch a deer? He had failed completely, and now he had to face his father. He felt sick. His throat was parched. He needed a drink of water to rehydrate after his mad sprint, but his canteen was in his rucksack, which he had left back in the clearing. All he had with him right now was his .22 hunting rifle and the spare cartridges in his coat pocket. He had to go back and face his father and uncle. There was nothing else for it.

After a few minutes rest, Edward turned around to retrace his steps, only to realise he was totally lost. He began to panic.

"DAD!" he screamed out. "UNCLE JOHN!" he yelled. "WHERE ARE YOU?"

There was no reply, and he began to walk.

Hours had passed. He was still hopelessly lost. He had wandered aimlessly through the woods, occasionally calling out for his father and uncle. He kept getting the distinct feeling that he was walking around in circles. He'd tried to overcome his panic and think logically about his predicament. He looked for any landmarks which would help to guide him, but there was nothing but more trees. His uncle John had the map and the compass. Edward had nothing. He tried to visualise the map in his head. He saw the forest and the river, the clearing and the farmhouse. He tried his hardest to remember, but without knowing his current location, it was all hopeless.

The forest had been frightening enough before, but now he was on his own…and it would be dark soon.

The light was fading fast. The sun was falling behind the tree line and soon the entire forest would be cloaked in darkness.

Edward's hope was also fading. He began to fear that he would never make it out of this vast wood. There had been a brief but heavy deluge about half an hour ago. He had initially been grateful for the rainfall, as the water had allowed him to quench his thirst. But now he was soaked to the skin, wet, cold, miserable and hungry.

The last slivers of daylight faded away to nothing and he remembered how hopeful and excited he'd felt at sunrise, but now the onset of night provoked dark fears in his young and impressionable mind.

This morning he had dispelled such childish terrors from his head, foolish thoughts of ogres, trolls and goblins, but now he wasn't so sure. Who was to say that monsters didn't exist in this world? He had read supposedly true accounts of spirits, ghouls, vampires and werewolves. It was easy to dispel such outlandish stories back in London, but not here, not now.

He walked on. He was tired, but he didn't dare to rest, to close his eyes, in fear he would never wake up again.

There was a slight breeze in the air. The leaves above his head rustled in the wind. Every sound frightened him.

The moon slipped out from behind a cloud to offer some welcome illumination. He looked up into the sky and saw the stars.

Then it struck him. He thought back to his school days in England when his geography teacher addressed the class on the subject of nautical navigation. Ancient sailors had used the stars in the night sky for navigation, in the days before more sophisticated techniques were invented. Suddenly all those memories from long ago came flooding back.

He located Ursa Minor, otherwise known as the 'Little Bear'. The brightest star in this constellation was Polaris, or the 'North Star'. He recalled that Polaris appeared within one degree of the Celestial North Pole. Its position in the night sky was north of the compass.

He created a visual image of the map in his head, based on memory. He recalled the forest to the north, the vast Pripet marshes to the south, and the agricultural land in the centre.

They had trekked north from the farm this morning. If Edward walked south, with the North Star always directly behind him, he would surely reach the edge of the forest eventually. Once he was out of the woods, his chances of finding his way home would increase significantly.

He felt a renewed vigour and hope as he strode forward, heading southwards. He hadn't gotten very far before he heard it, a heavy rustling in the undergrowth, only a few yards from him. He was frozen with fear as he imagined an unspeakable monster stalking him, a vile creature preparing to ambush him and devour his body.

Only then did he remember the hunting rifle slung over his right shoulder. The gun was his only defence.

The rustling grew louder and got closer. Edward could not see anything, but he raised his weapon and opened fire.

*BOOM!*

Then he started to run, sprinting as hard as his tired legs would carry him, but always heading south. It was some minutes later before he felt safe enough to stop. He turned around and listened carefully. It was too dark to see much. He could not hear a thing.

He regained his breath and moved on. Then all hell broke loose. A chilling animalistic growl was quickly followed by the sound of something large crashing through the undergrowth. He looked up in time to see a huge and ferocious brown bear coming straight at him. Edward was overcome by terror, and he realised then that he was surely only seconds away from a horrible death.

Mustering all the courage he could, he lifted his rifle, aimed at the animal's centre mass and pulled the trigger.

Nothing happened. He suddenly realised that he hadn't reloaded the rifle after the last shot, and now the bear was on him.

It struck out with its mighty paw. The sharp claws cut into the side of Edward's vulnerable torso. He screamed out in pain and shock. He fell backwards, dropping his rifle as he did so. And now the bear was right on top of him. Edward smelt wet fur and the stench of raw meat. He closed his eyes, knowing the end was near. A second later, he felt an unbearable pain in his right shoulder. Next, he felt himself being physically lifted up. He opened his eyes, and, to his horror, saw the mighty bear biting into his flesh.

That was when he felt a surge of pure adrenaline. He kicked and punched out, but his feeble blows were nothing to the powerful animal. Miraculously, the bear did release him from its deathlike grip. It opened its jaws, and Edward's broken body fell heavily down to the forest floor. His respite would be brief. The beast stood up on two legs - standing tall in front of its prey, poised to deliver the killer blow. Edward was hurt badly and bleeding heavily. He couldn't run or fight, so he had little choice but to accept his inevitable fate.

But then he heard shouts – the shouts of men. They were close, Edward was sure of it. The bear was temporarily distracted. It turned around to face this new adversary. Was this real? Edward didn't know. Was he suffering a delusion due to blood loss? Or was he already dead? An almighty booming sound reverberated through the forest. A gunshot? The bear appeared to be stunned.

BOOM!

A second shot rang out. The bear roared in agony. Fresh blood poured from a wound in its torso. The animal was defeated. It ignored Edward and limped away from the scene, retreating back into the forest.

Edward looked through his red haze of pain. He saw a figure approach, with a smoking shotgun in his hands. It was Uncle John. Was he dreaming? Was this really his uncle, or his guardian angel? He didn't get the chance to find out. A moment later the immense pain overcame him, and everything went black.

# 13/ 'Affair'

YVONNE HADN'T WANTED HER son to go on the hunting trip. She didn't care what Andrew and John did. They were both grown men and so were capable of making their own decisions – and their own mistakes. But Edward was still a child, no matter what anyone said. Yvonne knew her son. He was an innocent and naïve boy with a good heart. His father was a bad influence on him, but Andrew held sway over their son. He would follow his father anywhere, and that's what worried Yvonne.

She had hugged him tightly that morning, not wanting to let him go. Edward had pushed her away. Yvonne understood, of course. He was a 16 year old boy, and it was embarrassing for him to be molly-coddled by his mother. She understood this, but her son's coldness still hurt.

She had stood on the front porch to watch them leave – the trio of so-called hunters: two foolish men and one naïve boy. Her heart sank as she watched the three disappear from view when they entered the forest. What awaited them in those woods? Yvonne's maternal instincts were acting up. She had a bad feeling on that morning, but there was little she could do except pray that her son returned safely. The men would be gone for many hours, and Yvonne knew she would be better occupying herself with work, rather than sitting about worrying.

She re-entered the farmhouse and returned to the kitchen. She found Maria, their domestic servant, clearing the plates from the kitchen table and she instinctively went to help the old woman, but Maria shooed her away.

She had to admire the elderly woman's commitment to her work and her steadfast determination. Even so, it didn't seem right that she sit back, while poor old Maria worked herself into an early grave. When Yvonne looked at Maria she saw a hunched back and a shrunken body, covered from head-to-toe in a black dress and shawl.

Yvonne left the kitchen abruptly. She contemplated ascending the rickety staircase and going up to wake her daughter – but she decided against it. She would let Julie sleep on for another half hour or so. It wouldn't make much difference one way or another.

She was worried about her daughter. She knew that Julie wasn't adjusting to their new life. The girl had been very unhappy about leaving London. Yvonne realised this. Her feelings were understandable. Julie was forced to leave behind her life, her school and her friends. Yvonne also suspected there was a boy involved. A mother could always tell. She was just disappointed that her daughter didn't confide in her anymore.

The incident in Warsaw had been horrible. She had been worried sick about both of her children, even though they'd only been missing for a short time. She soon established that Julie had been the one who'd run away. Edward had simply been following her, trying to persuade his sister to go back with him. This wasn't a great surprise. Julie had always been the rebellious child. What Yvonne didn't understand was why her daughter had taken such a perilous risk to run away in such a dangerous place. She had asked Julie as much after she'd been brought back to the train carriage by Muller's men. Her daughter's answer had been full of anger and spite. She'd looked her mother straight in the eye, and told her that she hated their entire family, and never wanted to see any of them ever again.

Those words had hurt. Sometimes it was tough being a mother.

Julie hadn't been the same since her escapades in the ruins of the Polish capital. In the weeks since that day Julie had fallen into a state of apparent depression, and it was a constant challenge persuading her to do anything productive, or to make her wash, eat or even get out of bed. And then there were the nightmares. Julie had clearly been experiencing frighteningly vivid dreams, and she would wake up screaming night after night. Yvonne had asked her about the nightmares, but Julie wouldn't talk about them.

She didn't believe her daughter's account of the happenings back in Warsaw. She didn't think Julie was deliberately lying, but she reckoned the girl had fallen victim to her overactive imagination.

Yvonne knew the Nazis were bad, but she couldn't believe that they would murder children in cold blood. However, the important point was that Julie believed she had witnessed an horrific massacre, and this delusion was fuelling her depression and night terrors. She reckoned Julie needed some structure in her life. In a few weeks Julie would be attending her first term at the German speaking school in the nearest colonial settlement and Yvonne hoped to see her daughter making new friends and excelling at her studies. This was her daughter's only hope now.

Yvonne entered the main room of the farmhouse and she got to work. They had all chipped in to clean and repair the house, but their new home was still barely liveable. The fireplace had been cleared out, and the debris and soot had been removed from the chimney. The fire was already set. She would need to heat water for the work ahead. The decrepit old furniture in the room had been repaired wherever possible, although a few of the chairs had been so infested with woodworm that they had to be burnt. Most of the vermin were gone now. The men had laid down traps, which had caught most of the rats.

Yvonne's main task today was to scrub the walls in an attempt to remove the years' worth of mould and grime. It was a tough, tedious and dirty job which she hated. She lit the fire and heated a tin bucket of water. When she completed this task, she took the bucket of hot water over to the far wall and went to work with a sponge. How had her life come to this? she wondered.

She had enjoyed a comfortable and happy childhood, and had dreamed of a better life – better than this anyway. What had she done to deserve such a fate? Just one bad mistake she'd made as a silly little girl - a 16 year old virgin who didn't know any better. She had fallen for and married the wrong man, and she'd spent the rest of her life paying for this error. It was so unfair.

Dismissing the thought, she got down on her knees and started to scrub. She'd been working for about three-quarters of an hour before he entered the room. The man approached her from behind. He was soft on his feet, so Yvonne did not hear him coming. She almost jumped out of her skin when he called out her name.

"Excuse me, Mrs. Preston," he said, in an impeccably polite tone of voice. "I didn't mean to surprise you."

Yvonne turned her head and looked up at the figure standing over her – a young man with a toned and fit body and the aesthetically pleasing facial features…and his eyes - so bright and intellectual, so full of compassion. It was just a shame about those filthy clothes of his.

"No need to apologise, Sergei. I'm afraid my nerves are shot these days."

Sergei looked puzzled.

"I don't understand," he said, with a heavy accent. "What is this shooting of the nerves you speak of?"

Yvonne smiled faintly. She had to remember that Sergei was not a native English speaker. He didn't understand all of the nuances and sayings of the language.

"Never mind," she replied.

Only then did Yvonne notice the axe Sergei was holding in his right hand. She felt slightly unnerved by the close proximity of the sharpened tool.

"Have you been chopping logs?" she asked nervously.

"Yes," Sergei replied, with a reassuring smile. "We have gathered much wood to see your family through the winter."

"Thank you," Yvonne replied sincerely.

She liked Sergei, and not just because of his good looks. He was a polite and thoughtful young man who worked hard for their family. He was also someone to talk to. It was very lonely for Yvonne out here, in this foreign land. She thanked God that Sergei spoke very good English. Her husband didn't like the young Belorussian, but this was another positive point as far as Yvonne was concerned. It was just a pity about those smelly old clothes and his dishevelled appearance.

Suddenly, Yvonne had a moment of inspiration.

"No offence, Sergei," she said, in a light-hearted tone of voice, "but I think you could do with a good bath and a change of clothes."

She was worried that the young man would be offended by her comment, but instead he smiled and laughed.

"I believe you are right, Mrs. Preston. Unfortunately I do not have any other clothes, and it has been much time since I was last able to bathe."

"Well," Yvonne answered, with a smile on her face, "I believe there is something I can do on both counts. Maria and I can heat water and you can bathe in the tub upstairs. As for clothes…I think you're about the same height and size as my husband. He brought with him several sets of work clothes and a couple of old suits which he hasn't worn in years. He won't even miss these clothes, if I give them to you."

The grin disappeared from Sergei's face. He lowered his head and muttered a subdued reply under his breath.

"You are too kind, Mrs. Preston, but I'm afraid such things are not possible. A Slav cannot bathe in the same water as an Aryan. Such things are forbidden under German Racial Laws. As for your husband's clothes, I'm afraid your act of generosity could be dangerous for me. If Mr. Preston saw me wearing his suit he could accuse me of theft. This crime warrants a death sentence here in the Reichskommissariat, if the accused is a Slav."

Yvonne was genuinely shocked by Sergei's response.

"My God!" she exclaimed. "I've never heard such craziness in all my life!"

She paused for a moment in order to think it over. *The hell with it,* she thought. "Don't worry," she reassured him. "Andrew will never find out. On the off chance that he does recognise the clothes, I will take full responsibility and say you knew nothing about it. I know how to deal with my husband."

"Well," muttered Sergei, with some uncertainty still in his voice, "If you're certain…"

"I insist," Yvonne replied firmly. "I'll ask Maria to start heating the water, and I'll fetch the clothes."

Sergei nodded his head and smiled faintly. Yvonne felt good to be helping the boy, and maybe this dull day would become just a little more interesting.

Half an hour later, Sergei was enjoying his first bath in many a moon. Yvonne was sitting downstairs in the living room, as she waited for him to finish his wash. She'd handed him a fresh set of clothes to wear, and had laid out the rest of the outfits in his living quarters, which were located in the damp and dusty cellar of the farmhouse.

As Yvonne waited, her imagination started to run wild. She couldn't stop thinking about the naked young man bathing upstairs. She imagined his pale skin and toned muscles washed clean by the water. She obsessed over Sergei and fantasised about being with him – dreaming that she was touching, caressing and kissing his nude form. She felt like a giddy schoolgirl experiencing her first crush, her first sexual arousal.

*This is silly*, she thought. *You're being ridiculous, Yvonne Preston! Sergei is only a few years older than Edward, for God's sake!*

She tried to banish such impure thoughts from her mind, but this proved to be nearly impossible. What on earth was the matter with her? She heard footsteps emanating from the floor above. Sergei must have finished his bath. She imagined him climbing out of the tub, the water dripping off his naked body, as he picked up a towel to dry himself with. She imagined Sergei's manhood swinging back and forth as he walked. She wondered what it looked like. She had only ever seen Andrew's, so she had nothing to compare it to. She blushed. Such an impure mind she had developed. But surely such urges were only natural? And she certainly hadn't been getting any satisfaction from Andrew for a

211

long time. And, after all, she'd been faithful to her husband for all these years, and still he treated her like dirt.

He would have finished drying himself by now. Sergei would be putting on his underwear and Andrew's shirt and trousers. He'd be fully dressed by the time he came downstairs.

A part of Yvonne regretted the fact that she hadn't sneaked upstairs, in order to peek through the bathroom door and admire the boy's nude form, to see his manhood before he had gotten dressed. It was probably just as well that she hadn't done so. Such activities were bordering on the perverted. A lady had to maintain her dignity, after all…but maybe she didn't want to behave like a lady anymore.

When Sergei walked back into the room he looked like a new man. Her husband's old work clothes were a bit small on the boy. The shirt was about a size too tight and the trouser legs about an inch too short. Nevertheless, the outfit was a considerable improvement on the smelly old rags he'd been wearing before. Yvonne would have to throw his old rags on to the fire. Sergei's face was clean and his wet hair was slicked back. He looked more attractive than ever, and he had a big grin on his face.

"You look well," said Yvonne, in a deliberate understatement.

"Thank you, Mrs. Preston," he said. "You are most kind."

"It's not a problem," Yvonne replied with a smile. "And please, call me Yvonne."

"Ye-von," pronounced Sergei. "I am forever grateful, but now I must return to work."

"Not so soon, surely?" Yvonne replied, perhaps a little too quickly. In truth, she didn't want Sergei to leave her just yet. "Can you not take a break from your labours? Why not join me for a cup of tea?"

"This sounds good," answered Sergei. "But perhaps you would care to join me for the traditional morning drink of my country."

Yvonne was confused. "What do you mean?" she asked.

Sergei's grin grew wider.

"Will you be so good to accompany me out to the back, Yvonne?"

She was curious, but also somewhat suspicious. Nevertheless, the allure of this handsome and charming young Belorussian was enough to draw her in.

"Yes," she finally replied.

Two minutes later the couple entered the storage shed at the back of the farmhouse. It was an old and decrepit building, much like every other structure on the farm. The wood was rotting and the roof didn't look particularly stable. Nevertheless, the old building had something of a rustic charm to it. The place was tranquil and calm. Yvonne liked this.

"Do you come here often?" she asked jokingly.

Sergei apparently didn't understand her joke, as he answered her factitious question in a deadpan voice.

"Yes, I often come here for a peaceful time, when I have finished my daily work, of course. There is a bunk in the back of the shed, and sometimes I sleep out here. It is such a pleasant thing, to enjoy a fine summer's evening outdoors. Don't you agree?"

"Yes," Yvonne answered cheerfully. "So, why have you brought me out here?"

"Ah yes," replied Sergei, as if he had suddenly remembered the true purpose of their visit. He pointed to a shoddy table and a couple of old chairs in the corner of the barn. "Please, take a seat Yvonne."

She accepted his invitation and walked over to the chair. She took a seat and tried to relax. Meanwhile, Sergei went to the back room of the barn. Yvonne sat and waited for him to return. Suddenly, a wave of panic and paranoia hit her. She realised that she knew next to nothing about Sergei. Who was to say what his true intentions were? He might have deliberately lured her out here with a malicious intent in his head. He might intend to attack her, to rape her. Or maybe he was one of the Soviet partisans John had warned her about. Sergei might be a secret terrorist, left behind to wreak bloody havoc upon the settlers. He could be fetching a knife or a gun right now. Perhaps he intended to murder her.

Yvonne felt a raw terror deep in the pit of her stomach before managing to regain her composure. *Stop being so bloody ridiculous*, she told herself. First, she had lusted after the boy, and now she imagined him a killer. She didn't know what was happening to her.

She calmed herself somewhat, but her hair still stood up on end whenever he re-entered the room. To her great relief, Sergei came bearing not a weapon, but a glass bottle in one hand and two tin mugs in the other.

"Here it is," he said, "our traditional morning drink, for the two of us to share."

Yvonne looked on in puzzlement, gazing at the clear liquid contained in the glass decanter. And then it dawned on her.

"Vodka!" she blurted out in surprise.

"Da, Vodka," Sergei replied, as he took the other seat and set the bottle and mugs down on the table.

"But surely it's too early for hard liquor?" she exclaimed.

"In my country we start the day with vodka," Sergei replied. "The drink puts warmth in our bellies and gives us the strength to work, fight...and love."

Yvonne couldn't help but smile. She didn't feel quite right about drinking at this time in the morning, but she also didn't wish to offend Sergei by turning down his offer of hospitality. Besides, when in Rome, as they say... She accepted the mug, cautiously sniffing the strong alcohol contained within it. She and Sergei clinked their cups in a toast, and then they drank.

Yvonne felt the rough and powerful spirit force its way down her throat. She experienced the promised fire in her belly as the alcohol had the desired effect. But the vodka was almost too much for her and she coughed and spluttered as her body reacted. Sergei was unsympathetic. In fact, he laughed at her.

"My apologies, Yvonne," he said, after he'd stopped sniggering. "The vodka is homemade, and not of the best vintage."

Yvonne felt embarrassed. She decided to change the subject. "You speak English so well, Sergei. Where did you learn the language?"

"You are too kind," he answered, whilst pouring them both another drink. "Before coming here, I worked for two years for an Irish family living in Riga. Duffy was the family's name. I learnt English from them. I always had a talent for languages from a young age. I learnt German at school, and, at one time, I had hoped to study European languages in Moscow or Leningrad. Alas, it was not to be…"

Sergei had spoken the last sentence with a terrible sadness in his eyes.

"What happened?" she asked him, even though she reckoned she already knew the answer.

"Two things," Sergei answered, with a barely suppressed anger in his voice. "First, Stalin's Purges, and then the Nazi invasion. These twin catastrophes destroyed the Motherland. My country has been ravished, our people enslaved. Everything was taken from us…every last shred of hope, torn away."

Yvonne didn't know what to say. She felt Sergei's pain, and she couldn't imagine what the poor boy had been through, during his short but clearly very traumatic life. What had happened in this country? What had the Germans done to these people?

In truth, Yvonne didn't wish to know the answer. The truth was too horrific, and perhaps Sergei himself didn't care to relive it. Instead, Yvonne decided to be tactful and attempt to change the subject.

"Do you originally come from this area?" she asked.

"Yes," Sergei replied solemnly. "My family had a small farm only two miles from here. I lived there until the German invasion. I knew the people who occupied this farmhouse before the war. Malakhov was the family's name. The father was a widower. A kindly old man. He had two strong sons and three pretty young daughters. One night, the NKVD came for Mr. Malakhov. He was accused of being a 'kulak', a bourgeoisie peasant, if such a thing exists. Stalin's secret police arrested Malakhov and sent him to a gulag camp in Siberia. The rest of the family disappeared soon after. I never saw any of them again."

"And what of your own family?" Yvonne asked, as her curiosity got the better of her.

Sergei shook his head as he replied. His voice betrayed his immense grief. "All gone…the Nazis took everything from me…"

A terrible sadness seemed to overcome him and he took another large gulp of vodka from his mug.

215

"Why did you come here?" he enquired, looking directly into Yvonne's eyes.

The question sounded more like an accusation. She'd been put on the spot and was nervous and felt guilty. After all, this was Sergei's country, and her family had come here as invaders and conquerors, stealing his people's land. She decided to answer truthfully.

"I had no choice."

Sergei nodded his head in an apparent show of understanding. "Your husband?" he asked.

"Yes," Yvonne answered. "My husband is a cruel man. He said he would take my children and leave me behind. I thought of running away with Edward and Julie…but I knew he would find me if I did so. I didn't want to come to this country, but I had to."

Sergei smiled faintly, retaining eye contact as he did so – his youthful eyes, so full of intelligence and compassion.

"Most of us have few real choices in life," he said thoughtfully. "We can only make the best of the circumstances we find ourselves thrown into."

Yvonne felt a wave of intense emotions. This young man had been through hell, but still he felt empathy for her – an English mother and her children. Her eyes began to well up. Sergei reacted to her show of emotion. He reached across the table and took her hand in his. She felt his touch, and she liked it. Their eyes met. She was lost in his gaze, as her desire overcame all reason. Yvonne acted on pure instinct. She leaned across and put her lips against his, kissing him passionately. She met no resistance. In fact, Sergei did reciprocate. He put his hands on her body, feeling her waist and then working his way downwards. She opened her mouth and felt his tongue against hers. Yvonne experienced an intense longing rising up from deep inside her - a lustful desire, the like of which she had not felt for many a year.

To her disappointment, Sergei suddenly broke off the kiss. But he did so for a good reason. The man whispered in her ear, reminding her of the bunk in the back, and coyly asking whether she wished to come to bed with him. She only had to think about this for a second. She had come this far, and could not stop now.

"Yes," she answered firmly.

The young man took her by the hand and led her to his makeshift bedchambers. The bunk wasn't much to look at – nothing more than an old mattress and a blanket set in the corner of the barn. She didn't care though. There was only one thing on her mind right now. She wanted him so badly – his kiss and his touch, and something else.

Sergei kissed her hard on the mouth, as he pushed her down onto the mattress. Even now, he was still a gentleman. He asked her if she wanted him to continue. Yvonne said yes, without even a second's hesitation. He gently pulled at the shoulder straps of her dress, carefully slipping the outfit down over her body, before removing it completely. At the same time he tore off his own shirt and undid his trousers. Yvonne couldn't believe that this was really happening. Her fantasy was fast becoming a reality. His naked body was even more exquisite than she had imagined. She reached out to touch his chest, to run her fingers across his toned biceps and muscles. He reached behind her back and undid her brassiere.

Yvonne experienced a powerful arousal, much more intense than anything she had ever felt with her husband. Her nipples stood up. He leaned down to kiss her breasts and she groaned with delight. He removed his underwear. She saw his manhood for the first time – hard and erect. It was much larger than Andrew's. She helped him to pull down her panties. His touch was tender but firm. He asked if he could go inside her. Yvonne nodded her head in the affirmative. He entered her. She moaned in ecstasy, as her whole body awakened to sheer pleasure.

Yvonne woke up abruptly. Her slumber had been interrupted by the light patter of raindrops falling on the roof. She felt a blind panic as she struggled to remember where she was. Her body was naked under the blanket. Sergei was beside her on the mattress, still fast asleep.

She couldn't help but smile when she recalled the passionate day they had spent together in bed. They had made love over and over again. They had done things together that she had never experienced before. He had pleasured her in ways she'd never

217

thought possible. Hours had passed. It had just been the two of them – cut off from the world, bodies and souls intertwined.

On a couple of occasions she had heard her daughter's voice calling out for her. Julie had apparently been searching for her throughout the day. Each time, she and Sergei had stayed perfectly silent and waited until she went away. She felt somewhat bad, but she didn't want anything to interrupt her day of unbridled passion.

But now day had become night, and her lust had turned into regret and fear. During the throws of their passionate love making, she had forgotten all about the boys and their hunting trip. They had planned to return by sunset. She was terrified of getting caught with Sergei, naked in his bed. What had she been thinking of? Andrew would kill both of them, if he found out what they'd done.

She quickly got out from under the blanket and gathered up her clothes. She dressed and left the barn without waking Sergei. She ran across the grass towards the farmhouse. It was dark, but lanterns were lit in the main house, so she used the light to guide her. She had been gone all day, and her absence had surely been noticed – certainly by Julie. She hoped that the men hadn't arrived back yet. She entered the house and called out. There was no reply. The whole place seemed abandoned, but then she heard men crying out and she ran onto the porch and saw Andrew and John, their faces frozen with fear.

Edward was with them, too. He was motionless on the ground by his father's feet and was covered in blood.

Yvonne screamed. Her head was spinning. She collapsed. Everything went dark.

# 14/ 'Nightmare'

JULIE PRESTON HADN'T BEEN sleeping properly for several weeks now. The traumatic events she had experienced were trapped inside her head, and the horrific memories she vividly recalled meant it was all but impossible for her to rest. She didn't want to sleep; she didn't even want to close her eyes. Every time she did so, she saw the poor man getting savagely beaten on that back street in Berlin, she relived the brutal murder of Abraham and his friends in the ruins of Warsaw, and she recalled the vision of a terrible, almighty fire engulfing the landscape, its intense light more powerful than the sun. And now, a new horror haunted her dreams. She imagined the savage animal attack on her brother – the powerful bear slashing at Edward with its claws, and biting into him with its sharp teeth.

Julie hadn't witnessed the attack, but she had seen Edward's body after he was carried home by her father and uncle. His clothes were covered in blood, his face was pale and his eyes closed. Julie had thought her brother was dead. The girl shuddered every time she thought back to that terrible moment. Edward had survived the attack, but only just. Julie didn't know what exactly had happened out there in the woods, but she could imagine how scary that must have been for Edward.

John had found him just in the nick of time. He had shot the bear and rescued Edward, dressing his wounds and stopping the worst of the bleeding.

Julie had used the emergency radio to call for help and Edward had been rushed to a nearby field hospital for treatment. His parents had accompanied him, leaving her with Uncle John.

That had been 24 hours ago, and there was no word yet on Edward's condition. She was sick with worry. She also felt incredibly guilty. She had treated her older brother so badly. She had effectively disowned him. He wasn't perfect, but he was still family, and Julie loved him. But now she may never get the chance to tell him so.

She lay in bed and stared up at the ceiling, feeling a dreadful sense of déjà-vu as she did so. The last few weeks had been an endless nightmare. She had been torn from her home, separated from the love of her life and thrown into this living hell. She felt so alone…so scared. As far as she was concerned, there seemed to be no hope left. There was no chance of escape, no possibility of salvation.

Last night she had lain awake for hours before finally falling into a half slumber, and then her nightmares began.

She was looking on helplessly as red-eyed Nazi demons savagely attacked helpless pensioners and small children. She tried to intervene, to help the victims, but was unable to move. The Nazi monsters laughed at her as they continued to mercilessly beat their victims. Their sadistic cruelty knew no bounds.

She saw Abraham and the other children back in Warsaw – the innocents machine-gunned down by pitiless fascist killers – the many bullets ripping through their bodies, a deluge of gunfire which seemed to go on forever…and, in the end, the blood-soaked and broken Abraham looking up at her with his lifeless eyes, and him mouthing just one word: *Why?*

She dreamt that the whole family were together in the farmhouse, eating dinner. Edward had fully recovered from his injuries. They were all together and everyone was happy. It was a jovial dinner, with all the family chatting and laughing with one another, seemingly without a care in the world. But suddenly their peaceful meal was interrupted. The attack was instantaneous. The beast suddenly appeared inside the room, as if it had materialised from thin air. It was the bear. It had returned to finish the job. But there was something else. The beast had hatred in its eyes. The creature was pursuing a vendetta, and its purpose was to kill the entire family. Julie could only watch on in abject horror as it savagely tore them apart, limb from limb. And then the beast turned on her, its mouth full of blood and its eyes consumed by a killer's rage. It stood over her, poised to attack. She screamed in terror.

Then she woke up.

Today passed by in a blur. Sergei and the other Russian workers had gone to work as usual, and John had sat by the radio transmitter, waiting for news that never came. She had done very little other than wander the grounds in a half awake daze, trying in vain to find something to take her mind off the trauma of the previous evening. And now it was night time once again.

She was dozing by the early hours, and finally she fell asleep. She dreamt as she always did. She found herself outside the house. It was black, with the only light coming from the moon and the stars. Why was she outside after dark? It wasn't safe out here. There were bears, wolves and partisans in the forest, and any one of these enemies would be happy to maim or kill her.

She was on her own. The rest of the family were nowhere to be seen, but she was not afraid...until she saw the little girl.

The girl was glowing; her light illuminating the dark evening. Her hair was long and her dress was white. She looked as if she was going to attend her first communion. She waved, urging Julie to follow her, and then she turned and ran back towards the forest.

Julie followed, but then the girl vanished from sight, and she found herself lost in the depths of the forest. Dark and sinister trees surrounded her on every side. She could hear the branches creaking and leaves rustling. It was as if the woods were alive. The trees were creeping towards her. Their branches became like arms, grasping out to grab hold of her helpless body. She screamed. At that moment she awoke in her bed, her body soaked in a terror-induced sweat.

Another nightmare…but what did it mean?

Suddenly, Julie was startled by a soft sound emanating from outside her bedroom window. She stayed perfectly silent and listened intently. It sounded just like a child sobbing. Julie felt a cold chill creeping up her spine. Almost paralysed by fear, she pulled her sheet tightly over her body, as if imagining that the blanket would offer her some protection.

She was in no doubt now that the sound was that of a small child crying. How could this be possible? There weren't any children here. There weren't even any other people around for miles.

Julie decided that she must be dreaming. She was still asleep – this was the only logical explanation. She pinched herself. It hurt. She was awake after all and she imagined that the old farmhouse might be haunted. The crying child may be the ghost of a former occupant. She had never really believed in ghouls, spirits and supernatural beings, but how could anyone be sure that such things did not exist?

There was only one way she could be sure. She would have to see for herself. She carefully removed her covers and climbed off her mattress before creeping across the bedroom floor to the partially boarded up window. She peeped out through the gaps in the wooden planks and gasped when she saw the little girl.

She was standing on the grass, directly below the bedroom window. She had stopped crying. The child was looking up at Julie and she quickly realised it was the same girl from her dream. She looked exactly the same, right down to her long black hair and tattered white communion dress, but she was no longer surrounded by the aura of bright light.

Julie was very scared, but she couldn't take her eyes off the girl who eventually turned and slowly walked back towards the woods. As she did so, she raised both hands into a horizontal position and carefully put one foot in front of the other as if playfully mimicking the actions of a tightrope walker.

Then she began to hum loudly. It was a tune Julie did not recognise, but the melody sounded dark and sinister. Even so, she felt an inexplicable urge to pursue the child into the night.

222

She dressed quickly, creeping out of her bedroom and quietly ascending the stair-case. Julie reached the hallway, took a deep breath and opened the front door just in time to see the little girl approach the edge of the forest.

She was skipping and still humming loudly as if she had not a care in the world and Julie moved slowly towards her, reaching the edge of the woods moments after the child had disappeared behind the trees.

Julie had spent her whole life living in the city of London and to her the forest was a frightening place, the dark trees holding a foreboding presence. She paused and listened to the girl's humming and then moved off again in the direction of the sound, zigzagging between the trees, always fearful that she would lose her way or her footing.

Eventually she came to a clearing in the forest and stopped. She stifled a scream. The little girl standing directly in front of her was still and silent and then she raised her right arm and pointed to what appeared to be a large carefully constructed mound of stones set in the middle of the clearing, and partly illuminated by the moonlight. Julie wondered who had placed them there, and why.

Just then, the silence was shattered by the piercing howl of a wolf. The howl became a chorus and Julie realised to her horror that there had to be a pack nearby. She turned away from the girl for but a moment and when she looked back in her direction just seconds later the child was nowhere to be seen.

Julie was on her own. She began to panic, and when the howls of the wolf pack grew in intensity, she took to her heels and ran for her life.

Her heart was beating fast. Cold sweat poured down her forehead. She kept picturing her brother's mangled and broken body. She didn't want to end up like that, so she picked up her pace, dodging in between the trees, trying her best to find her way in the dark. Her right foot hit something solid, and suddenly she fell to the forest floor face first, feeling an excruciating pain in her ankle.

She used her hands to push herself up and that's when she saw a dark figure running towards her. She opened her mouth and screamed in terror before the blackness engulfed her.

223

# 15/ 'Discovery'

JOHN PRESTON HAD STOOD vigil until the break of dawn, not having slept a wink all night. He was extremely tired, but he didn't falter, determined to stand guard and defend the farmhouse from whomever or whatever lurked in the forest.

He had sat for hours on the front porch with a loaded Mauser rifle laid across his lap. It had been almost four hours since he had found Julie.

He had discovered her missing shortly after 2am, when he had gone upstairs and peeked into her room, only to find her bed empty. He had meticulously searched every room in the house and then had begun to panic.

Just twenty four hours previously, he had brought home the bloodied body of his nephew, after his and Andrew's negligence had resulted in Edward's mauling by a vicious wild bear. And now, yet another catastrophe had occurred. He had been entrusted by Andrew and Yvonne to look after Julie, while the couple stayed with Edward at the hospital

John couldn't think of any good reason why his niece would have left the farmhouse after dark, especially given what had happened to her brother. He had been awake all night, sitting by the radio receiver in the back room. He'd waited all day for news from the field hospital on Edward's condition. No one had contacted him, and every call he had made to the military station had been abruptly cut short by an unsympathetic Wehrmacht communications officer; it had all been extremely frustrating.

Concerned about Julie's disappearance, he had armed himself with the Mauser rifle and a holstered Luger pistol, and he'd gone outside to search for her.

It hadn't been long before John entered the forest and a short time later had heard Julie's screams when she had fallen in the darkness and temporarily blacked out.

He'd had to carry her back to the farmhouse, all the time having to listen to her mumbling about a little girl in a white dress. It hadn't made any sense to him then, and still didn't now.

With Julie now asleep and recovering from her ordeal, John went back out on to the porch and stared across the open fields toward the forest; it was a truly terrifying and dark place. He had never been so relieved to see the sun rising to herald a new day.

Now physically and emotionally exhausted, he knew it would be sensible to get a few hours rest, but he was still troubled by the events of the past night. He had dismissed the story of the girl in white, but what had really drawn Julie to the woods? What was the mound of stones in the clearing she'd talked about?

He decided that he would seek out the location and see if it really did exist.

Armed with his rifle, he began his solo trek to the forest, trying to retrace his steps from the night before. Even in daylight, it was still a foreboding place, but soon he reached the spot where he had discovered Julie.

That had been relatively easy; the hard part was to locate the mound of stones and for some time he found himself walking round in circles.

He was about to call it a day when he stumbled into the clearing and at once spotted the stone structure; it was just as Julie had described - approximately six foot tall, shaped like a pyramid and built from dozens of rocks and stones of various shapes and sizes. Somebody had gone to a lot of time and effort to construct it, but for what purpose?

Suddenly, there was movement away to his right. He raised

his rifle ready to defend himself and then gasped in disbelief. It was her.

The little girl in white was standing about fifty yards in front of him. She was just as Julie had said.

He met her gaze, but had little idea of what to do next. Moments passed before he finally mustered the strength to call out to the child.

"Hello!" he shouted. "Are you all right? What's your name? Where are your parents? Are you lost?"

The girl didn't respond to any of his questions. She didn't move. John found it all very bizarre.

Suddenly, the girl lifted up her right arm and pointed towards the stone pyramid. Then she fell on to her knees and lowered both hands into the dirt, lifting up a pile of soil for John to see. Seconds later, the soil slipped through her fingers.

John got the distinct impression that the child was attempting to communicate a message to him, but then quite suddenly, the girl turned away and started to sprint back into the forest.

"Hey wait!" John shouted, as he started to chase after her.

He ran past the tree line, but stopped abruptly when he lost sight of the girl. He scanned the forest for several minutes, but to no avail. The child had disappeared.

He contemplated searching for her, but quickly decided against it and returned to the farmhouse to grab a spade, after which he retraced his steps back to the clearing, stopping only when he reached the mound of stones and rocks.

He removed the rifle from his shoulder and placed it on the grass, glancing this way and that, sensing he was being watched from afar. Was the little girl still hiding in the forest? Was she spying on him right now? John didn't know. He couldn't see anybody or anything, so he began digging at the foot of the mound, for what, he wasn't at all certain.

It wasn't long before his spade struck something hard. He used his boot to clear away some loose soil, exposing the skeletonised remains of a human arm. He dug deeper, eventually unearthing the decomposing body of a woman.

In life, she had been dressed in a floral patterned frock, now tattered and torn and just about recognisable.

He briefly examined the remains to discover she had been shot through the head. Murdered, John reckoned, executed, perhaps, a victim of the war.

His eyes were drawn to the remnants of a pile of blankets still clutched in the woman's right hand. He recoiled in horror when he pulled back the tattered old blanket, for wrapped in them was the mummified body of an infant. It had clearly died in its mother's arms.

John felt physically sick. He retched, managing to swallow his bile. After composing himself, he picked up his shovel and began digging again. Over the next couple of hours he uncovered many more bodies. There were men and women and children, all evidently shot in the head, and buried in a mass grave.

A massacre had obviously taken place here and he was certain more digging would expose hundreds, maybe thousands, of corpses.

It was all beginning to make sense to him now. The ruined and abandoned towns and cities, the miles after miles of empty countryside, the cryptic conversations he'd shared with Henrich Muller.

Everything the Nazis had told them was lies. The Slavic and Jewish populations of these countries hadn't simply gotten up one day and marched hundreds of miles to the East. Millions of people hadn't moved to the east of the Ural Mountains. They weren't living in newly constructed settlements built in the vast wastelands of Siberia. They were dead. The Nazis had murdered them all. Sure, they had kept a proportion of the population alive to serve as slave labour, people like Sergei and the others, but the rest had surely been slaughtered.

The East was probably full of mass grave sites such as this. Had the Fascists shot all of their victims? This seemed unlikely. Summary executions by firing squad – this method seemed too inefficient for the Germans. Surely they had developed some better means of mass murder. Perhaps they had starved millions of Slavs to death. John had heard stories of mass famines breaking out across Russia during the war. Had these famines been a part of a deliberate plan, orchestrated by the Nazi bureaucrats back in Berlin? This seemed plausible.

John felt ill. He realised that he'd uncovered something truly terrible – possibly the worst act of murderous genocide in human history. It was almost too horrific to believe.

He spent the next few hours returning the corpses to their original resting places, vowing never to tell of what he had uncovered in this awful field of death.

He picked up his shovel and his rifle and made the lonely hike back to the farmhouse as the sun began to set, fearing what fresh horrors may befall his family in the coming days.

# 16/ 'Breaking Point'

YVONNE PRESTON ARRIVED BACK at the farmhouse at midday on the Wednesday afternoon. She got a lift in the back of a German armoured car, complete with the standard escort of armed Wehrmacht soldiers.

She had spent three days and three nights in the chaotic German military field hospital, sleeping in a cot out in the corridor, as she maintained a constant vigil at her son's bedside.

The first night had been the most frightening. The ambulance journey had been hell. She had held Edward's ice cold hand throughout the drive, and she had whispered words of reassurance and comfort into his ear, even though he probably could not hear her in his semi-conscious state.

She had thought her son would die. His injuries had seemed so severe. She had never felt so scared in her whole life.

When they finally arrived at the hospital, Edward was immediately rushed into surgical theatre. She and Andrew had sat up through the night and into the next morning, as they impatiently waited for news.

The delay was unbearable. Yvonne hardly spoke a word to her husband throughout those tense and anxious hours. She couldn't even bear to look at him. It was Andrew's fault, after all. He should never have brought her son out into that dangerous forest. And now, after disaster had struck, Andrew had nothing useful to contribute. He had no answers, and no means to mend his son's broken and bloodied body. He was such a foolish, stupid little man. Yvonne despised him so much.

In the end, a doctor had come to speak with them early the next morning – a thin, bald headed German wearing thick spectacles and a long white coat. Yvonne's heart had almost burst through her chest when she saw the man approach. She was so sure the news was going to be bad. The doctor's face was so grim.

The surgeon spoke patchy English and so his report was frustratingly slow, but, eventually, they were able to establish what had occurred in the theatre during the night.

The medical team had performed surgery on Edward's shoulder, which was where the beast had bitten into him. He had also received a transfusion to replace the large amount of blood he'd lost after the attack. Following the operation, Edward's condition was stabilised, and he was out of immediate danger.

Yvonne felt an enormous relief, as if all of her prayers had been answered.

'Thank God!' her husband had exclaimed, after the doctor had delivered the good news.

Yvonne had shot Andrew an angry glare. She wondered whether her husband was more relieved that his only son and heir would live, or because Edward had survived in spite of his father's gross stupidity. Yvonne didn't know, nor did she particularly care. She had stayed with her son for the next two days and nights. She'd been there when Edward regained consciousness. Seeing him open up his eyes had been one of the happiest moments of her life.

She sat with him as he regained his strength. She'd comforted him, read to him, fed him his meals and helped him in and out of bed whenever he needed to use the toilet. It was like he was her little boy once again.

Edward had been too proud to hug his mother on the morning of the hunt, but now he depended on her for almost everything. His progress had been good. He had needed over 50 stitches as a result of the attack. It would take time to heal, but the doctors expected him to make close to a full recovery.

His scars would be for life, though.

Edward had been much stronger when Yvonne left the hospital. Well, she hadn't left, as much as she'd been kicked out. The nurses had told her repeatedly that there was no need for her to stay by her son's side, since he was now out of danger, but she was having none of it. How dare anyone tell her that she couldn't stay with her boy, to look after him in his hour of need! Besides, Yvonne would never leave him alone in a place like this, a hospital run by Nazis, of all people!

On the third morning, the doctor had come to Yvonne and had told her she must leave, as her continued presence was disrupting the staff's day-to-day work. She'd told him this was ridiculous, and she wasn't going anywhere. In the end, they'd sent for two burly military policemen to escort her out. At that point, she had given in to the inevitable, but before leaving, she had embraced Edward and kissed him on the cheek, saying, 'I love you.'

Andrew had returned to the farm the previous day. He hadn't slept in the hospital after the first night. Instead, he had been billeted in the Wehrmacht barracks adjoined to the field hospital. He had come to visit Edward only a couple of times over the two previous days, not staying for long on either occasion.

He'd had no clue how to deal with his son's hospitalisation. He came in and made scathing jokes about Edward's poor shooting skills and his lack of direction. He'd also had a go at Yvonne, accusing her of 'molly-coddling' Edward, and of fussing too much over him.

A harsh word or two from his wife had been enough to shut him up. Yvonne didn't fear him like she used to. His obsessive pursuit of his insane fantasises had pushed his family through the Gates of Hell.

For perhaps the first time in his life, Andrew realised he was wrong. Yvonne could see the guilt in his eyes, even though he would never admit to feeling it.

She climbed out of the back of the armoured half-truck, feeling relieved to see the sunlight once again. She made sure to politely thank both German military policemen who had accompanied her.

The soldiers met her with cold and emotionless glares. Were they born this way, she wondered, or was the humanity beaten out of them during their training?

To think that her husband had wanted to turn Edward into one of these soulless storm troopers - over her dead body!

She strode across the gravel pathway to the farmhouse, fighting off dreadful memories of that terrible night when Edward had been attacked.

Yvonne remembered fainting when she saw his blood soaked body in John's arms. Julie had revived her on that night.

Yvonne had hardly given her daughter a thought over the last few days. What kind of mother was she? Julie hadn't been doing too well the last time she saw her – what with the bouts of depression, sleepless nights, constant nightmares and the mental trauma she had suffered, and she had been left to deal with all of this alone.

Yvonne was feeling very guilty just being back here, and not just because of her neglect of her daughter.

The front door was ajar. She cautiously walked inside, as if expecting some catastrophe to befall her as soon as she entered. She called out for Julie, for John and lastly for Andrew. None of them answered. Instead, she was greeted in the hallway by the last person she wanted to see right now.

Sergei appeared much the way she remembered him from their last meeting. True enough, his face and his hands were dirtier. Presumably the young man had not been able to partake of another bath since the weekend. Sergei still wore Andrew's old shirt and trousers. He'd been naked the last time she'd seen him.

She still felt extremely guilty about what they'd done on that fateful day. She didn't feel particularly bad about cheating on her husband. She didn't love Andrew anymore. If anything, she had come to despise him. Nevertheless, she did fear what her husband would do, if he ever found out about her day of unbridled passion shared with young Sergei. However, the real reason for Yvonne's immense guilt was clear to her. She had been in bed with Sergei whilst her son had been in mortal danger. They'd been making love while Edward was wandering alone in the woods, lost and scared.

Yvonne had been asleep at the exact time her only boy was being mauled by the vicious bear. It gave her a cold shudder every time she thought back to that night. And seeing Sergei again brought all the memories flooding back.

Yvonne had hoped to avoid her one-time lover, but she knew she'd have to face him at some point. A part of her felt very guilty, but, to her shame, she also experienced an intense longing when she set eyes upon the beautiful Belorussian boy. She remembered everything from that day – every sordid detail of their passionate encounter. And she still felt a strong longing for him. When Sergei smiled, her heart pounded.

"Yvonne," he said, in his heavily accented English. "It is very good to see you."

He moved forward, as if meaning to embrace her. Yvonne fought her strong instinct to reciprocate. She stepped back and shook her head, retaining a cold and stand-offish demeanour. Sergei looked visibly hurt by her rejection, but he quickly regained his composure.

"Your son," he said. "How is his health?"

"Edward's doing better," Yvonne replied, with a forced smile on her lips. "He's out of danger and the doctors expect him to make a full recovery."

"This is good news, Yvonne," he replied. "When will they allow him to come home?"

She appreciated Sergei's concern, but didn't wish to continue this awkward conversation for much longer, lest the feelings she held for the man get the better of her.

"Where is everyone?" she asked, deliberately changing the subject.

"They are all out in the fields," answered Sergei. "Mr Preston wished to inspect the farm, and he brought Miss Julie with him, as he felt she needs…how do you say?…fresh air."

Yvonne rolled her eyes in annoyance. This was bloody typical of Andrew. His stupidity had put their son in hospital and now he was bossing Julie about. She felt a fresh fury rising within her. She would kill her husband if he allowed anything to happen to her daughter.

Yvonne tried hard to control her anger. She very much wanted to see her daughter, but their reunion would now have to wait.

"And what about my brother-in-law?" she asked. "Where is John?"

"Sergeant Preston has stepped out," replied Sergei. Yvonne vaguely noted his use of John's former rank held in the British Army. "He has been taking walks out in the forest most days. We rarely see the sergeant during the daylight hours."

Yvonne nodded her head. She felt her strength failing. She had been forced to leave her stricken son behind. And she had come back to this dump – this decrepit house which was falling down around their heads. She wanted to see her daughter, to make sure she was okay. She also wished to speak with John, to thank him for saving Edward's life, and to seek his comfort and support. But there was no one here to greet her...nobody except for Sergei.

Yvonne had been strong for the last few days. She'd had to be, for Edward's sake. But now she was home, she couldn't hold it in any longer.

All of a sudden, she burst into tears. She cried aloud as the tears rolled down her cheeks. The suddenness of her emotional outbreak seemed to take Sergei by surprise. She looked to him through tear-filled eyes, yearning for his comfort...for his love. Sergei held back for a moment. He looked awkward and uncomfortable, but not for long.

He stepped forward, put an arm around her and pulled her close in a warm embrace. She didn't push him away. Instead, she rested her head on his chest and dried her eyes on his soft shirt.

"I'm sorry," she sobbed. "So sorry....you have suffered through so much in your life. You've lost your family in such terrible circumstances...and yet, you care about me, don't you?"

"It is true," Sergei replied emotionally. "I have grown very fond of you, Yvonne. We are very different people, from different lands, but I believe you are a kind and honest woman...a true beauty on the outside and the inside. I greatly enjoyed our day spent together – our passion shared. I have thought of you every waking moment since...you have been in my dreams, Yvonne..."

Those were the words she had secretly yearned for. Her heart beat faster and she felt goose bumps all over her body. She knew it was wrong, but she felt unable to stop herself; her intense passion and desire overwhelmed every other emotion.

She looked into Sergei's deep blue eyes and saw just how besotted he was with her. He wanted her, desiring both her body and her soul. She now realised just how good it felt to be desired – to be loved. He moved in to kiss her, his lips hungrily seeking out hers. She closed her eyes and opened her mouth. She experienced a moment of pure ecstasy when their tongues met. She didn't want to end the kiss. She didn't want to open her eyes and return to harsh reality – but yet, she did so.

It was only then that she saw him. Her passion and lust was instantly replaced by shock and fear. Her eyes widened in terror. She opened her mouth to speak, but no words came out. She broke the embrace and pushed Sergei away. He looked at her in confusion.

Andrew had returned home early from the fields. He had left his troublesome daughter with Yuri and Ivan, the Slavic workers. She'd been a pain recently, and John said she'd been playing up whilst they were up at the hospital. A day's hard graft would do the girl the world of good. She'd been limping around and complaining all morning about a sprained ankle, but Andrew didn't believe a word of it. He'd grown sick of her constant whinging. She needed to learn that her father wasn't going to tolerate her bad behaviour any longer.

At first, he couldn't be sure what was happening. He'd thought Yvonne was upset. He could see that she'd been crying and Sergei had his hands on her. *The Slav's vile hands on his wife!* Andrew was overcome with rage.

He'd looked around, searching for something to use as a weapon and found a discarded plank of wood. He'd picked it up, ready to strike the boy, and that's when he had seen the smile on Yvonne's face.

She'd been looking into Sergei's eyes. He saw them embrace. He saw them kissing. He clenched his teeth, screwed up his eyes and tightened his grip on the plank of wood, feeling more anger than he'd ever done before. His wife's betrayal was shocking and unbelievable.

Yvonne had seen him approach, which was when she'd broken away from Sergei.

Sergei didn't see him coming. Andrew struck out with the wooden plank, smashing the weapon against his enemy's skull. Sergei cried out in shock and pain, and he fell to the floor.

Andrew raised the plank once more for a second strike, but Yvonne grabbed it, before her husband lashed out with his fist. He punched her hard in the nose, drawing blood. He grabbed her firmly by the hair, ignoring her screams of pain and protest as he dragged her across the floor before throwing her into a broom cupboard, pushing a chair up against the door to prevent her escaping.

Pumped up with rage, he turned his attentions back to Sergei who'd managed to get back on to his feet, blood now seeping from his head wound.

"Oh no you don't, you filthy animal!" Andrew shouted, as he launched a fresh attack.

He struck out with the wooden plank, hitting Sergei's left shoulder. The Russian cried out in agony. Andrew didn't care. Sergei fell back to the ground. Andrew smashed the plank against his victim's spine over and over again, until finally the wood broke in two.

Only then did Andrew remember he had a Luger pistol in the holster around his waist. He withdrew it and took aim.

"Any last words, you subhuman swine?" he asked, glaring down at Sergei. The boy's face was bloodied, but his eyes were defiant and his lips were sealed.

Andrew stepped back and prepared to pull the trigger, but suddenly, someone grabbed the gun and pushed him away.

It was his brother John.

"What the hell are you doing?" John screamed. "Have you gone bloody mad?"

"Keep out of this, brother!" Andrew snapped back. "You don't know what this bastard has done! He...he has to die!"

"I won't permit it," John said firmly. "I won't allow you to murder this man. You'll have to go through me first."

Andrew briefly considered doing just that. But, when he glared into his brother's intense and determined eyes, his strength failed him. He lowered his gun and backed away, effectively admitting a humiliating defeat.

Yvonne shouted through the blocked door, as she begged John to come to her aid. Andrew ignored them both, as he stormed out of the farmhouse, slamming the front door so hard behind him that it almost fell off its hinges.

His brother had prevented him from killing Sergei, but his murderous rage had not diminished. The gun was still in his right hand, loaded and ready to fire.

He stomped out onto the gravel pathway, blinking as he adjusted his eyes to the summer's sun. He used his left hand to remove a cigarette from the pack in his pocket. Next, he placed the fag in his mouth and attempted to light it, but his hand was still shaking. Feeling frustrated, he turned abruptly to his left, spotting three figures standing on the grass, the other members of his Slavic workforce.

Andrew was furious with them. Yuri and Ivan were supposed to be out in the fields working, and Maria should be in the kitchen, preparing lunch for the family. "What the hell are you all doing out here?" he asked angrily. "Why are you not working? Does no one obey my bloody orders?"

None of them responded. They just stood there, staring at him. And then it dawned on him. They had known all along. They knew Sergei had been playing around with his wife, and yet nobody had told him so. It was all one big conspiracy, a plot against him. Andrew hated them all. Enough was enough.

"I'll teach you bastards!" he screamed. "I'll show you what happens to those who betray me!"

Andrew saw red. His fury was so intense that it overpowered all other emotions. He marched up to Maria and raised his gun. The old woman didn't flinch, or even blink. He pulled the trigger.

*BOOM!*

The bullet tore through the woman's skull, producing a gruesome cloud of blood, bone and fragments of brain. He looked on awestruck for a moment, as Maria's lifeless body fell into the dirt. Yuri reacted in a blind panic. He charged at Andrew, his arms opened up, as if he meant to embrace him.

"Bloody hell!" Andrew swore.

Yuri's hands were on him. He pushed the gun against the Russian's body and pulled the trigger, firing three times in quick succession. The bullets tore through Yuri's chest and stomach. He screamed out in agony before falling down to the ground in a heap.

Andrew then turned around and saw young Ivan sprinting away from the bloody scene. He fired a shot after him, but the bullet went high and wide and Ivan kept on running.

Andrew took a deep breath and re-aimed. He had the fleeing boy in his sights. It would be so easy to shoot him in the back. All he needed to do was squeeze the trigger, but in that moment, he had a vision of his son Edward at play, running through idyllic green fields, his heart filled with a child's joy, and he lowered his gun, allowing Ivan to disappear from view into the forest beyond.

Andrew carefully placed the Luger pistol back into his holster and turned to survey the limp and bloodied bodies of Yuri and Maria. It felt like some kind of terrible nightmare from which he would awake at any moment now. But no; there was no escape from the awful reality of what he had just done.

He slowly walked back towards the farmhouse, carefully opening the door and entering the building. He found his brother and his wife sitting on the staircase. Yvonne was crying, and her upper lip and chin were covered in dried blood. John was holding and comforting her.

"What the devil were you shooting at?" John asked.

Andrew did not answer. He looked down at the pool of blood on the floor and the broken wooden plank which lay beside it. This was the spot where he'd savagely beaten his wife's lover, only minutes before. The last time Andrew had seen him, the Russian had been broken and bleeding on the floor....but now, Sergei was gone.

# 17 / 'Assault'

JOHN PRESTON HAD SPENT the previous day dealing with the aftermath of his brother's blood-thirsty rampage. Andrew's crimes were truly appalling.

Of course, John had seen Andrew's dark side before. He'd had a violent and nasty streak ever since childhood and John remembered how his brother behaved in Palestine, where he regularly abused and beat Jewish and Arab suspects alike. Nevertheless, John had never imagined that his brother was capable of cold blooded murder. He didn't know exactly what had occurred to provoke such a murderous rage, although he had his suspicions.

Whatever had happened between Yvonne and Sergei wasn't his business. John didn't condone adultery but, then again, Andrew hadn't been a good husband to her over the years. He could understand why his brother had gotten angry, given the circumstances. Nevertheless, the alleged adultery certainly did not justify the extremity of his violent reaction. John had arrived home just in the nick of time. If he hadn't stopped his brother, Andrew would surely have killed Sergei, and probably Yvonne as well.

Maria was a weak old woman and Yuri was slow witted and harmless. Both were unarmed and posed no possible threat to Andrew. He was shocked that his brother could be so cruel and callous.

239

The killing of unarmed civilians was dishonourable and inexcusable, and, as far as John was concerned, his brother's actions made him as bad as the Nazi death squads.

He found Andrew sitting alone in his bedroom, staring blankly at the wall, and realised his brother was still in a state of shock.

He barely responded to John's presence, or to his questions. He asked his brother why he'd done the terrible deed, but Andrew wasn't able to provide a coherent answer. He had mumbled something about 'the boy', and letting him go. John presumed he was referring to Ivan, who was missing after the attack. To John's relief, Andrew had given up his Luger pistol without any objection. He seemed to be glad to get rid of the deadly weapon. John no longer trusted his brother, so he decided to lock the bedroom door to keep him trapped inside. Again, Andrew did not complain. He appeared to be totally disconnected from reality.

John's next task was to deal with the bodies. He dragged both corpses off the grass, and brought them inside one of the disused sheds, covering them with a piece of discarded tarp.

He then pondered over what to do next. The obvious course of action was to report the shooting to the German authorities, but he was loathe to do so. That could result in Andrew being hanged for murder. On the other hand, he couldn't protect his brother forever; Andrew would have to answer for his crime sooner or later.

Finally, John made his decision. He made the call to the Wehrmacht barracks, using the two-way radio located in the backroom. He was deliberately vague in his explanation of what had occurred. He simply informed the Germans that there had been an incident on the farm which had resulted in two of their workers being killed, and the other two fleeing from the scene.

The Wehrmacht lieutenant who took the call was surprisingly nonplussed by the whole affair. He seemed largely uninterested. He was more concerned about Sergei and Ivan being missing and said that a patrol would come out to the farm on Friday to collect the bodies and then conduct a search of the forest.

And so, that was that. John realised that he'd been foolish to think the Nazis would care about dead Slavs. Why would they?

The Germans had already wiped out millions of innocent people in this country. John had seen first-hand evidence of this mass genocide. And, from the Nazi perspective, what difference did two more shootings make in the grand scheme of things? The Nazis treated the Slavic workers no better than livestock – animals that could be shot down at will by their Aryan masters. This was 'Lebensraum', the Fascist Empire where even murder was tolerated, as long as the right people were murdered. John was disgusted, but there was nothing he could do.

Another night, another dusk to dawn vigil; John had sat on the porch with a Mauser rifle on his lap and a Luger pistol in his holster. He'd kept a close watch on the darkened forest, fighting off the powerful urge to sleep, whilst he maintained a state of readiness.

John had reckoned either Sergei or Ivan might have returned to the farmhouse during the night. The boy was likely running scared, but Sergei may well return with the intention of seeking revenge on his attacker. Andrew had committed a terrible crime, but he was still John's brother, and he had a duty to protect him.

On a couple of occasions during the night, John thought he'd seen movement in the tree line. Both times, he'd jumped up from his chair and aimed his rifle…but there was nobody out there. Or so it seemed.

In the morning John went back inside the farmhouse. He proceeded to the backroom, laid down his rifle on the desk and checked the radio set, ensuring the device was switched on. Next, he entered the kitchen and began to prepare tea and breakfast for the family. He shouted up to Yvonne and Julie, hoping they would make the effort. It was so hard to maintain the illusion of normality under such dire circumstances.

Andrew was still locked up in the master bedroom on the second floor. John brought him breakfast on a tray, finding him lying on top of the bed, fully clothed and staring up at the ceiling. The room stank of stale cigarette smoke.

Andrew barely acknowledged his brother's presence as the tray was placed on the bedside table. John then vacated the room, making sure to lock the door behind him, considering his brother a danger to himself and to others.

He went back downstairs to the kitchen to discover that neither Yvonne nor Julie had emerged from their rooms. He shook his head in despair. It was going to be tough pulling this family back together.

He tossed the keys down on the kitchen table, poured himself a mug of tea and took it outside on to the porch where he continued to ponder the situation.

His thoughts were interrupted by the sound of an approaching vehicle, a Volkswagewerk Kubelwagen, the equivalent of the American made jeep. It was carrying a two people, both dressed in the grey uniforms of the Wehrmacht.

The car came to a halt about twenty yards from the house, and the two occupants jumped out. It was only then that John recognised Jan van der Merwe and Pieter Steyn, the two South Africans who the family had met on the final morning of their train journey through Eastern Europe.

John groaned inwardly. Steyn gave him a sarcastic smile and a mocking 'thumbs up'.

"Well, well…there's our old pal Sergeant Preston, heroic soldier of the British Empire. Great to see you again, old chap," Steyn said.

"Steyn, van der Merwe," replied John, nodding his head, his tone deliberately cool.

He recalled that his brother Andrew had got on rather well with the Boer cousins, no doubt because they were white supremacists and Waffen SS soldiers, who shared many of Andrew's racist beliefs. His brother had invited the two to come and visit the Preston homestead during their next period of leave from the Wehrmacht. John had thought nothing more of it, since he didn't expect the cousins to take up the offer. But now they were here, and their timing couldn't have been any worse.

John didn't care for either of the South Africans. He would have to find a way to get rid of them. As the men strolled towards the farmhouse, John noted both were armed with MP-40 submachine guns, causally slung over their shoulders.

242

"So, this is the Preston homestead," Van der Merwe said. "Not bad, although it could do with a lick of paint. Where's your brother?"

John was trying to think of a satisfactory answer, but he was suddenly distracted. He saw a flash of light in the far tree line, followed a split second later by an almighty bang. John reacted instinctively, as he recognised the distinctive sharp crack of a rifle shot. An agonised cry rang out. He looked up just in time to see van der Merwe fall. The bullet had torn through his back and exited through his chest, leaving a large and bloody hole in his tunic uniform. The man collapsed to the ground like a lifeless rag doll.

"Jan!" screamed Steyn, "Jan…you've been shot!"

Steyn dropped down to his knees and grabbed hold of van der Merwe, but the man was already dead.

John also dropped to his knees, pulling his pistol out of its holster and scanning the tree line, quickly identifying the gunman's position.

The shooter emerged from the forest and sprinted across the empty ground, his sights focussed on the South Africans' vehicle. He carried an elongated wooden rifle, but did not wear a uniform. He was dressed in the dark brown garb and flat cap of the Russian peasantry and John realised he must be one of the Soviet partisans Muller had warned him about.

Still over one hundred metres away, the gunman was well beyond the range of John's pistol and he could only watch on impotently as the partisan raised his rifle, preparing to fire again.

"Steyn!" John cried. "Watch out!"

The South African was still holding onto the lifeless body of his comrade, and didn't acknowledge John's warning. Only when a bullet whizzed over his head, missing him by inches, did the Boer soldier come back to reality. He dropped his cousin's corpse and picked up his MP-40.

"You bastard!" Steyn screamed emotionally. "You murdering swine!"

The South African opened up with his submachine gun, spraying automatic fire in the general direction of the advancing partisan. Steyn missed his target, but the barrage of bullets gave the

Russian a fright. The man quickly dropped down to the ground, searching for cover as John looked back across the field and, to his horror, saw more men emerging from the forest.

Two armed partisans advanced past the tree line. They were soon followed by a third, and then a fourth. All of them opened fire simultaneously. Bullets tore into the parked vehicle, as Steyn screamed and ducked for cover. John spotted a gunman sprinting towards the farmhouse itself, firing wildly from a submachine gun as he came. Bullets slammed into the porch and hit the wall behind him.

John struggled to control the surge of panic he suddenly experienced. He ducked down behind cover and raised his pistol. He waited until the gunman came into range and fired from a distance of about 50 foot. He squeezed the trigger and felt the kick back of the pistol. Two shots, fired in quick succession. He missed both times, but the bullets were close enough to their target to make the man think twice. The machine gun wielding partisan was forced to drop to the ground, thus temporarily halting his advance. John now had a brief window of opportunity, and he knew he needed to act fast.

Steyn was holding his own. He was firing on the advancing Russians with his MP-40, keeping the enemy at bay. There were too many of them however, and it was obvious to John that they could not hold this position. He waited for a break in the gunfire before shouting out to the South African. "Steyn! We must retreat into the house. You have to move from there. Run to me and I'll cover you."

The Boer let off one last burst of automatic gunfire before he began to sprint towards the farmhouse. John aimed his pistol in the general direction of the advancing Russians. He fired four shots, spaced out by a few seconds. He didn't expect to hit anyone, just to keep their heads down. The machine gun wielding partisan fired from ground level. The bullets tore into the soil, just inches from Steyn's feet.

He kept running. John was sure his comrade was going to get hit, but, miraculously, the South African made it to the relative safety of the front porch, tripping on the steps.

John grabbed a hold of Steyn's jacket and pulled him inside, slamming the door shut, as yet more of the partisans' bullets slammed into the walls of the building.

A second later, there was an almighty explosion when a bullet struck the Volkswagewerk Kubelwagen, igniting the vehicle's fuel tank.

John glanced across the hallway to the bottom of the staircase. Yvonne and Julie were standing there, hand in hand. They both looked completely terrified.

"John," Yvonne cried out, "what the hell is going on out there?"

"Partisans," John replied, with a firm and steady voice. "Both of you, get to the back of the house. Go to the radio room. I'll meet you there."

"Where the devil are you going to?" Yvonne demanded.

"I'm going to get Andrew," John replied. "He's still locked in the bedroom."

His sister-in-law nodded her head.

"Don't be long," she said, before both she and Julie fled from the hallway to the rear of the house.

John made off to fetch Andrew, but was distracted by banging in the adjacent living room. Pieter Steyn was frantically tearing down the wooden planks which shielded the glassless window frame. He was using the butt of his MP-40 to smash the wood to give him a clear view of the front porch.

"Don't be a fool, Steyn," John cried out. "You can't stop them all."

But the South African wasn't listening. He was overcome by a bloodlust, and sought vengeance for his dead cousin. He opened fire on an advancing enemy, mercilessly cutting the partisan on the porch to pieces.

Steyn let out a vicious cry of triumph, but his victory was to be short-lived. As he was reloading his machine gun a hand grenade was tossed into the farmhouse. John spotted it first and dived behind a wall seconds before an explosion filled the room, temporarily deafening him. When he came back up for air, he saw that Steyn had taken the full force of the blast.

There was nothing he could for him, so he made for the staircase with the intention of freeing Andrew from the locked bedroom. It was only then that he remembered the keys to the room were still lying on the kitchen table. He went to retrieve them only to discover them missing. A second later, he heard a frightened cry coming from the rear of the house.

"Uncle John...come quickly!"

It was Julie.

He raced to her aid and found both her and Yvonne in a state of panic.

"Look!" said Julie, as she pointed to the desk in the corner of the room.

The German made radio set had been deliberately smashed beyond repair. The family's only means of communicating with the nearby Wehrmacht military base had been rendered useless.

Worse still, his Mauser bolt-action rifle and Andrew's Luger pistol were missing.

Andrew was sitting alone in his bedroom when he was startled by the sudden and distinctive boom of automatic gunfire. It had been a long and hellish night. He couldn't sleep a wink because, every time he closed his eyes, he saw the bloodied corpses of his two victims.

Instead, he'd laid on the mattress and chain smoked all night. He had never killed another human being before. Sure, he'd beaten up suspects in Palestine and had fired the odd pot shot at Zionist snipers, but he'd never actually got 'up close and personal' to pull the trigger.

He had always thought he'd enjoy the act of killing. It was a man's natural instinct, after all. He'd never imagined experiencing an emotional reaction whilst taking a life. All his boasts of Aryan manhood seemed foolish now.

Lost in his own sombre thoughts, he was hurtled back to reality when he heard the first gunshots. A number of bullets slammed into the wall just below his window, and he became concerned about his family's safety.

There was more gunfire and two large explosions. It sounded like a bloody warzone out there!

When a relative calm returned, he heard footsteps on the other side of the locked bedroom door, and when a key was slipped into the lock he imagined John had come to his rescue.

Not so.

The door opened and standing there was the boy. Ivan had a pistol in his hand and it was aimed at him.

"What the hell are you doing, you stupid boy?" Andrew cried out. "Put down that gun immediately! Don't you realise it's bloody dangerous?"

Ivan smiled. It was not a boyish grin, but rather the cold and cruel smirk of a killer.

*BOOM!*

Andrew felt like a blazing hot knife had cut into his belly. He looked down and was horrified to see his own blood pouring from the bullet wound to his stomach. He screamed aloud in shock and agony. He managed to stay on his feet and struggled to lift his head.

"Please," he pleaded.

Ivan pulled the trigger again…and again.

*BOOM!*

*BOOM!*

Two shots fired in quick succession. The bullets tore into Andrew's exposed torso. He squealed as he fell backwards, collapsing helplessly on the bed. He stared up at the ceiling – unable to move, and struggling to breath. In his final moments, he thought of his children and prayed for their survival.

John heard the gunshots and instinctively knew his brother was in trouble. Without a thought, he sprinted out of the radio room and through the kitchen, ignoring the panicked cries of Yvonne and Julie.

He felt a throbbing pain in his thigh, but he fought through it and ran into the hallway and sprinted for the staircase, but he never made it.

Two men burst through the front doorway, one armed with a revolver and the other a rifle. John reacted in an instant. He swung around and fired two shots from the hip. Both men collapsed as the bullets tore through their bodies. They screamed in agony as they fell.

The first wave was defeated, but more partisans would soon follow. John saw another figure in the doorway and went to open fire, but he'd used up all his bullets.

*Shit!*

A large and bearded partisan climbed over his two wounded comrades, screaming a chilling battle cry as he brandished a hefty machine pistol, firing wildly in John's direction. John ducked down and fled from the hallway, retreating back into the rear of the house.

He did not expect to survive what was to come.

Yvonne held on tightly to her daughter. Julie's body shuddered every time she heard the gunshots. Yvonne was as terrified as her youngest child, but she had to stay strong. She would fight tooth and nail to protect Julie, because she knew what those animals would do to her if they got their filthy hands on her.

If it came down to it, Yvonne would submit to assault and rape herself, rather than let such a horrific fate befall her 14 year old daughter. She cried out in terror when she heard gunshots from the hallway and seconds later John darted into the room.

"Get moving!" he cried. "Run to the back door and flee for your lives! I'll keep them at bay for as long as I can."

Yvonne didn't need to be told twice. She grabbed hold of her daughter's hand but met with resistance.

"But, we can't leave uncle behind!" Julie exclaimed.

"Don't worry about me," John replied firmly, as he put on a brave face to reassure the girl. "I'll be right behind you."

Julie didn't look convinced, but Yvonne tugged her arm and screamed in her ear...and then they were both running, hand in hand.

They soon reached the back door, ignoring the crashing sounds and shouts coming from behind them. Yvonne flung the door open and both women sprinted out into the sunlight. They didn't get far. Yvonne stopped abruptly when she cast her eyes on the three figures standing before her, shabby Russian peasants wearing red sashes, and armed with a variety of different guns. All

248

three were young men who barely looked old enough to shave, but, when Yvonne looked down the barrels of their guns, she felt a cold shudder running through her whole body.

She stepped forward, deliberately putting herself between the gunmen and her daughter. One of the partisans spoke to his comrades in their native tongue. His comment provoked a chorus of hard sniggers from his companions. Yvonne couldn't understand the words, but she was unsettled by the men's cruel and mocking laughter. Their eyes were hungry and filled with hatred.

She considered telling Julie to make a run for it, but she knew the men would surely shoot them both. There was no escape.

A moment later, she was distracted by a ruckus behind her. John was being physically shoved out of the back door by a large bearded man brandishing a pistol. He swore fiercely in Russian as he pushed the barrel of the gun into John's back, forcing him forwards.

The gunman was accompanied by a young boy who was similarly armed. It was Ivan.

Yvonne knew that the end was close. Deep down, she'd always known they would die in this place. She just hoped that it would be quick. If she could trade her own life for her daughter's, she would do so in an instant.

And what would become of poor Edward? Right now, he was lying in a hospital bed, totally unaware of what was happening to his family. He'd be left all alone in a foreign and dangerous land and Yvonne couldn't bear to think about it. She wanted to scream to the high heavens, to fight tooth and nail with these Soviet terrorists, but she knew such actions would be futile, and would only prolong their suffering.

Then, to her surprise, the partisans stood back. A moment later another figure appeared on the scene. He limped around the side of the house and nodded to his comrades, before speaking to them in their native tongue. The man spoke with authority, and the level of deference the others gave him suggested that he was their leader. Then the man turned his head, and Yvonne saw his face for the first time.

It was Sergei.

Her young lover had returned, except now he wore the red sash of the partisans, and he carried a large silver coloured revolver in his belt. He walked with a limp and was clearly in pain, no doubt as a result of the savage beating he'd received from her husband.

Yvonne felt relieved that he was alive, but confused and fearful by his presence here, angry at his deceit.

"You?" John said angrily, shooting Sergei an accusing look.

"Yes, me," Sergei replied defiantly.

"You were with them all along," John said, as he acknowledged the obvious truth.

"Yes," Sergei answered.

"And what of my brother?" John demanded. "Is he gone?"

"Your brother is dead."

John lowered his head. A pained look came over his face, but all Yvonne felt was relief. In truth, she was glad Andrew was dead, even though she had been married to him for almost 17 years.

"Kill me if you will, but let the women go," John pleaded. "They've done you no harm."

"No more people will die today. Enough blood has been shed already," said Sergei, glancing across to Yvonne. "Your time here has come to an end. We will show you mercy, even though our enemies have shown us none. You were ignorant when you came here, but now you know the truth, do you not?"

"I do," John answered solemnly.

"We have a network of resistance cells, from here up to the Baltic coastline," explained Sergei. "We will take your family as far as the sea, and will arrange to have you smuggled on board a ship to Sweden. From there, you can travel back to England."

"And why would you do this for us?" John demanded. His tone of voice was still suspicious and hostile.

"For one reason," Sergei answered. "So that you can tell your countrymen what you have seen here. You must tell the truth…reveal to the world exactly what the Germans have done to my country, to my people…"

"I see," John replied, in a more thoughtful tone.

"But Sergei," Yvonne cried, "you must know I will not

leave my son behind…not in a million years!"

"I know this, Yvonne. We have agents working in the German hospital. We will rescue Edward and bring him to you. This I promise you, Yvonne…you must trust me now."

Yvonne looked deeply into her lover's eyes, and she saw no signs of deceit. But, then again, Sergei had lied to her before, and she had never suspected a thing. She was in an impossible position. She was separated from her son, and had no way to get to him. On the other hand, her daughter was here, and she needed protection right now.

Julie's face was pale white. She was clearly terrified and perhaps still in a state of shock, after hearing of her father's death. In the end there was no other choice. She had to trust Sergei, and believe that he would be true to his word.

She nodded her head and said, "Okay."

Just then, everyone's attention was drawn up to the sky above where a German spotter plane came into view, circling overhead.

"The Nazi troops will be here shortly," said Sergei. "We must retreat to the woods. Let's go!"

Yvonne took one last look at the old farmhouse. It had been their home for only a few short weeks, but, during this time, the Preston's had been through hell and back.

This was to be Andrew's final resting place. Yvonne couldn't feel sorry for him. He had made his choices, and paid the ultimate price.

Without further thought, she took her daughter by the hand and followed John and the others as they headed for the salvation of the forest.

# EPILOGUE/ 'Rattenkrieg'

SERGEI BARKOV, COMMANDING OFFICER of the 17th Independent partisan company, Belorussian Front, Red Army, sat on a hard wooden bench inside of the underground bunker, which functioned as the ramshackle headquarters for his severely depleted force.

He had a PPsh-41 submachine gun laid across his lap. The SMG was one of several thousand built in the Ural factories and smuggled into the occupied territories, for use by the partisan units operating deep behind enemy lines. He kept a tight hold on the Soviet made weapon, expecting to go into battle at a moment's notice.

Right now, the German infantry were patrolling the woods, searching for any signs of the partisan unit. They would sweep the forest until dusk, leaving no stone unturned in their effort to root out and destroy the remaining resistance fighters.

Sergei knew that their network of subterranean bunkers was well hidden. The Germans had searched these forests many times before, and, to date, they had found nothing. Nevertheless, there was always a chance that the Hitlerites would get lucky and stumble on them one day. This was a serious concern, but Sergei could do little to negate that threat. If it came down to it, he and his men would fight to the death; better that than allow themselves to be captured, because Sergei knew what the Germans did to partisan prisoners – brutal torture followed by a slow and painful execution by hanging. He'd lost many friends and comrades this way.

He looked around the small bunker, with its walls of earth and timber support beams. The dugout was one of a network which held the full number of the unit, along with their supplies, weapons and ammunitions. He shared this particular bunker with four other individuals, two of whom were men under his command: Joseph and Vladimir, teenage partisans, hot headed young men who had both lost their families during the war, like so many others.

The teenagers were typical of most of the men under Sergei's command. They'd been raised in a country devastated by war and bloody genocide. They had known nothing but bloodshed, chaos and violence since their early years. Most of the partisans wanted nothing more than to kill every German or German ally they could get their hands on. That was why Sergei's orders were so unpopular with most of his comrades – because, it had been his plan to spare the lives of the Preston family.

It had also been a hard plan to sell to his Commanding Officer. The district command had been sceptical. The standard orders were to kill all settlers whenever the opportunity arose. 'Scorched Earth' was the Soviet policy now – make the lands uninhabitable for the invader…grind the Germans into the ground - terrorise their women and children and never allow the swine a moment's peace.

Sergei's original orders had been just that. He was meant to infiltrate the settlers' home, posing as a slave worker. He would remain on the plantation long enough to gain the family's trust – and then he would muster his men and they would kill them all. This was the original mission, but things had changed.

Sergei had used the German radio set to communicate with his Command. He'd waited until the family were asleep or out of the house before he made the calls. How ironic, that the German's own technology should be used against them in this way. It was by this method that he'd communicated his new plan. At first, his CO had thought Sergei had gone insane. His orders were to murder all of the family, including the children. And instead, Sergei was asking to spare the English, and to use the resistance network to smuggle them through the occupied territories, across the Baltic Sea and into neutral Sweden.

In the end, it was the Division's Political Commissar who had pushed to implement Sergei's unorthodox plan of action. The Commissar was a survivor of the Stalinist era – a loyal Party man, even though the Communist Party hardly existed anymore, not in this part of the country at least. Nevertheless, the Commissar in question still appreciated an opportunity for a good propaganda victory. If the Preston's made it back to London, they could tell their story to the English press. Sergeant Preston knew the truth. He had seen the bodies with his own two eyes. The Germans could no longer cover up the atrocities they had committed here in the Soviet Republics. Soon, the whole world would know the truth...and maybe, just maybe, other countries would stand up and join the fight.

The real hope was America. The Yankees were an industrious and technologically advanced people, and their country was very wealthy. If they could get the Americans on side....victory could be possible. For Sergei, this was a glimmer of hope, but his reality right now was this god-forsaken bunker and the SS dogs patrolling the forest above.

Sergei looked across to the other two occupants who shared the dugout with them.

Ivan.

And the little girl in a tattered white communion dress.

Boys like Ivan were thrown into the fray, forced to become killers before they even reached adolescence. Sergei didn't like using children, but the partisans were desperately short on recruits; they needed every man – or boy - they could get.

Ivan had become a man today. He'd performed bravely on the field of battle and he'd liquidated his enemy without hesitation. Sergei was proud of the boy. He would tell Ivan as much, but only after this current crisis was over.

The young girl had been found wandering through the wood late one night, a few months back now. She was a pretty child, with long dark hair and hazelnut eyes. They didn't know her name, but the men and women in the unit called her 'Anastasia', after the Tsarist princess.

They'd taken the girl under their wing, looking after her and feeding her. She never spoke and had a worrying habit of sneaking out of the bunker late at night to wander through the forest, alone in the dark.

Anastasia was a troubled and odd child, but she was Sergei's responsibility now. They had to look after the children, as they were the only hope left for the Motherland.

Once a man gave up on compassion and kindness, he was no longer human. Sergei had almost forgotten this truth, but then he'd met Yvonne.

His feelings for the Englishwoman were the real reason behind his change of plan. His illicit liaison with her had not been planned. He hadn't fallen in love with the woman at first sight; far from it. At first, he'd seen her as a legitimate target for assassination. After all, she and her family were the invaders. They had come to the Motherland with the intention of stealing their lands, and building their new homes with slave labour. Sergei had hated the Preston's and had been quite prepared to kill them all. But his feelings had changed over the subsequent days and weeks.

He considered Andrew Preston a vile creature, a fascist swine who hated the Slavic peoples, considering them as no better than livestock. Preston was typical of the Nazi sympathisers who came to settle in the occupied territories.

Sergei had no qualms about executing the man, especially after he'd witnessed his treatment of Yvonne.

Andrew's brother John had seemed different however. He was much more respectful than his younger sibling, and appeared not to share Andrew's fascist beliefs. Nevertheless, John was a former sergeant in the English Army. The man was a trained and experienced soldier, and thus a threat. Sergei could easily have justified his assassination, but he held back because of Yvonne.

Yvonne had been kind to Sergei. He hadn't expected that since the Nazis had never shown him anything but cruelty. She'd allowed him to bathe and she gave him good clothes to wear. He hadn't intended to seduce her, it had just happened. It had been a

255

day of sheer bliss, and afterwards, against all odds, he had found himself caring about the family.

He felt concern for Edward after the young man had been mauled by a bear. He worried about Julie when the girl woke up screaming during the night. And most of all, he yearned for Yvonne to return to him. But there was no future for the couple. Sergei had always known this. The best he could do was save Yvonne and her family. Sergei had seen Yvonne, Julie and John to safety, and he'd made a commitment to help Edward. He'd promised his lover to rescue her son from the Wehrmacht field hospital and he intended to keep his promise, no matter how difficult it would be to infiltrate the German base.

He would personally lead the mission.

Sergei and his men saw the Preston's to safety, rushing them through the forest, using the hidden pathways which only the partisans knew. Their party reached the relay point and handed over responsibility for the family to the special squad sent by the Divisional HQ.

As they parted, Yvonne gave Sergei a tender kiss on the lips, before whispering, 'thank you'.

Sergei didn't know what to say. He wanted to stay with her, but his place was with his men. Even so, he considered himself lucky, because he'd experienced love, if only for a short time.

He would remember Yvonne for the rest of his life.

After the hand-over, Sergei turned his attention to the task in hand: how to rescue Edward.

He was pondering the operation when his thoughts were disturbed by the thump of boots, the shouts of men and the barks of several dogs on the forest floor above their bunker.

The barking grew louder. The jackboots were right above them now. The enemy were on top of them, combing the forest floor inch by inch. How long would it be before they found the hidden shutter door?

Sergei looked to his men. Joseph and Vladimir grabbed their rifles, affixing bayonets, as they stared up at the ceiling of the dugout. He raised a finger to his lips, urging the men to stay quiet.

Then he glanced across to where Ivan and Anastasia were sat side by side. Ivan had a Luger pistol in his hand. His eyes were wide, and his forehead was covered in sweat. Anastasia, though, appeared unconcerned and apparently disconnected from reality, even though an attack was imminent.

Sergei's heart was beating fast as he lifted his submachine gun and cocked the weapon. His men followed his lead.

They were prepared for battle.


Captain Henrich Muller had volunteered to lead the anti-partisan sweep of the isolated Belorussian forest. This was his first combat command in many years and had happened by pure coincidence.

He had been temporarily billeted in the Wehrmacht frontier post when the mobilisation order came through. He'd just finished escorting yet another English family out to the frontier – the Dales from Yorkshire. They'd taken up a plantation about twenty miles to the west of here. It was just a standard liaison mission no different from the dozens of others he'd completed since the end of the war. This was all he was good for now, according to the OKH Command at least.

He'd been waiting at the barracks for the next convoy heading back up to Minsk, when the call was received. There were reports of a partisan attack to the east of the base. A reconnaissance plane had spotted a number of armed men assaulting an isolated farmhouse belonging to the English Preston family, and the order had come through for a counter-attack. The rapid response company was mobilised for action.

Unfortunately, the OC of the unit was off base on a week's home leave. The company needed a commander, and Muller just happened to be on base and at a loose end.

The rapid response company was already recognised as an elite anti-partisan unit, and Muller was a veteran combat officer who had fought in Moscow and Stalingrad, amongst other battles. Therefore, when the call came in, he was ordered to take the command.

Muller's own feelings about the mission were mixed. It had been years since his last combat command, and a part of him had never wanted to see battle again. He'd already witnessed enough bloodshed to last a lifetime. On the other hand, he was a trained and experienced soldier, and warfare was in his blood. He had no love for the Nazis, but he was forever loyal to his country, and he would do his duty by the Fatherland.

There was another good reason why Captain Muller had wanted command of this operation: he had a soft spot for the Preston family. He had to try to rescue them. He owed it to Sergeant Preston.

In was late in the morning when 120 armed Wehrmacht troops entered the forest. Muller studied the map and divided his company into four platoons, each tasked with combing a specific area of the forest.

Each section was allocated half-a-dozen German Shepherds. Their chances of finding anything were slight – it was a vast primordial forest after all. Nevertheless, the tracker dogs might pick up a scent.

Muller trotted through the woods with his staff officer, a young Lieutenant named Hoch, and a squad of heavily armed enlisted men. The soldiers in this company were fired up and ready for combat. The men were angry. They'd all seen the bodies of their murdered fellow soldiers back at the farmhouse. There was a time when the Wehrmacht would inflict merciless and bloody reprisals in response to all partisan attacks carried out along the Eastern Frontier. The killing of a German soldier could provoke the summary executions of between 50 and 100 Russian peasants. If a Wehrmacht officer was killed, the dead man's troops might wipe out a nearby village or two...but that was during the war. The trouble these days was that there weren't many Russian peasants left to shoot. Most of the local population were already dead, and those left alive almost all worked for the German occupiers in some capacity.

Muller and his countrymen had ravaged this country, all but eradicating the Slavic people – but still the partisans fought on. Not that he could blame the Russians. If the Fatherland was invaded and the German people slaughtered, he too would fight the enemy until his last breath. But, the Soviet partisans were in dire straits now, short on men and weapons, and forced to hide underneath the ground. The real war was still to come. America had the atomic bomb, and now, so did Germany.

The prospect of these terrible weapons frightened Muller immensely. He imagined entire cities engulfed by atomic flames, and tens of thousands wiped out in a second. He tried not to dwell on such horrors. Right now, he needed to focus on the mission at hand.

Muller looked ahead and saw nothing but trees. He listened intently and heard the sound of dogs barking excitedly. A moment later a German soldier emerged from behind the trees, shouting as he ran.

"Hauptmann," he cried, "Captain Muller...the dogs have found something. We have discovered a clearing in the woods just a couple of hundred yards from here. We believe the partisans are hiding beneath the forest floor."

"Tell your lieutenant to pull back the dogs – they make too much noise," replied Muller. "Comb the area carefully and search for a trapdoor or dugout entrance. If you find one wait for us to arrive. Do not use hand grenades under any circumstances. The enemy may be holding hostages. Do you understand, soldier?"

"Yes sir," the private replied sharply and left.

Muller removed his Walther P38 pistol from its holster. He cocked the gun, making it ready to fire.

"Let's go," he said, turning to his men.

They were marching into the clearing when they heard the first gunshots.

When they arrived on the scene, a partisan armed with a submachine gun was emerging through a hatch from beneath the ground. Muller thought he recognised the man, but he couldn't be sure.

The partisan wasted no time and opened fire, killing three of Muller's men in an instant, before trying to make good his escape, but he was met by a hail of bullets and died before hitting the ground.

Two more partisans emerged from the bunker, both brandishing bolt-loaded rifles with fixed bayonets, but they were heavily outnumbered and were cut down by Muller's men without mercy.

What happened next took Muller by surprise. He was visibly shocked when a young boy and girl emerged from the dug-out. He watched in confusion as the children ran hand in hand towards the tree line. Muller ordered his men to hold fire. But then he spotted the boy was armed...too late.

The boy opened up on his men, leaving them no option but to return fire. As a bullet tore through the boy's chest, killing him instantly, the girl stopped in her tracks and turned to stare directly at Muller himself.

He lifted up his pistol and aimed. The girl didn't even flinch. She wasn't afraid. The men were watching him now. They expected their officer to act.

It was better this way, Muller rationalised, better for the child to die quickly and painlessly, rather than hand her over to those brutes in the Einsatzgruppen. He felt a last twinge of conscience as he looked the girl in the eye, but it wasn't enough to stop him. Orders were orders and Muller would do his duty, no matter how ugly those duties were. It wasn't like it was his first time.

He took a deep breath and squeezed on the trigger, knowing he would be forever condemned.

Evil had triumphed, and darkness ruled supreme.

§

# POSTSCRIPT

*The Times, 3rd September 1948*

FAMILY RETURNS HOME WITH EXTRAORDINARY
STORY OF LIFE IN NAZI-OCCUPIED EUROPE

By W. F. Deedes

LONDON – Three members of the Preston family, John, his sister-in-law Yvonne and teenage niece Julie today appeared at an impromptu press conference at Brick Lane in East London, organised by the Socialist Worker's Party.

The trio were part of a five strong group which left Dover in July of this year with the apparent intention of defecting to Hitler's Germany. The Preston's' are one of hundreds of British families to have immigrated to the German-controlled continent in recent months, but the three are the only known UK citizens to have returned safely to their home country.

Mr John Preston, formerly a sergeant in the British Army and a veteran of the Battle of Dunkirk, was widely condemned by UK politicians and newspapers following a published photograph which appeared to show him giving a Nazi-style salute to a Wehrmacht General at the site of the June 1940 battle. Mr Preston today claimed that this salute was given under duress.

He went on to describe the family's epic train journey through Europe in which they witnessed many scenes of Nazi brutality, modern day slavery and evidence of widespread war crimes and atrocities. Mr Preston's vividly retold account included detailed descriptions of depopulated and ruined cities, ravaged countryside and hidden mass graves.

Mr Preston's younger brother Andrew, a former member of the British Union of Fascists and outspoken admirer of Herr Hitler, was allegedly killed in Eastern Europe during an armed confrontation with Russian partisans. The ex-sergeant claims that the same group of partisans aided the family's escape from the German controlled province, transporting the trio to the Baltic coast and helping them board a merchant ship sailing to neutral Stockholm.

The conference ended with a heartfelt and teary-eyed appeal from Yvonne Preston, whose eldest son Edward (aged 16) is being held in a German military hospital in Belarus, apparently against his will. In an emotional address Mrs Preston pleaded for assistance from the Foreign Office and International Red Cross in order to bring her son home.

Prime Minister Anthony Eden spoke at Downing Street only a matter of hours after the press conference, promising a strong response from the government in light of the Preston family's claims. Mr Eden announced an interim ban on all British and Commonwealth emigration into German-controlled territories pending a full investigation and parliamentary inquiry. However, former Prime Minister Lord Halifax advised caution, claiming that the Preston family's 'outlandish' account bears all the hallmarks of 'Bolshevik black propaganda'.

The German Ambassador in London was unavailable for comment.

## About the Author

Mark Lynch has lived in Northern Ireland all his life, studied History & Politics at Queen's University Belfast and maintains a keen interest in both of these subjects.

He currently works as an office administrator in Belfast city centre and enjoys reading both fiction and non-fiction, but is particularly keen on the science fiction genre and its sub genres, such as alternative history and space colonisation. This is his fifth book.

He is currently working on his next novel.

**Also currently available from David J Publishing:**

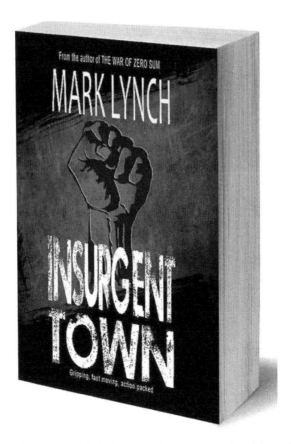

The riveting follow-up to Mark Lynch's debut 'alternative history' thriller THE WAR OF ZERO SUM It's July 1969 and the struggle continues as Sean McCann and Josie Ferguson return to the Soviet-controlled North East of Ireland. Josie is determined to avenge the death of her father, while Sean reluctantly re-joins the underground resistance in Belfast.

But neither reckon on the dogged determination of Special Branch's Alec Lynch who wants McCann dead or alive. And so begins a deadly game of cat and mouse, played out against the backdrop of a city in a state of open rebellion against Russian rule as Protestants and Catholics unite to fight a common enemy.

Action packed, fast moving, thought provoking, INSURGENT TOWN picks up where THE WAR OF ZERO SUM left off. It is a gripping alternative look at what could have happened had the Irish Troubles developed differently in the late 1960s.

Imagine how the Irish Troubles might have developed differently if the historical context of the late 1960's was significantly altered.

Europe 1969. The failure of the Western Alliance has allowed the Soviet Union to expand its borders to the North Atlantic. The United Kingdom no longer exists and Her Majesty's Government has long since been overthrown.

Ireland remains divided, with the North controlled by the Communists and the South effectively an American client state. Two mighty armies glare at each other across a heavily fortified border, which the locals have grimly christened as the 'Shamrock Curtain.' In the midst of this chaos is Sean McCann, a young Belfast man with a chequered past who is drawn into a war which is not of his making.

This is a gripping, fast moving, action packed, thought provoking and well researched debut novel from a promising new Northern Ireland author.

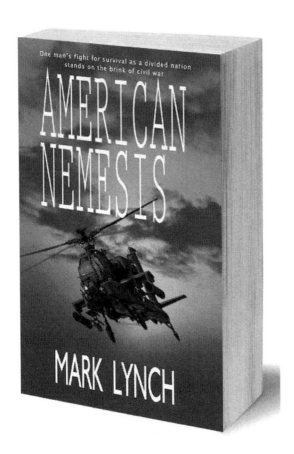

It's July 2030. The American States are no longer united, as the 'Tea Party' Republicans have seceded from the Union to form a new nation, the Confederated Christian States of America. For a decade the two ideological rivals have faced off against each other across the intra-American frontier. It's an uneasy truce that begins to crumble as a tragic incident pushes both sides to the very brink.

Joshua Hamilton is a liberal with a history of political activism. Regarded as a traitor by the ultra-conservative population of the Arizona Strip where he lives, he has been blacklisted by the government security apparatus.

His plans to cross the border to start a new life in the remnant United States are thrown into disarray when the brutal murder of a friend forces him to re-evaluate his priorities.

As America creeps closer to a potentially catastrophic civil war, he finds himself embroiled in a high risk mission. If the operation succeeds he will gain everything he desires. If it fails, his life will be over.